YEAR'S BEST
AOTEAROA
NEW ZEALAND
SCIENCE
FICTION
& FANTASY

YEAR'S BEST AOTEAROA NEW ZEALAND SCIENCE FICTION & FANTASY

V3 / EDITED BY MARIE HODGKINSON

PAPER ROAD PRESS

Year's Best Aotearoa New Zealand Science Fiction and Fantasy: Volume III
edited by Marie Hodgkinson

First published in paperback and ebook in 2021
ISBNs: paperback 978-1-99-115030-1
ebook 978-1-99-115031-8

Paper Road Press
paperroadpress.co.nz

Cover art by and © Rebekah Tisch 2020
Cover and internal design by Marie Hodgkinson

CONTENTS

INTRODUCTION

The third volume of this anthology series arrives into a time of constantly changing travel and border restrictions. While the rest of the world opens up, Aotearoa and our neighbours across the ditch are more likely to be transported on the wings of imagination than via more literal means.

Fortunate, then, that the barriers to sharing the written and spoken word are so low even as we get such a clear reminder of the physical barrier of distance. Far from being cut off from the rest of the SFF world, writers from Aotearoa continue to share their words and worlds around the globe. The stories in this anthology are only a small selection of the incredible writing from local authors over the past year, published online and in print in venues that range from traditional anthologies to Instagram Live storytelling events.

This is the longest of these anthologies yet, and this is the shortest introduction. These stories have been around the world and come back home – I'll let them speak for themselves.

—Marie

NEW ZEALAND GOTHIC

JACK REMIEL COTTRELL

You are waiting for a bus. One drives by, empty. The second is cancelled as the bus arrives. The third is driven by an eldritch horror with an infinite number of limbs. It does not know the route.

You glance at listings of vacant houses to rent. The moment you look closer they are occupied. They have always been occupied.

"Clean and green," the cows low. Rivers run an unearthly viridian. The water is rumoured to grant eternal life. The water is rumoured to kill instantly.

Road cones grow sentient. They whisper secrets about you.

You have to sign up for a RealMe account. The captcha asks you to identify shifting pictures of ancient runes. As you click the squares, it comes to you that you are not real. You never were.

The path between the domestic and international terminals is a test of virtue. The sages say only the pure of heart may enter. The oracles counter that only the pure of heart may leave. The truth is closely guarded by those souls stranded in the smokers' hut.

"We must build up not out." "We must build up not out." Towers stretch into oblivion. Many children have never touched the ground.

Clothing in the capital grows darker by the day. Soon every jacket is its own black hole, sucking in tourists who disembark from gargantuan cruise ships.

The motorways are under construction. They are always under construction. They stretch to unimagined planes of torment and ecstasy. They will allow you to reach those dimensions seven minutes faster.

The country is mentioned in a blockbuster movie. The populace rises up to cheer as one. You do not know what you are cheering for. You do not know that there is a movie. You are in the movie.

SYNAESTHETE

MELANIE HARDING-SHAW

The first time I remember noticing a flash in someone's eyes was the day I started preschool. The shadow of black and red in the teacher's eyes matched the feathers lining the korowai cloak of the girl sitting next to her who was leaving that day to start school. I thought that was clever. The flashes had always been there, of course. In the eyes of my parents and the adults who came to visit. When I was old enough to wonder, I thought they must be spirit animals. Guardians, perhaps. I was oblivious in the way that many children are. Or maybe I just didn't want to see.

I can remember the first time I looked in the mirror to search my own out. Staring into the depths of my eyes and feeling a moment of panic that there was nothing there before I saw the shadowed outline, the hint of movement from the rise and fall of its breath. I shouted at the mirror to try and wake it, but it did not stir. I sometimes wonder what would have happened if I had succeeded in waking it that day. It was only when I closed my eyes and saw the after-image on my eyelids that I could make out the shape. A hound as black as my pupils curled in sleep. It wasn't until puberty hit that I started to realise the truth.

#

Scotty was the first boy I thought I wanted to kiss. I didn't tell anyone because all the girls wanted to kiss him and it was ridiculous to think he might pick me. I just stared at the back of his head in class. Admired the casual swagger that somehow came across even when he was sitting still.

And then the party. Those first gulps of cheap and burning vodka. Stumbling into a bedroom, and there he was. His casual swagger, now a stagger. His hands pulling me closer. The sudden sickening realisation that I did not want *this*.

I pushed him away in panic. "No!"

"I've seen the way you look at me," he slurred.

I shook my head, and stepped back.

"Freak."

My stomach churned with dread and my frantic eyes met his, searching for a sign that this would not make my life 'over'. That I would be able to show my face at school on Monday. The thing is, I didn't usually meet people's eyes. Somewhere between kindergarten and that party, I had realised no one else saw the flashes and I had decided I would not see them either. I watched their mouths instead: the twitch of hidden amusement at one corner or the downturned edges of lost patience. Maybe I would have been prepared if I had been watching eyes all those years. If I had let myself accustom to my changing sight.

I stared into Scotty's eyes and I saw the rabid peacock tearing at his brain. Clawed feet scratching gouges down his amygdala as its sharp beak wrenched at optic nerves stretched so tight his eyes might pop out the back of their sockets. The bird's majestic iridescent wings spread wide, bloodstained and razor sharp as they beat within his skull, slicing the soft tissues like the cutty grasses that used to catch our unwary arms as we walked to the beach.

I stood in that room and I screamed and I did not stop screaming until the ambulance came. I could not show my face at school that Monday or any Monday after.

#

It was weeks before I could even step foot outside my room. Weeks before I could bring myself to cry on my mother's shoulder. I watched her mouth as I crept out into the lounge. I saw her fear for me in the tightness of her lips. I heard the tentative tremor in her voice, the uncertainty that she might say the wrong thing and make it worse. I kept my eyes down, scared of the coloured flashes lurking higher.

I sat beside her and leaned my head on her shoulder. I felt the comforting weight of her arm around me. I couldn't see her face from there. I was safe.

"I love you," she whispered.

I didn't say anything. I could feel a tendril creeping down my face, caressing me. Each time it pulled away, I felt pinpoints of my cheek stretch outwards one by one. Tiny circles of pain. Not a tendril, but a tentacle. I jerked upright to stare at her, despite knowing better. I didn't notice the metallic reflections of the octopus's eyes within hers at first. I was too distracted by its tentacles tearing off the features of her face to shove them into its beak. I could see glimpses of her flesh further in. Pieces of her nose and ears being ground down by a tongue covered in rows of teeth.

I tore myself away and ran back to my room, the sound of

her voice calling after me muffled by the squelching of those tentacles rending her faceless.

I could feel a sickening movement in my eyes, the first stirrings of a slumbering animal. I broke every mirror in the house.

#

My therapist thought that writing might give me an outlet, and it did. I chatted to other writers online. I could communicate, be supportive, and have value; and I did not have to see their faces. As I grew more confident, I could even meet them sometimes. I would sit and stare down at my paper, focusing only on the letters I was forming on the page. I would laugh at their jokes, offer solace for their trials. But, it is a hard thing to look away from the pain in a friend's voice.

There came a day when I lost focus. I glanced up for a moment as I spoke.

"You are doing it! You are a writer already!" I tried to say.

My words were cut short by a missile smashing into my nose. I covered my face in my hands, but not before I saw my friend's eyes bulging outwards with the pressure of a thousand cuckoo's eggs. The mother bird invisible inside their skull but for the sound of her beak clacking in sinister pleasure. I staggered to my feet as a stream of projectiles flew at me, beating me backwards. I caught a glimpse of my friend as I ran away. Unimaginable pressure sending eggs erupting from their scalp like pumice flying from flesh volcanoes. Their red blood lava oozing from the open wounds.

The squeaking sound of hound's teeth worrying at my synapses, not unlike the noise of biting into halloumi, echoed in my mind and drove me running home.

#

So, I locked myself away from the world once more, reaching out only through my keyboard and the screen. Groceries delivered to my door. Feet dragging, shoulders hunched, and the smell of loneliness permeating every space. The ache of claws and teeth inside my skull never left me and I wondered if there was anything left there and what that hound would feast on once it was stripped bare. There was a single mirror in my subsidised apartment. I had covered it with rainbow lines of duct tape. The colours made me feel like it was a choice; an interior design quirk that I could remove any time I wanted. I never did.

You can't stay inside forever, though. The day I met Sid, I was walking to the letterbox. She was walking her dog, a golden terrier. Even with my eyes cast down, I noticed her nails reflecting in the sun. They were the most beautiful nails I'd ever seen; works of art with rainbow chrome colours shifting as she walked. I didn't know it then, but people often stared at Sid. She didn't match what they expected to see. She didn't match who they expected her to be.

I stared at Sid, too, and maybe she saw the horror in my eyes because she looked away. Her shoulders hunched slightly against the blow she thought might come, just like mine. Everyone I met had something eating away at them. Sid was different, though. The thing consuming her was not inside her skull like mine. Its human mouth was latched onto her legs gnawing on an Achilles tendon while the weight of its body dragged behind her each step she took. As I watched, its jaws loosened but only so that its rooster talons could tear chunks from her calves. It was the cruel alpha, driving her away. A monster denying her the right to live.

Somehow, she strode on despite the creature hanging off her

that was part human, part beast and all the cruelty of the world. I watched her pained footsteps almost pass my gate and I couldn't take it anymore.

"Hi," I cried out, and she turned around, uncertain.

I could feel the gnawing in my own brain pause.

"Hi," she said.

I stood and stared at this beautiful woman, the horror of her parasite now hidden behind her legs. I tried to imagine how to convey to her that I was different, too. I didn't have the words. I reached up and buried my face in my hands. My dank, unwashed hair fell forward to hide my face as sobs shook my body.

She didn't see my dirty nails clawing into my eyes, tearing out the creature I could feel inside. And I am certain she did not see the black hound that I threw to the ground between us. Its teeth were bared in a snarl and its muscles were poised to leap back up; to savage my face before digging a hole back into my brain as if my frontal lobe was freshly mown grass begging for its claws.

She saw the red scratches down my cheeks, though. She saw the tears. She reached out to me, a stranger, and she hugged me in the street.

"Do you want to come for a walk?" she asked.

I nodded.

#

There is a forest at the end of my street where I had never ventured. At the entrance was a sign: 'Dogs must be kept on a leash.'

Sid saw me reading it. "It's to protect the birds, our taonga. We can't let dogs roam free or they will destroy them," she said.

Sid set off towards the trees. I looked at the black hound stalking beside me. I could still see the vestiges of my brain tissues on his snout, my blood colouring his whiskers. Then I looked at the almost human creature ahead of me, clinging to Sid's shoes. It had lost its grip when I started walking beside her, shrunk back a little. It was still horrifying, but now it was no bigger than the playful terrier trotting by her side.

I glared at the black dog, looked deep into his eyes. We can't let dogs roam free or they will destroy what is precious to us. I bared my teeth and planted both feet firmly on the track. His snarl faltered, his ears pressed down to his skull, and his tail twitched downwards until it was pressed tightly up under his belly.

I pointed at Sid's creature and he streaked towards it, slamming his head into its side and sending it careening into the shadows of the undergrowth where it peered at us cowering. When he returned to me, I reached down to touch him with a trembling hand, to finally feel that coarse black fur. He tried to snap at my fingers, to crunch the tiny bones in his powerful jaws. I slapped his nose and grabbed the leash lying across his back. I had never even noticed it was there.

"Are you coming?" Sid asked from up ahead, her steps now gloriously unconstrained.

"Yes."

She smiled at me. I could tell because of the tiny creases forming by her eyes. In their glossy depths, I could just make out the reflection of the silver fronds of a young ponga fern beside the track.

KŌHUIA

T TE TAU

Ōreo saw a faint impression in the blanket of moss that lay across the path, an outline created by the weight of a foot that had broken through to the mud. She crouched low, pushed aside ferns that brushed her face and prompted the lens over her right retina to turn on. It brought the imprint into focus and filled in missing information, sketching out the faint outline of a person, someone taller than herself. She swiveled to look back down the trail and stiffened at the sound of rustling leaf litter. Birds called to each other as they returned to roost for the night. No one else could be this far in, she was pretty sure, not without her knowing about it. She'd been so careful. The blocker she'd taken – the pill to keep Hiria out of her head – meant no one could check in on her.

The tree guarding the bones of Ōreo's mother lay ahead, hidden behind a curtain of kareao. She'd left before dawn without a whisper to anyone. By now, they'd be worried that she wouldn't be back in time for the release. Night came early to the forest, and even though sunlight still dusted the leaves above the canopy, its thick cover prevented light from reaching the ground below. The trek was mostly uphill and along ridges to her mother's tree. Occasionally the track dipped into gullies and past streams where she'd refilled her water bottle.

A gust of wind with a chill on its edges washed through the canopy. The undergrowth crunched and snapped as Ōreo pushed through the bush, her eyes felt hot and dry. Finally, the giant they called her mother's tree stood above her. Ōreo's lens adjusted to compensate for the dark. It allowed her to see the epiphytes carpeting the trunk, networked together in thick arteries and delicate veins. The waka kōiwi holding her mother's bones was visible from the ground, the deeply carved lines standing out from the branches. By this time next year, the climbers would have it fully entombed. Her mother's tree was one of the oldest. It had seen the fire that destroyed Te Tapere Nui o Whatonga and had lived two hundred years since. The tree rose high over the canopy observing the forest creep outwards again, reclaiming the grassland through the work of planter bots and people.

She instructed her lens to do a heat scan of the area. Fine silvery gridded lines appeared in front of her, tracing the ground's surface and then the trees. The lines brushed over different-sized objects in the canopy, birds preparing to roost for the night, kererū, kōkako and hīhi. A large, round body that she guessed belonged to a whēkau nestled into a gap in the trunk of her mother's tree. Her mum would like that it had chosen her tree. Ōreo wished she could ask it to scout around to find whoever had made that footprint.

She cleared a few fallen branches and laid some ponga fern fronds across each other to give her a soft surface. As Ōreo did this, she tried to push away intrusive thoughts of tomorrow, the thousands of interested people all linked in with their endless questions. They'd want to know about her mother. Ōreo was quite good at relaying what Hiria told her, straight from the prompt on her lens. Hiria was great at encouraging her in real-time; "That's an 89% sincerity score. Pretty good, you'd make a better actor than a biologist I've always said." It was an instinctive thing to reach out for Hiria, inherent and habitual. Ōreo was doing it now, reaching out with a mental arm to signal the AI. But for the moment, it was severed, cut off by the pill. Hiria would have told her who had made the footprint the instant the thought had entered her head.

The crisp air bit at the exposed areas of Ōreo's skin, her neck and face. She picked up fallen branches and snapped dead ones from small trees, stacking them next to the pile of fern fronds a couple of metres from her mother's tree. The twigs flashed to life as she lit them, orange flames bouncing off the giant trunk; the interwoven vines and plants creating an elaborate shawl across its lower branches. Lydia's body had been lowered into the tree by helicopter. She'd said herself that she didn't want anyone breaking their backs to carry her there. "Build a platform and lower me onto it. Easy! Just feed me to the birds," she'd croaked to the worried faces gathered around her bed. "You'll just have to make sure it's a giant tree fit for a giant woman!"

The cold nipped at her again, and with alarm she realised that she was feeling it through her clothes. Her jumpsuit was thin but regulated her temperature, the network of soft green cells collecting energy from the day. The home display on her lens flickered and went out. She sunk into a crouched position next to the fire, trying to think past the panic sweeping through her body. The thin material was a layer of ice against her skin.

The whēkau above sent out a shrill call to let others know it was awake. Ōreo flinched at the sound. Without the use of her internal light, the darkness closed in on the weak flames. Ōreo dragged the pile of fern fronds to the base of her mother's tree where the roots created an indent at the bottom. She felt better having the monster tree at her back and the tiny fire between her and the rest of the forest. Her bag was on the ground somewhere, hidden in leaf litter and out of reach. In the bag was a tightly wrapped bundle, the reason for her visit.

Ōreo was stocktaking specimens in an old freezer when she found the body of the kōhuia raised by her mother. She'd called her Tiro Pī because the baby bird seemed suspicious of the hand puppet she used to feed her but went along with it anyway. Ōreo had quietly decided to bury Tiro Pī close to her mother. The team would never have agreed, and so she hadn't told them.

Ōreo threw a log on the fire and watched the flames recoil from the damp wood before leaning back into the nook to wait for sleep. She wished she could send a message up through the epiphytes to her mother's bones, tell her how they were releasing the kōhuia all at once and that it was a stupid idea. Lydia would have disapproved of that too she thought, safer to do it in smaller quantities. But now they had one hundred and fifty birds living in the secured area. They'd had less than half that amount when Lydia died. The birds were doing so well everyone said. Ōreo blew on her fingers and tucked them under her armpits. Hiria would've been giving her a running commentary of stats if she requested it: all the vital signs, and the unvital ones. She'd be telling her to get up and move around, jog on the spot, that she needed to be more resilient like her mother. Hiria wasn't supposed to relay the messages that lurked in your subconscious, but sometimes she did.

Ōreo was pulled from her thoughts by the cries of startled

birds in a tree nearby. She remembered the footprint and that whoever made it could be watching her from beyond the clearing. She wished the blocker would wear off now; she was ready for Hiria to send for help. Every sound beyond the fire echoed, masking whether it was human or animal. The glowing embers faded.

Ōreo awoke to another cry – this time a kārearea searching for its breakfast. It was still mostly dark, but the light had a blueness that revealed the outline of trees beyond the clearing. Her body was a frozen lump and as she tried to move her toes sharp jolts of pain assured her they were attached but not happy. She could taste bile on her cardboard tongue. Pushing the fronds aside, she moved, stiff and clumsy from her bed. Mosquitos had found her, and the squadron followed as she felt around for her bag. The usual synapses reached out for Hiria and still found no response.

Something cracked behind her in the undergrowth, a sound that she knew could only be made by the weight of a human. She clambered back towards the tree and turned. The figure was crouched low, and she could see eyes peering from the face of a man. She could see that he held a rope with a bundle tied to the end of it. Rays of light soaked through the clearing, and Ōreo could make out the person's dark and curly hair. He wore a blanket of layered fibres that flicked up at the ends. Her eyes rested on the bundle dangling from the rope and saw a mass of black feathers, the cord wrapped around clawed feet. She could see three heads, one of them had a long curved beak flanked by wattles on either side. The realisation of what she was looking at hit her like a branch in the face.

"Kōhuia?" she exclaimed. "You killed them?!" Ōreo's hand scrambled for something to protect herself, finding only a detached tree frond, which she held out limp in front of her. At the same time, she edged forward; she had to see. He threw the birds at her as if to stop her from coming any closer. They landed at her feet, and she crouched down to pick them up. The birds were larger than the ones she was used to handling. She could see now that they weren't kōhuia at all but something much, much more confusing.

Ōreo brushed her shaking fingers over the leathery orange wattles, a colour they hadn't achieved in the lab. The bodies of the birds were cold. Her tears rolled off the surface of the feathers into the dirt. She looked back up at the man, wondering how afraid of him she needed to be.

"Where did you find these?!" Her voice sounded strangled, the panic sucking air from her lungs. They couldn't be from this part of the forest or any forest that she knew. Ōreo lifted out the stiff wings, uncurling the recently immobilised feet. Live huia hadn't been here for almost two hundred years. These were a deep black, not the grey-blue of hybrid kōhuia. She couldn't believe that someone had unravelled the genetic mechanisms underlying the orange wattles and not passed the information on to their lab.

She pressed him again, "Where did you find these huia?!"

He remained silent and fear gleamed from the whites of his eyes.

She could feel herself shaking but kept her voice steady. "Nō hea ēnei Huia?"

"Nō konei."

"Ehara!" she yelled back at him.

Startled, he edged backwards and said something under his breath. His words flowed around and over each other like a flock of birds changing direction. They were both familiar and unfamiliar, and the effect was disconcerting.

His eyes trailed over her jumpsuit.

"He tūrehu koe?"

"Tūrehu me? Tūrehu yourself!" Ōreo was stunned that he didn't recognise her. Who was this caveman?!

"Why the hell would you think I'm a tūrehu?" Ōreo said in Māori, trying to think past the fog that gathered in her head.

His attention turned to something nearby and he signalled her to be quiet. In a smooth motion, he pulled the string of dead birds back to him and tied the cord to his belt. The chirping of the birds above was growing louder as the day lightened. He seemed to be listening to something beyond the clearing, something that Ōreo couldn't isolate from the frenzy of chattering bird talk.

She became aware again of how cold it was, her thin jumpsuit sucking it all in. She wanted to get moving; to go home. If she could convince the man to let her have the birds, she'd be out of there. Her eyes drifted back to the dead huia now hanging from his belt, wondering why they hadn't been able to determine the genetic mechanisms underpinning the wattle colour. The memory felt undefined like a doughy ball, changing shape as she pressed for it. Out of the many obstacles they'd faced in piecing together a genome for kōhuia, orange wattles seemed minor. They used chimera kōkako, with huia DNA from museum specimens inserted into their primordial germ cells. Two chimera kōkako mated together produced kōhuia offspring, a bird the same size and shape as a huia but with blue-grey feathers and bright blue wattles.

The man whistled a crisp bird call that cut through the cold

air. Ōreo closed her eyes to listen closer – the sound indistin-
guishable from any made by a bird. A moment later, an identical
call was returned from only a few metres away. A large female
huia hopped onto the lowest branch of a young sapling.

Ōreo looked on, her brain struggling to keep up. The movements of this bird were slower than kōhuia. The kōhuia tended
to act and sound more like kōkako who liked to ghost through
the forest, but this bird seemed more curious than wary. Kōhuia
also flew more than their huia ancestors who preferred to fly
short distances from tree to tree or hop along the ground. Ōreo
forced herself to look away from the huia and back at the man.
Both of them, relics from the past, as if *she* was the one out of
place.

In a quick movement, the man picked up a thin shaft on the
ground that Ōreo hadn't noticed before. Fluid, the spear left his
hand on a path towards the huia. She leaped forward to intercept
it, and the spear embedded itself in the palm of her hand. In the
corner of her eye, she could see it jutting out.

The man looked bewildered as he edged towards her, his
palms raised. The nerves in her hand prickled, sending shock
waves up her arm. She forced herself to look down and saw
that the stick, about seventy centimetres long, was more like a
long dart than a spear. Ōreo sunk to the ground, feeling woozy.
As he grabbed her hand, the sharp smell of wood smoke and
feathers floated around her. The spear was wedged into the fatty
pad of her thumb, the tip protruding about two centimetres. He
dropped her hand to rest in her lap while he looked through the
contents of his belt. It was woven from harakeke only one or two
millimetres thick. The single piece was folded into the centre
four times to create a pouch, and the ends plaited together to

make the belt tie. He pulled out a thick pad of soft moss that she recognised as angiangi, along with a shell filled with a fatty balm or gel. She wanted to inspect it, but the man picked up her hand again and gave the spear a quick tug. Blood filled the hole but didn't spill over. He dipped the moss into the balm and then pressed it to the hole in her hand.

"Māu e pupuri," he said.

She held the moss to the wound and felt it throb in response to the pressure.

Inside the folded belt was a bundle of soft-looking leather strips that Ōreo thought might be bird skin. She noticed scars, criss-crossed pink lines against his dark skin as if sharp claws had torn at him. He was older than she'd initially thought, seeing lines appear around his eyes and across a concerned forehead.

"Nō hea koe?" She forced herself to ask.

He glanced at her then shook his head, speaking slowly as if she might not understand.

"Kāore au mō te kī atu, he tūrehu kē koe."

"I'm not a tūrehu! My mother is Lydia Ngātapu for god's sake!" Ōreo waited for him to nod in recognition as everyone else did. Her mother – practically the princess Te Puea of genetic rescue – was well known for her work. But he said nothing while wrapping the soft leather around her hand before tucking the end under itself.

Ōreo flexed her fingers. The bandage was tight, but not enough to cut off the circulation.

Something rustled in the leaves and she saw that another huia had joined them, this one a male. The other bird – probably its partner – didn't seem at all bothered by the humans. The idea of killing one of these birds was repulsive and would be to anyone she knew – but not to this guy, who acted like she was the one being weird about it.

"What are you going to do with those birds?" She nodded towards the pile of dead huia. Ōreo had seen paintings of a time when huia lived in the tens of thousands; they had been used to make accessories, a whole head pushed through an earlobe with the body hanging behind, draped over the wearer's shoulder.

The man ignored her, turning his attention to the huia prying a chunk of soft bark from a rotten log. He called them again, the long and short notes mimicking theirs perfectly. The birds continued their foraging but seemed to keep him in their line of sight. The melody of his call started to take form in her head, each note lighting up behind her eyes. She stood up and took some shaky steps to her mother's tree, the sound digging up a memory. She was a kid at the old Pūkaha wildlife reserve standing outside the old aviary called Free Flight. A recorded voice played loudly over speakers, a mihi to the forest and its guardians. Then a bird call whistled by a man. It danced along the same notes.

"Kei te wehe au." He gathered up his things and stood. Ōreo felt a tinge of relief quickly replaced by panic; he'd be killing more birds.

"Ka hemo au i te hiakai." Ōreo blurted out. "Māku ngā huia?"

He frowned and pulled at the rope on his belt. The knot unravelled and the three dead huia landed on the ground with a thump, and he was gone. Ōreo felt an urge to go after him. It was like the man had walked out of a hole in the hillside, bringing birds along behind him. She reassured herself that once she was home and reconnected with Hiria, it would be easy to track him down. She had evidence to prove that she hadn't lost her mind in the forest, that at least was something. Dizziness hit as the pain from her hand spread through her body. Ōreo took some shaky steps around the clearing to search for her bag, remembering that the dead and defrosted kōhuia was still in there. After kicking at piles of leaf litter and ferns and finding nothing, she wondered if the man might have taken it while she slept. Although that seemed unlikely if he really thought she *was* a tūrehu.

She looked up into her mother's tree to where the waka kōiwi sat between the tightly wound vines. Her eyes wandered from branch to branch, but the deeply carved patterns were no longer visible. The box was gone. She sat at the base of the tree on her pile of fern fronds, the dead birds resting at her feet. Home was starting to feel very far away.

Ōreo sent another thought out to Hiria, a faint and feeble distress call. She'd wanted to be free of her, and that's what she imagined Hiria whispering to her now; "Anā! Kua wātea koe. That's what you wanted, wasn't it?" It occurred to her that perhaps this was all Hiria, a punishment for blocking the AI. But even Hiria couldn't simulate the pain in her hand and the deep throb in her head.

The birds lay heavy at her feet, their dead eyes covered in a watery glaze. It occurred to her that she'd never seen their real eyes before, just the plastic beads of reconstructed museum specimens. She leaned her head back hard against the tree as dots of light swam in the darkness behind her half-closed eyes. She wondered if she stayed there long enough and let the vines grow over her, a helicopter might eventually arrive carrying her mother's bones.

Ōreo knew that she needed to start walking. She stood up, using the trunk of her mother's tree to steady herself and slung the birds over her shoulder. The forest grew darker with each downhill step, and by midday, the sun barely pierced through the leaves. Although her eyes couldn't see much, her ears soaked in the multitude of bird conversations layering the air, dense and spectacular. The path had also become very narrow, and Ōreo had to put one foot in front of the other to stay on it. It was unreasonable to think the place was different, except it was. The severity of the darkness reminded her of descriptions of the forest before it was burned out of existence, such as the need for torches while the daylight was restrained beyond the canopy. She wondered again if Hiria could have orchestrated this situation. Although she did like to punish in the form of snarky comments, this was beyond her scope, as an AI she lacked the purpose.

The simulated environments that Ōreo had experienced were just like any other story, you choose to be immersed in it and could opt out at any time. There was no opt out of this scenario that Ōreo could see.

By the time Ōreo reached the area that should have been the car park with signposted directions to the different whare within the kainga, she didn't expect it to be there. From the hill behind where the small village had been, she saw columns of grey smoke against the darkening pink sky, signs of another papa kainga. Given the tūrehu status she'd earned with the man, approaching the village seemed like a bad idea. The three huia were heavy. They pulled her towards the ground and the rope had rubbed her shoulder raw. Hunger punched at Ōreo's stomach, echoed by the ache in her hand. She thought about how she'd lied to the man about wanting to eat the birds when in reality she'd eat her own wounded hand first. This wasn't reality though was it? Not hers anyway.

There was an area further up the hill that she knew well, large boulders piled onto the hillside. Ōreo and her cousins played behind the rocks as kids. She would go there, make a fire and, maybe even, cook the huia over it.

DEATH CONFETTI

ZOË MEAGER

Death actually just climbed into the cannon himself, so that was pretty profound and everything. Before he got in, he stood there for a moment admiring the view from the end of the New Brighton Pier. Everything smelled of fish guts and we'd all just sung *Auld Lang Syne* and everything had gone quiet; even the seagulls were looking at us sideways. I was thinking *We should have got him to climb into the cannon as we were singing, or got him to climb in and then sung and then BOOM, but not this, this is just awkward*. Then Tim, who was in charge of lighting the fuse, said "Rotary hoe then," which made it worse, and then Death whipped off his cloak and stood there, balls to the sea, his arms flung up and his cloak whip-whopping away across the waves. His skeleton made the shape of a large Y. Death did a couple of knee-bends and rattled into the cannon. "Yay," came his wee voice from inside the barrel, "I'm excited as, thanks guys!" Death had really come to terms with himself. Then he gave this dry cough and was probably thinking *There's still time, I could jump out and scythe a few of these pricks before I go*, and no one would have blamed him, I mean, would you? We all wanted him dead, basically. Tim flicked his Bic and the fuse was lit, we got a big

BOOM and a billion shattered pieces of Death burst out in a fiery spasm. When the scythe shot out still intact, we thought *Ooh, that could do some damage.* There was this dude thrashing around in a wetsuit a couple of dozen metres out, and then, no dude. Death would have smiled at that, we thought. From the sandy shore a dog barked vigilantly and alternately, at one half of the dude, then the other, while all the little bits of Death floated down around us. Black snow landing on our eyelashes and bejandaled toes, black snow sifting into the crevices of our stubbies and glancing off the brims of our beers. We each of us got a different part. Graeme got a dot in the shape of a V-Dub Beetle on his cheek – his beauty mark, he called it. Mine was stuck on that fleshy pad between finger and thumb and looked just like a full-stop. "What're the ladies up to?" Andy asked, spinning Death's watch around and around his wrist. "Are they seeing theirs?" And I said, "Yeah, quality time for them too I guess," but I didn't say anything more. I knew they were meeting Her in the dapples of Thomson Park, and it wasn't the kind of thing they wanted blabbed around.

FOR WANT OF HUMAN PARTS

CASEY LUCAS

A woman takes the subway most mornings. She wears bold, bright colours. She curls her hair. She is beautiful, smooth, and human, and her skin is flush with veins and her veins are flush with life. Bone Pile watches her go from its place in the storm drain, a backlog of washed-up parts and autumn leaves and trash. The woman always arrives when the hands on the clock across the street are pointing at certain angles. Some days Bone Pile is lucky and she walks past its resting place twice.

The woman cuts down the street in her high-heeled shoes and descends to St. Patrick Station with her blood-red lipstick and victory rolls. The flare of her skirts and the streak of her eyeliner remind Bone Pile of a bygone era, not that it knows what a bygone era is. But something about her feels like home. Like a place Bone Pile can still remember.

It has to meet her.

But in order to meet her, it must rebuild itself. For years it has rattled through gutters and drains, scuttling through tunnels and pipes to avoid the wary eyes of humans. To escape the glare of the sun. So few of its original parts are left, and it does not know where on its journey it even lost them.

Some time ago, Bone Pile tumbled down into this place, washed through gutter after gutter until enough pieces tumbled inside to lodge in this grate. This gave Bone Pile, for the first time in decades, a view to the outside world. The world has changed since Bone Pile walked alive upon it, and in what remains of its brain, Bone Pile attempts to reconcile the fragments of its memories with this too-new too-fast too-bright reality.

Bone Pile waits until dark. Then, with a shudder, it stretches free of the plastered wads of leaves and newspaper that have cocooned it to the storm drain's wall. The flaky stuff peels away, cracking, and with a creak and a flex Bone Pile uncurls. It is a slithering length of vertebrae woven through with old hair and garbage, curls of ribcage clinging stubbornly amid the mess. Its jaw flaps uselessly, the mandible swaying low and detached from what remains of its caved-in skull. Four cracked knuckles grip and twitch as it tests its strength.

Bone Pile needs another hand.

Out into the dark and silent street it sends its seeking ribs. Twisted together with knots of rotted cloth, its ribcage scuttles spider-like out into the night. Bone Pile watches it go. Each skittering step the ribs take saps more energy from Bone Pile until it slouches, exhausted, resting its cracked and battered brow against the concrete. Go, it tells its ribs. I will be here when you return.

Ribcage is careful as it creeps across the asphalt. It remembers the time it strayed too close to living eyes. The shrieks, the stomps, the feeling of being disarticulated and kicked to pieces by a frenzied, terrified human.

Discarded in a gutter, fabric shredded by the wind, lies an umbrella. Ribcage feels along its aluminium fingers, testing the strength of its joints. It delights at the spring and snap of the hinge mechanism that pops the umbrella open, the squeal of metal as it bends.

This will do.

*

Bone Pile strokes Ribcage with its remaining fingers after Ribcage drags the umbrella home. With patience, it peels the fabric into strips and binds its sagging joints. It assimilates the material, strains against it, testing the bounds of its supports. Cracking the umbrella's metal frame, breaking it down into its base parts, it sheaths metal rods into its skeleton, twisting them just so, sliding them up and in past rubber-band tendons and bottle-cap joints.

Bone Pile curls against itself, nestling among the newspapers, and sleeps. Sleep will knit its new body together, and when it wakes it will be stronger.

*

For the next four days, the woman with the blood-red lips does not appear. It has been so long since Bone Pile was alive that it does not miss life, but it finds it misses her.

Over those four chilly autumn nights, Bone Pile prepares. It gathers more into itself: the cracked remnants of a push-broom make a serviceable leg, woven through with bungee cords salvaged from a dumpster. It can crawl through the pipes with ease now, broadening its search for new pieces, so that when the woman returns it will be ready.

At the bottom of a plunging sewer shaft, it discovers scattered metatarsals and the fractured halves of a kneecap. Bone Pile cradles the patella in its new, creaky-umbrella hand and wonders:

Was this a part of me?

It is now.

*

When the woman with the blood-red lips finally returns, Bone Pile shudders with relief. The hands on the clock say the right time now, and it now remembers what those hands mean: eight twenty. She is wearing a brilliant purple peacoat. The wool of it looks soft. Bone Pile longs to touch it. It drags its scratchy push-broom foot along the tunnel wall, rasping, and a thought occurs in the remnants of its mind: her clothes are beautiful. Bone Pile needs clothes.

The clothes that find their way into Bone Pile's domain will not do. Their colours are drab, faded by sun and drowned in sewage. This far below ground, everything seems to end up brown. Bone Pile needs eyes that can see more colours than brown, so it gorges itself on rats and strings together a garland of their nerves, tiny eyeballs peeking every which way, and dons them as a crown. It can see in all directions now.

Come sundown, Bone Pile shivers up to the streets.

The best place to find human clothing is on humans.

Humans have hurt Bone Pile before, but it does not want to hurt them. It rasps its way free of the storm drain, levering slowly on its new-found joints until it can hunch in against itself, a protective crouch. There are no humans in sight.

Seeking with its many new-found eyes, Bone Pile comes across a human who seems to be resting. She leans against the door of a car, speaking loudly to someone unseen. She is wearing a charcoal-coloured raincoat and a plush blue plaid scarf. The wool of the scarf looks so soft that Bone Pile momentarily both remembers and misses what it feels like to have skin.

Bone Pile is certain it remembers how to speak. It will ask the woman for her coat and her scarf.

"TSSSSSSSSSSSSSS," hisses Bone Pile from its semblance of a mouth.

The woman looks up. For a moment she stares, as if she cannot quite comprehend what she is seeing, then she screams until she's out of voice. Bone Pile reaches out, an attempt to assure the woman that it means her no harm. Its fingers just barely touch the woollen yarn of that bright blue scarf and the moment of contact sends the woman into a spasm of motion.

Still screaming, the gurgling inner-workings of a human throat too complicated for Bone Pile, she thrashes free of those comforting hands and stumbles off down the street. She screams the word "MONSTER" into the glowing box she holds inside her hand. A voice rattles back, too far away to understand, and it sounds like the radio.

Radio. Bone Pile remembers the radio. Voices and music carried from faraway places to its waiting ears, ears that could once hold earrings and whispers both. Somewhere there's music, how faint the tune.

The scarf dangles from Bone Pile's fingers. It did not mean to scare her.

As it turns to shuffle home, Bone Pile catches sight of itself in the side mirror of the car. The tangled, tufted skull, the dangling toothless jaw, the coronet of eyes. Bone Pile needs a better face. It snaps the mirror from the car with a single twist of its umbrella-hinge hand and clambers downward, towards home. It thinks about radio as it collapses into sleep.

*

Radio wasn't always yelling voices that sounded far away. Sometimes, radio was the crack of a baseball bat and the sounds of thousands cheering. During the best times, radio was music.

Bone Pile feels ready. It does not internalise the word monster. It refuses. It internalises music. Or perhaps it simply remembers. Les Paul and Mary Ford. The Tennessee Waltz. Elvis Presley. Those words rattle in its head like a handful of loose teeth.

The next time it sees the woman with blood-red lips, Bone Pile will say hello.

*

When it finally sees her, the shiver that quakes through Bone Pile is almost enough to dislodge a couple bottle caps. But it straightens itself out. It curls its fingers, digging at the wall in an attempt to soothe its anxiety. Nerves roil where its stomach might once have been. Fluttering blinks strobe down its crown of eyes. Bone Pile adjusts the scarf about its throat, covers its half-hinged jaw, and takes a moment to trace its bony phalanges over its newly-acquired face.

Bone Pile shuffles to the storm drain, watching the woman's feet. Today she is wearing neon orange heels that click-clack pleasantly with her every step, and the sound of it is music to Bone Pile's sensory organs.

It seeks its feelers out through the grate to greet her.

"TSSSSSSSSSSSSS," hisses Bone Pile.

The woman keeps walking. She doesn't even look down.

She walks right past the grate as if she hadn't heard a thing.

Something cracks in Bone Pile's chest, near where it has built itself a sternum from an old bicycle seat. Bone Pile remembers this part of being alive: the sting of rejection, the cold creeping loneliness of going unnoticed. Of trying and being ignored.

Bone Pile needs a voice.

*

Bone Pile finds its voice in a human's purse. A couple of them sit, drunk, on a curb. They're mashing their mouths together, hands wandering places that hands wouldn't have gone in public back when Bone Pile was a human, and frustration tightens the hitches of Bone Pile's bungee cords and whistles through its empty throat like steam through a kettle. It surges at them, wailing, frustrated, but the hollow tube of its debris oesophagus merely hisses air.

"TSSSSSSSSSSS."

Horrified, screaming, the humans stumble away in such a hurry that they leave all their belongings behind.

Bone Pile sinks atop the things they've left, subsuming them. It feeds on half-finished hamburgers left in two brown paper bags: meat and carbohydrates and paper, a rich feast of proteins. It gropes its human bone fingers through the woman's handbag, exploring the interior, the many shapes inside that are familiar yet not.

Down the pipes, lurking out of sight, Bone Pile weaves itself a set of vocal cords from dental floss. It jingles a set of keys in its umbrella-claw fingers, remembering what keys felt like in a human appendage. Keys lead to places. Keys open things.

Bone Pile remembers walking through a door. A man was waiting on the other side. Bone Pile was so excited to meet him. A stirring of excitement it has never felt for anyone but the woman with blood-red lips.

Bone Pile may be a monster, but more and more these days, it remembers when it was not.

"How high the moon ... is the name of the song ... how high the moon." Bone Pile sings, the minty fresh twang of its dental-floss voice like the crunch of dry leaves underfoot.

*

Bone Pile cannot work up the nerve to sing to the woman when it first sees her. Too much morning. Too much light. Too many others who might see. It lets her walk past. If she takes the subway home that evening, today will be the day. Something inside its dregs gives a nervous quiver and it shivers up from the storm drain and down a nearby alley, waiting.

The sky has long since grown dark when Bone Pile spots the woman once more. She walks up from St. Patrick Station in that brilliant purple coat again, and before Bone Pile can contain itself, it's jingling the keys to get her attention. Its hand trembles, eager, and she jerks her head towards the sound.

From above ground, Bone Pile can see all of her. She is more than beautiful – she is colour and sound and life. From the click of her heels to the red of her lips, she's like a glimpse into a past that Bone Pile only just now understands it had.

"H-hello," Bone Pile whispers.

The woman squints. She can't quite see into the alley, recessed from streetlamps as it is. She takes a couple steps forward. Bone Pile shivers. Please don't let her be afraid.

"Is someone there?"

Bone Pile has not had a human conversation in forty years. Bone Pile was never good at conversations to begin with. It remembers tense afternoons at home, silently working in the kitchen, praying its husband would keep to himself. Bone Pile had a husband.

"I'm here," it wheezes. It reaches for her. Reaches for a vision of itself that it had forgotten.

Oh no. No. She's screaming just like the others. Bone Pile stammers, shuffling back – it knows not to chase her, even as it aches to reassure her. The woman parts her blood-red mouth but no sound comes out. Her soft-looking skin goes pale.

"Please," Bone Pile stammers. "I won't, I won't, I won't—"

But by the time it says "hurt you" she has run off down the street. She screams more, and each scream twists through Bone Pile like a knife. Bone Pile remembers in an abstract way that it knows exactly how it feels to be stabbed. How it had real organs once, and under the right hand they shredded so easily.

Slinking, dejected, back towards home, Bone Pile does not look up. It does not realise the woman's screams have drawn attention.

"What the fuck—" A human man stands there in the alley's mouth. Bone Pile has run right into him. Either he is not so scared or he channels his fear in a way the others do not, because instead of running he charges.

Bone Pile is swept off its feet as the man tackles it to the ground. The impact is shattering. Knucklebones rattle away along the sidewalk. Bone Pile's rat-eye crown slips sideways and it goes blind.

The man strikes at it by reflex and when his fists collide with Bone Pile's body, parts fly free in a shower of detritus. The bicycle seat tumbles free of Bone Pile's chest. The dental floss frays. With a horrified groan, Bone Pile attempts to wriggle loose. The man seems to realise what he's just put his fists into, because his voice rises into a shrill wail of terror too, and for a moment he and Bone Pile are screaming together.

He swings again and this time his fist connects with Bone Pile's shiny new face, the special face it built just for today. The glass of the car side-mirror shatters. Blood erupts from the man's knuckles. He jerks back, stunned, and this is when Bone Pile can make its escape.

Lurching sideways with all its might, Bone Pile tries to drag itself towards the storm drain. Its legs are tangled with the man's, so it twists the remnants of its spine and leaves them behind. The push-broom clatters lifeless to the ground.

Shivering uncontrollably, its consciousness made animal by fear, Bone Pile retreats into the darkness of the sewers. So far from many of its parts, it grows sluggish. It can no longer see the same way that it could, missing its borrowed eyes. It feels its way deep into the dark and settles into a pool of putrid water. The flow of sewage seeps through the hole cracked in Bone Pile's skull and it misses the woman and it misses its life and every action comes slower than the last.

Bone Pile is so, so tired.

*

It is a crisp spring morning, the last grasp of winter not quite having let go. Kelly Chabot stands with her hands in her pockets, staring down the mouth of an alleyway. It leads to the back of a beauty salon. Apart from a dumpster and the cracked and broken remnants of an old broom on the ground, there isn't much to look at.

She knows exactly how many days it's been since she saw the creature. And it was a creature, she tells herself. She's certain.

One hundred and forty-nine days ago, a creature tried to lure her into this alley to…

To what?

That's the part she can't answer. She was certain it was going to kill her with those gnashing metal claws. And the smell. The smell…

But in her dreams she hears its voice. How afraid it sounded. How if anything it sounded like it was pleading with her. How the whole incident had started with a meek and gentle hello.

She took a different route to work for the longest time, but now in the spring sunlight she feels like she can face this place again. And there's nothing sinister about it at all.

Stepping out of the alley, she looks up and down the road. Sparsely populated this time of day. She turns a look across the street. The bank across the way sports a squat little clock tower which informs her it's one in the afternoon.

While her eyes are occupied by the clock tower, she trips, foot hitching on a lip of concrete on the sidewalk. She catches herself, arms akimbo, and looks down by reflex.

There in the gutter, the shards of a shattered mirror reflect her wide eyes and her startled, open mouth. Just as that same glass reflected her face when embedded in the horrifying, guts-and-garbage body of that thing. Kelly staggers back from the storm drain, far enough away that she's out of ankle-grabbing range, but now that she's come all this way she can't not look.

She crouches down, cautious, cagey, creeping forward a little at a time and peeking through the half-rotted grate. Then she sees it. She recoils in disgust when she spies a snapped-off piece of what can only be a human jawbone tangled in the leaves and trash.

Kelly does the right thing. She slips her phone out of her pocket and calls the police.

*

It's doubtful anyone will ever figure out how Ingrid Martel died, but at least they found enough teeth to identify her by, even if it took almost a year.

Kelly stands outside Batham and Sons Funeral Home in Five Points. There are few cars in the parking lot and the elegant wooden doors are propped invitingly open, as if in silent supplication to passers-by. A plea to fill the pews, to not let this woman's final procession pass through an empty room.

Ingrid Martel doesn't have many living relatives. The daughter who submitted her missing persons report died back in ninety-nine. And the more Kelly thinks on it, the more she supposes that even being blood related to Ingrid might mean little to people these days. She vanished so long ago. None of the people inside this building ever met her.

And Kelly doesn't know her either. So why is she even here?

She can't explain it. The strange tug she feels in her stomach when she thinks back to that night in the alley, the gleaming metal hand outstretched towards her.

She wants to look inside. She imagines the interior of the funeral home, all warm-toned wood and tasteful flowers. Lilies, maybe. She imagines a portrait of Ingrid in a glossy wooden frame: a blond-curled beauty with a gentle smile and shy eyes. She imagines all this while standing on the street outside because she can't bear to take that first step through the door.

When she closes her eyes, she sees a hand outstretched towards her own. A hand of snapped-off mangled metal and garbage. It is crazy – it is absolutely stark raving bonkers – to think that Ingrid beckoned her into that alley somehow.

Yet when Kelly steps into the parlour, she can't stop staring at the coffin. She imagines the bones inside, wonders just how many the police had found.

She wonders whether they are truly inert.

HOW TO GET A GIRLFRIEND (WHEN YOU'RE A TERRIFYING MONSTER)

MARIE CARDNO

In the constantly changing void of the Endless Dimension, there is no such thing as *people*. There is only one person – or perhaps 'being' would be a better word. The constant, hungering entity that both is and fills the entire dimension: the Endless itself. Fragments of the Endless sometimes fracture off, spattering free like bubbles in a galactic pot of porridge, but they are quickly absorbed again, and anything they learned or thought or felt while they were separated is gobbled back up into the hungering one-ness.

Except for one.

She didn't remember how it had happened. One moment, she hadn't been anything at all; the next, she was. She'd had *edges*. Something between the Endless and this new, separate thing that was *her*. And with those edges and this new her-ness, a sudden and desperate desire not to be sucked back into eternal obscurity.

The Endless wanted her back, no question about that. But she (she! An individual!) was still very small, and so long as she didn't *do* anything particularly noticeable, it was apparently difficult for the Endless to notice her.

The first time an interdimensional portal opened into the Endless, Trillin thought it would provide good cover. The portal was very noticeable; next to it, she was even more invisible. Even when the Endless manifested enormous eyeballs to peer at the portal, its gaze slid over her as though she didn't exist.

Excellent.

She didn't pay much attention to the portal the first few times it popped in and out of existence after that. It was enough that it attracted attention away from her, as she experimented with her edges and what she could do with the body – *her* body – inside them.

Until, one day, just as she had succeeded in creating a tentacle and was waving it around, the portal flared. The rippling surface between the five points that outlined its shape against the Endless changed colour as a shadow formed at its centre. The shadow darkened, grew larger, and something pushed through from the other side.

Not something. Trillin's edges sparked. A … a *someone.*

A someone with a flattish, paleish face, one blunt nose, two lidded eyes and a crest of dark hair. The bottom half of her face split, but not like aspects of the Endless split, forming and reforming along seams that changed position from moment to moment. This was an existing hole in the face, stretching wide as she stepped through the portal. Stepped through on legs. A body! A living body that moved through the world without changing its form!

Trillin was suddenly, horribly self-conscious. She manifested an eyeball on the end of her tentacle and used it to look down at herself. Her body was … not like the newcomer's. It had too many limbs to start with. Small, skittery limbs. She'd made a lot for practice, but now they were too many.

And now it had too many eyes, too, if the two that the new-comer had were the number people were meant to have.

And a tentacle.

The newcomer didn't have *any* tentacles.

She skittered down until only her tentacle-eye was visible over the solid surface that had formed in front of the portal. From there, she watched as the strange new being twisted its head this way and that, its mouth still stretched wide and its eyes darting around as though it was searching for something.

"Fantastic," the creature breathed, and stepped back through the portal.

Trillin's heart thudded. She suddenly had a heart to thud. It seemed to fill her entire body.

All at once, she knew two things.

First, she needed to make herself a better body.

Second ... she *had* to see that creature again.

Despite being separate from the Endless, Trillin still had its memories. At least, as many of them as could fit in her far smaller mind. She rifled through them as the portal dimmed. Before long, she found what she was looking for.

The portal-creature was what was known as a *human.*

The Endless had lots of memories of humans. Most of them were consumed memories from when a part of the Endless had split off, large enough to have its own goals and be able to carry them out. Most of the time, when a piece of the Endless got that big, its goals involved breaking through to another dimension and turning its inhabitants into mindless thralls. And it seemed like the dimension where these *humans* lived was a particular favourite.

This did make it difficult for Trillin to figure out what humans were like, given most of the memories involved screaming.

Still, there was enough in the memories to give her a good idea of what to do next.

If becoming an individual was the most exciting thing Trillin had ever done, the *human* was the most exciting thing she'd ever seen. And if she wanted it to stick around for longer next time … she probably shouldn't look like the sort of beings that had spent the last couple of millennia trying to terrorise its dimension.

She wasn't sure how much time passed as she concentrated. Two jointed arms, with five bony tentacles on the end of each. Two legs, also jointed, with shorter tentacles. A sort of oblongish shape in the middle. One head, two eyes…

Trillin was in the middle of trying to figure out how the limbs connected to the oblongish middle bit when the portal began to glow again.

She had a mouth by this point, so she was able to make a strangled "Aaargh" noise as she tried to pull the rest of her new body together. Arms, she told herself. Arms and … legs … and … how did noses work? How many eyes?

The portal blooped, and the human popped through again.

Trillin's heart fluttered. The human was so … *solid.* Its limbs knew exactly where they were meant to be and how their joint-edness worked. Its eyes were incredibly non-bulbous, and not even slightly on tentacles. And they were hardly bloodshot at all! Even their colour was exotically unchanging. Trillin felt as though she could stare into them for hours and not get even a glimpse of uncanny light suggesting a hidden being staring out at her, or a bubbling, glittering madness hinting at mysteries beyond all mortal ken.

Which was perfect.

Because as Trillin's heart was telling her, if anyone was going to make this human's eyes glimmer with unearthly madness, it was going to be her.

"Woo! Houston, we have landfall!" The human looked down to where its feet were resting on a coil of the Endless, which gooped slightly. "Well. Something-fall, anyway. Wow!" It picked up her feet one by one and Trillin watched, fascinated, as the human's body readjusted itself to allow for the movement without altering its shape.

The human had a skeleton underneath, didn't it? Trillin thought about adjusting her eyes to see through the human's surrounding flesh to the bones beneath, to see how they worked, but that seemed rude. They hardly knew each other. Trillin didn't know much about human customs, but skeletons had to be private, or else why would they be so carefully wrapped up?

If she were more powerful, and the human agreed, she could arrange the human's atoms for her, make her flesh invisible or insubstantial as fog…

If she were more powerful. Trillin felt the tug of the Endless, plucking at her edges.

Anyway, even if she *were* more powerful, that seemed like more of a — Trillin hunted through the impressions she'd gathered of human customs, outside the screaming — more of a 'third date' sort of thing.

"Gidday!" the human said, stretching its mouth over its teeth. Trillin waited for the smile to stretch all the way around the human's skull, revealing teeth where no teeth should be, and felt a thrill when she realised it wasn't going to happen. The human was completely, incredibly unchanging.

And looking at her.

Trillin gulped. Her new limbs wanted to curl inwards and drag her away somewhere to hide.

But…

She wanted the human to stick around, and step one of that was *look like something worth sticking around for*, which – well, the human hadn't run screaming at the sight of her, which was a start – and step two was … was…

Conversation.

The mouth she'd created went dry. Was it meant to do that?

She tried to say 'Hello', but all that came out was a low hiss.

"Are you the welcoming committee?" the human asked chirpily. Its eyes – no, Trillin thought, cross-referencing the human's appearance against the Endless's memories – *her* eyes travelled down the body Trillin had manifested. "Nice tentacles."

Trillin looked down at herself. Her heart sank. She knew she had trouble with legs, but she'd never gotten it this wrong before.

*

Sian's skin was still tingling from stepping through the portal. All the hair on her body and possibly the hair on her head, who knows, was standing on end. She imagined each hair trying to weave itself into her spelled boilersuit, like it wanted to escape and become part of this incredible … place. She'd have to shear herself out of her clothes when she got home. That would be worth a paper, at least. *Effects of Cross-Dimensional Travel on Leg Hair and its Interactions with Longjohns.*

She couldn't stop looking around. The first few times she'd portalled in, she'd stayed long enough to test the protection spells on her clothing and take a few initial samples. This time she'd finally gotten sign-off to stay longer. To go farther into this strange world than anyone had been ever before.

Anyone who'd come out again, anyway.

Everything here was so … so exactly what previous reports of this dimension had been, if you cut out the screaming. The air, if it was air, had a strange colour that shifted between deepwater green and lurid purple; the landscape bulged and lurched and twisted, and seemed to be somehow vastly distant and awkwardly close at the same time, as though the air and the land (was it land?) were changing places, one becoming the other in less time than it took for her to take a breath of what she really hoped *was* air.

Well, she wasn't dead yet.

Anyway, the constantly wobbling landscape wasn't the only thing that had caught her eye.

It would have been lying to say she dragged her eyes away from pulsing, frond-like growths on the horizon (or were they super close? It was all a bit *Magic School Bus Explores the Digestive System,* regardless). More like she was having to drag her eyes *to* the natural world she was meant to be studying, so that she didn't look like a total creep ogling the local who was hanging around near the portal.

She was meant to be studying the landscape, not its inhabitants.

Her ethics approval didn't cover interactions with locals.

Well, it did. But all it had said was 'DANGER! DO NOT INTERACT; IF APPROACHED, RUN' and she'd already ignored half of that by saying hi to her.

And she didn't *look* dangerous.

Okay, so she'd hissed at Sian after she'd said hi, but not in a scary way.

And—

Sian forced herself to stare at an undulating length of the landscape and clenched her fists. And she was *really hot.*

She was pretty sure inhabitants of the Endless Void weren't meant to be hot.

Terrifying, yes. Evil and desirous of nothing more than to wreak havoc on Earth and turn its inhabitants into mindless thralls, yes, yes, she'd read the literature on *that*. Freakishly horrible, etc. Apparently just looking at them was enough to drive people mad.

Sian didn't *feel* mad.

At least no more than usual, her usual self being the one who had begged and bothered her department's coven head to let her do her thesis on the Endless Void. The poor woman had probably weighed up the fallout between letting her do it and probably ending up dead, and not letting her and dealing with her continued campaign of bothering, and well – here she was.

Getting the hots for a creature from another dimension.

She glanced sideways. The local – seriously, she had to come up with a better word than that, but the only alternatives from the literature were even worse and she wasn't going to go around referring to her as a 'Godless atrocity of creation', even in her own head – anyway, she was shorter than Sian, mostly humanoid, but with an odd formlessness where the parts of her face and body met. As for her clothing ... honestly, Sian wasn't sure whether the nightgown-like shape muffling her body was *actually* clothing or some sort of natural lichenous covering, and she was surprised how much she wanted to find out which it was. Her skin was a pale purple, and her hair floated around her calm, watchful face like seaweed. And her eyes...

Wow.

She'd probably have to come up with something better than that for her report, but for now, 'wow' would have to do.

Sian weighed up her options. Much like her department coven head, she thought, she could either have another go at it now, or give up and spend the rest of her life yelling at herself about it.

She sidled closer.

"So," she said, casual as. "What brings you here to the endless whatever?"

The woman stared at her with those big, shimmering eyes.

"Guess I should say what brings me here, eh? Since I'm the one who's, uh, come here."

The woman blinked at her.

"My name's Sian, by the way."

The woman's lips parted. She blinked again – and new eyes appeared above and below her existing ones, to blink as well.

Sian couldn't stop her own eyes from going wide. "Wow! Are you – you can – I mean, shit, that's probably really rude to ask about, right?"

Come on, she thought privately. That's got to do it. Doesn't everyone like a chance to tell someone else they're behaving badly?

Especially if that someone was her, in her experience.

But the other woman still didn't say anything. Her extra eyes vanished, and her mouth pinched shut. Dark splodges appeared where her eyebrows would be, if she had eyebrows.

Sian's heart sank. "Ah well," she said, trying to sound cheerful for the – shit. The recording! She'd forgotten about it. Very right-ly, her assistant Jonesy had suggested that if the Endless Void did break her mind, an audio recording would be better value than whatever she could remember herself, so she was all wired up and later she'd have to come up with an excuse not to let Jonesy transcribe her failing to flirt with an other-dimensional being. Fan-fucking-tastic.

"Nice to meet you, anyway. But I'd better get on with it, eh," she said, again for the benefit of the bloody tape, and gave the rope attached to her harness three quick tugs. The rope extended back behind her through the portal where, unless something had gone terribly wrong or his latest undergrad booze-up had finally gotten to him, her student assistant Jonesy was keeping the portal steady until she returned.

The rope twitched in her hands. Three responding tugs from beyond the portal. Jonesy was up to the mark after all. Good-oh.

Sian unclipped an anchoring rig from her harness and at-tached it to the most solid-seeming outcrop of … well, not rock, but *something* … her side of the portal. She put all her weight on it to check it would hold fast, then shot one last smile at the purple-skinned woman.

"I'll leave this in your safe hands, shall I?" she declared sunni-ly and, before she could distract herself by checking whether the woman actually had hands or not – oh, God, what a thought, and one that raised far too many other thoughts – rappelled off the side of the portal.

*

Trillin watched the human disappear down into the Endless. *Sian.* She watched *Sian* rappel down into the Endless, and all the things she hadn't said to her before she left rolled around in her mind.

Maybe it was worth becoming one with the Endless again, just to have more space to hide from the memory of how completely she'd messed that up.

Plus she wouldn't be *her* anymore. The memories wouldn't be about *her* staring at Sian like a mindless fragment while she tried to make conversation with her. That silent, staring weirdo who'd accidentally created herself some extra eyes to stare with would just be a memory of something part of her had used to be.

She sagged. She sagged further, and more squishily, than Sian would have, with her straight bones and knee joints, and she glanced down at herself to see that her legs had turned into tentacles *again*. Existence eternal, how embarrassing.

She hadn't reckoned on how difficult it would be to keep her new shape while trying to figure out how to speak, let alone what to say. Whenever she almost got to the point of maybe actually producing the words 'Hello' or 'My name is Trillin', her insides had gone all wibbly. And her outsides, too.

This was *awful*. How did other fractures of the Endless manage it? The last one that Trillin knew of, from a few centuries ago, had entranced dozens of thralls before the humans had driven it back and the Endless had sucked it up again, and she couldn't even manage to *talk* to *one*?

Not that she wanted to enthral Sian. She wanted ... something new. Something she couldn't find experience of any part of the Endless ever being, or having.

But the humans it had encountered had. A special connection between two or more of them that sometimes helped them to escape the Endless, so that instead of their memories, all the

Endless had was the shadow of them slipping out of its clutches. There was one memory in particular that the Endless didn't like, at least to the extent it liked or didn't like anything. A woman standing over what remained of a fragment of the Endless right before the whole swallowed it up again, some sort of weapon in her hand, saying over her shoulder to the man behind her: "How's *that* for girlfriend material?"

The Endless might not have liked that memory, but Trillin did.

And she wasn't going to give up. She let her tentacles collapse under her for a few more minutes, then firmly straightened them up with an internal skeletal structure – *ankles*, she told herself, *and knees* – and stood up again.

She'd have another chance to speak to Sian when she came back. Right? Yes. She must be coming back at some point, Trillin reasoned, because she was attached to the rope and the rope was attached to the portal. And when she did come back, Trillin would say … something.

Something really good.

Smart. Witty. Maybe even … alluring.

Trillin wasn't entirely sure what alluring meant, but she suspected it was a big part of being girlfriend material.

She was about to start deciding what smart, witty and/or alluring things she could say to Sian when the rope snapped.

*

Sian lobbed another fireball at the monster as it charged towards her.

Damn it, this field trip had started off *so well*. If you ignored her failed attempt to chat up the purple woman, which she was absolutely going to do.

She'd lowered herself on the rope until the glow of the portal was a dim light far above her. The air was thicker down here – still perfectly breathable, thanks to the charms woven into her gear, but *dense*. And some of the supposedly solid ledges and outcrops of rock she tried to balance herself against were disconcertingly permeable. And floating. Basically, the Endless Void dimension equalled weird shit central, which she loved.

Until she finally landed on something properly solid, and it attacked her.

Well. Fine. In the interests of full disclosure and not losing her funding when someone noticed holes in her story, it hadn't *immediately* attacked her.

It was a quadruped the size of a Toyota Hilux, seemingly made up entirely of eyeballs and teeth. She'd landed on it approximately where its shoulders would have been, except they were teeth. Teeth that moved and ground beneath her feet so that for a moment she thought she was lunch, until she realised they were moving *away* from her feet. For a moment, she was standing on craggy skin, then for another, grosser moment she was standing on an eyeball that popped out from the skin and then that, too, slid away towards the front of the creature's head.

It took her another moment to figure out why that was.

The ute-sized monster was biting at an outcrop of soil and rock. As it tore pieces off, they … changed. They didn't fall like rocks should, even taking into account the strangely solid air; they twisted and reshaped themselves and by the time they hit the ground they weren't rocks anymore. They were little creatures. Tumbling, wriggling, scuffling little beasties that looked like what a rabbit might look like, if it had forgotten what it was.

And the monster Sian had landed on was eating them.

"Oi!" she'd shouted, and kicked it for good measure. "Pick on something your own size!"

It had. Hence, fireballs.

Sian threw herself sideways as the monster barrelled towards her, using her rope to swing herself wide. She didn't see whether her fireball did anything useful, but she got a face full of muck, and the monster missed her – good enough.

She summoned another fireball and loosed it above the monster's head. A warning shot, she told herself, already sketching out her trip report. A warning shot, not meant to do any damage.

It didn't do any damage at all, as it turned out.

The fireball seemed to forget what it was the moment it left her hand. It glooped in on itself, more liquid than fire; it grew hair, and lumpen limbs, then went all watery; by the time it hit the monster, it looked like a feathery fungal growth.

The monster snuffled at it, and one of its sets of teeth slid up its side to worry it loose.

"Fascinating," Sian whispered, trying to make sense of what she'd just seen. It was as though the changing nature of the world they were in had overwhelmed the spell.

She glanced down at herself. She didn't appear to have changed at all; even as the ground shifted beneath her feet, from something that felt like mud, to clinking gravel, to snakeskin smoothness, she remained herself.

She narrowed her eyes at the monster, half wary for another charge, half just inspecting it. It was a changing thing, too, but all on a theme. Teeth. Eyeballs. Dripping, slaggy skin that turned inside-out and revealed more teeth, which made her stomach lurch.

She appreciated that. It was nice to know that she still had a stomach, and that it could lurch. Point to her; Jonesy had been sure she would be soup by now.

Of course, she could still become soup in the very near future.

Most of the tiny creatures that the big one had scraped out of the landscape had scattered. Sian wondered where they'd gone, until she saw one literally get swallowed up by the ground. She gulped.

It made sense. They'd come out of the ground, and they were going back into it. But not into holes in the ground. It was as though they were transforming back into the landscape.

As though everything here was one giant single organism, and bits could occasionally pop free but were absorbed back into it.

For some reason she thought of the woman she'd seen near the portal. Was she a part of this *everything*? Would she meld back into the landscape as easily as the rabbit-things?

But not all of them were merging back again. One of them was running towards her. If you could call it running. Stumpy legs emerged from its body, hit the ground, and folded back up into its belly, instantly replaced by new legs that kept it tumbling forwards.

It hit Sian's leg and bounced off. She picked it up.

Picking up the local wildlife was definitely not covered in her ethics approval, but she was hardly going to be able to study these things if they all got eaten or dissolved before she got a look in, right? It was a … sample.

A really cute sample. It was sort of bread-shaped, covered in soft fur and oddly wriggly, as though it hadn't yet decided what shape it wanted to be. Not like Mr Big and Teeth over there, who was still gnawing on what was left of her ex-fireball.

Not like the purple woman. She knew what shape she wanted to be, too. Human-shaped. And…

Sian frowned. Every time she'd come through the portal, testing its stability and the wards on her clothing and equipment and the whole 'Can I even breathe in here?' question, there'd been something watching her. Something, or someone, human-shaped. It hadn't been the same every time, and Sian had thought that meant it was a different being every time, but maybe…

A roar cut through the air and Sian swore.

Right. Maybe, she was busy getting lost in her own thoughts when she should really be focusing on not dying.

The teeth-monster roared again, eyeballs bursting out from its skin and focusing on her with stomach-churning intensity. Teeth glittered in every inch of space, ready to rip and tear.

The hell with it, Sian thought. She had her bunny monster – uh, sample – and she'd seen enough here that she wouldn't have to pay for her own drinks for a year at least. Time to head home.

She pulled on her rope, releasing a spell that should have shot up the length of the rope back through the portal to where Jonesy was waiting, and let him know she was ready to come back, pronto.

Instead, the rope fell loose in her hand. She stared at it in horror. It wasn't just loose, it was *falling*. Slowly, through the thick air, in big, loose loops. Something must have cut through it, far above her.

The falling rope looked unreal. It looked like a computer animation gone wonky, or like gravity wasn't working properly anymore. Some of the loops weren't even falling *downwards*. They slithered and wound through the air like a sea snake shimmering through the tides, and not at all like a good dependable way to escape the predicament she'd found herself in.

Well.

Fuck…

The monster hit her dead on. She slammed into the ground and all the air smacked out of her. Then the huge weight on her was gone. She sucked in a breath that didn't fill as much of her lungs as she had hoped, and rolled over just in time to see the monster wheel around.

It stomped its feet angrily. The falling loops of Sian's rope were tangled around it, and it seemed confused (or maybe just enraged) by the fact that the rope was keeping its form. Which it promptly dealt with by biting through it.

And Sian hadn't even stood up yet.

She formed another spell in her mind. Fireball. Right, because that had worked so well last time. She let it drop, and pulled her magic in another direction.

The landscape here had sucked up the tiny bunny-creatures. Maybe it could do the same to the tooth monster.

She focused her magic on the ground. Which was surprisingly difficult. The ground *reacted* to her magic – pulling away, then pushing close, like it wanted to get a closer look. Creepy, but maybe she could use that.

The tooth monster lowered its head. Hundreds of jaws sprouted from it, each one lined with row upon row of shark-like teeth. Sian twisted her magic – and let it go.

The shapeless wave of power rushed towards the monster, and the ground followed it.

A tonne of dirt hit the monster like a tsunami. It disappeared beneath the rubble.

Sian scrambled to her feet. Barely. She'd put everything into that last rush of magic, and that left her with…

Herself. A big empty gap where her magic wasn't. And her escape rope, her only way home, still falling, still making lazy patterns in the too-solid air.

She took a deep breath. She could replenish her magic. There had to be power here, right? How else would everything in this world keep changing? Sure, she'd prefer to stretch out in her aunt's herb garden, letting the sun and the scents of a hundred green growing things fill her with their strength, but maybe weird goopy-land magic would have to do.

She reached out – and stopped.

Whatever power was in the land here had followed her magic. Followed it like it wanted to *devour* it. Like it was as hungry as the tooth monster.

Maybe … maybe she didn't want to invite that inside herself.

She groaned and stared at the rope, which was still falling. Maybe when it all came down, she could use it to secure herself to the floating rocks and undulating cliff faces and climb back up to the portal. Yes. That sounded like a plan. And since Jonesy wasn't here to tell her it was a fucking stupid plan, she might as well think it was a good one.

She just had to wait until the rest of the rope came down.

Sian found a suitable-looking probably-a-rock and collapsed onto it. It oozed slightly beneath her, and she buried her face in her hands.

That bloody rope had better finish falling down soon. Much more of this waiting and she might have to admit that—that—

She groaned. That there was probably a reason no one had ever found their way back from the Endless Void.

That her supervisor was going to have to have a Bad Conversation with her family.

That Jonesy was right, and she really should have done more testing with equipment that could instantly broadcast back to Earth, so that at least what she'd seen here might be of some use to future researchers instead of stuck on a memory drive stuck on her corpse for the rest of eternity.

Ugh.

This was why she always jumped straight in. If things went wrong, they tended to go wrong fast, and either she fixed them fast or, she'd always assumed, things went worst-case-scenario fast and then there was no point worrying about it.

She'd always managed to fix things fast in the past.

She'd never expected worst-case-scenario to be so *slow*.

Or the only fix she could see being so slow either, she reminded herself, because there *was* still a potential fix. Climb back up. You know, just freeclimb a few hundred metres of constantly moving vertical landscape. Easy.

The ground shifted. Sian lifted her head in time to see the mass of rubble where the landscape had swallowed the tooth monster begin to move.

More normal-to-this-dimension changes, Sian told herself.

Then the monster burst out.

Sian was on her feet before her brain registered more than an *oh, fuck*. The tooth monster wasn't dead. It was hugely, screamingly alive, and instead of melting into the rubble as it fought free, the rubble was melting into *it*. Making it bigger.

"Aargh," Sian said, eloquently. She tried to walk backwards, and fell over the rock she'd just been sitting on. The monster shook its head slowly from side to side. Its eyes didn't move at the same speed as the rest of it but slowly, they all focused on her.

"Aargh," Sian said, more quietly.

She was still cradling the bunny creature under one arm. It squeaked as she tucked it down the front of her boilersuit, then stayed still, a warm, trembling weight inside her shirt.

"All right," she said, clenching her jaw to stop her teeth chattering as she stared up at the monster. "Let's try this again."

The monster rushed her. She got out of the way – just – but it was bigger this time, and instead of slowing its charge and stopping before it turned, it spun on the spot. Sian was still trying to pull together a plan – she had no magic left, but maybe she could grab the rope, try to tie the thing up or choke it. But how could you choke something that changed its form as easy as breathing? God, she should have taken Jonesy up on his suggestion that she learn how to shoot, and brought along that old shotgun he lifted from his mum's farm—

And then there was no time to plan. The monster attacked; Sian ran, and feinted, and tried to get away, but she could already see how this was going to go.

She was getting tired. The monster wasn't.

And this really wasn't as fast an end as she might have hoped for.

She picked up a rock, meaning to use it as a weapon, and it squeaked and wriggled in her grasp. She dropped it, feeling sick. She couldn't use a living thing as a weapon – and not just because the monster would probably just eat it and become even bigger.

All she had left was the rope. She hefted a length of it, as though there was anything useful she could do with it, and the monster reared above her.

Just as she thought everything was over, something plummeted down from the sky and crashed straight into the monster.

*

She hadn't meant to land *on* the other fragment.

It had been bad enough trying to keep hold of herself as she fell through the Endless. She'd almost lost a limb to a sudden mist of Endless intention, and had fallen tentacle-first into the first whispers of fragmentary thoughts and plans all their own. Her awareness had stretched out, the edges becoming fuzzy as the line between *her* and *all* began to blur. She'd had to hold tight to *her*. As tightly as she was holding on to the end of the rope.

At one point she'd bounced off something and it had exploded into a thousand feathered snakes. She'd been tempted to absorb some of them – she was still so much smaller than most other things in the Endless – but then she'd fallen past them and it was probably a bad idea, anyway. Even if she was doing the absorbing rather than being absorbed, who knew what else she would pick up from them?

It occurred to her shortly after that she could have created wings for herself instead of just falling, but by then it was too late. She landed directly on the brutish fragment of the Endless that was standing over her human.

And it exploded.

All her tightly held edges splattered at the impact.

Hunger.

The creature she'd exploded into didn't have a mind, as such, but it had wants. It was all want. All consuming, hungering want, to eat and devour and become bigger so it could eat bigger things and become even bigger.

It felt … familiar.

Like parts of the Endless had been this before.

Trillin struggled to keep herself intact. But she was so much bigger than before. The bit of body she'd formed and reformed for herself was so much smaller than what she was now. And that was the only bit of body that was used to holding her mind. Used to keeping her mind what it had been, not –

She had been here a long time. Eating. Finding things to eat. She had been about to eat a small thing, newly scraped from the Endless, and then something bigger and better had come along…

They made eyes and stared out at the human.

Hunger.

They made teeth.

Hunger.

The human stepped back, but – it had done that before, too. They knew how to deal with that. Move faster. Wear it out. More work than the small things but a bigger feast.

Eat—

No!

Something rose up inside them, determined and angry. It wasn't *food*. It wasn't just any human. It was *her* human!

Trillin folded herself into existence. The hunger fell away. The rest of her body did, too, sloughing off the shape that was *hers* and melting back into the Endless.

She looked down at her human, with her own two eyes, which were in her human-shaped head.

Her human looked back, eyes wide and … somehow starry, although they hadn't changed their colour.

"Wow," Sian breathed. "That's a hell of a trick."

Trillin had her body back. Her human was alive. Now she just had to make some words.

"I ... sss…" she began.

Something moved on the human's chest. Her clothing bulged, and something pressed out from beneath the collar. Something furry and soft-looking.

Trillin couldn't help the disappointment that cut through her. "You changed," she said, and suddenly the words came too easily. "I thought you wouldn't. I've never known anyone who hasn't changed before."

"Changed?" Sian's eyebrows went up. She didn't seem to even notice the new part of herself until it pushed another head out from under her shirt. She tucked her human chin down to look at it. "Oh, this wee guy? No, he's not attached. Shit. I hope not."

She pulled it out and showed Trillin that the furry thing was another fragment, not part of herself succumbing to the Endless.

"Cute, eh? That, uh … the other guy was trying to eat it."

"Cute?"

Trillin stared at the fragment. It was tiny, and fluffy, and had made itself six tentative legs and two furry antennae on top of its head. It had one eye, then three, and settled on six.

It was too small to have a mind of its own. Trillin wondered if it even had desires of its own, like the creature she'd almost absorbed. Or maybe it was just a tiny bundle of fuzz, content to be carried around by its human.

Sian dug her fingers into its furry coat, and Trillin thought for a moment that she was trying to absorb it, but the fingers and the fuzzy crumb of Endless stayed distinct. Whole. Touching, but separate.

A new sensation stabbed through her. Why had she made

herself so big? Maybe if she'd been as small as the … cute … thing, Sian would—

The crumb stretched into the human's touch and formed a mouth to make a happy trilling sound.

"How did you do that?" she asked.

"What, giving it a scritch? Everything likes a scritch," Sian said, and added to the crumb: "You're like a cat, aren't you? Or a rabbit. A cat-rabbit. With, uh, lots of eyeballs. Which seems to be a trend, round these parts. Which reminds me of another trend, which is me distracting myself with dumb shit instead of focusing on what's important."

She looked up at Trillin, her eyes suddenly bright and sharp and somehow the same as ever. "Thank you," she said, her voice catching. "You just … saved my life. Out of nowhere. And I don't know who you are, or why you would do a thing like that, but … thank you."

Trillin ran through all her borrowed and inherited memories and couldn't find anything to say that didn't make her want to curl herself up into a tiny ball and roll away to safety. She couldn't laugh maniacally at Sian. Or turn herself into a duplicate of her, and taunt her. That would be … wrong.

"Oh. That's okay," she said, and then, after a few seconds of horrible silence: "My name is Trillin."

"I didn't think anything here had names," Sian said and then groaned and clutched her face in one hand. "Oh, for … that was awful. I'm sorry. To start with, that should've been any*one* here, and obviously people here have names if *you* have a name, and I just … there is a reason my supervisor very strongly suggested I run like hell rather than interact with anyone here and maybe it's got more to do with me being the world's worst diplomat than her being worried about me ending up an Endless chew toy." She groaned again. "Which is also ... probably ... bad thing to say..."

"But you're right," Trillin said. "The Endless doesn't have a name and fragments usually don't last long enough to have them. I made mine up."

Sian lowered her hand. "It's a very nice name," she said, her lips stretching very slightly.

She felt warm. "And most other fragments would try to eat you," she reassured her.

"Uh, cool. I mean, I do try to give the benefit of the doubt... Fragments?"

"Pieces that break off the Endless. Like me, and..." She gestured towards the crumb in Sian's arm. "And..." There was nothing left of the bigger fragment to gesture at, but Sian caught on.

"That big bastard?"

Trillin nodded. "The Endless doesn't want. Not much. Just to be all one thing. But when pieces fall off, they want things – to be more, or stronger, or just to be apart from the Endless as long as they can..."

"Sheesh." Her eyes flicked from the crumb, to Trillin, to the patch of Endless that Trillin was standing on, and – slowly – back up to Trillin. It was amazing, Trillin thought, how her eyes and her face could change so much without changing shape at all. "And which of those do you come under?"

This was another of those moments that seemed to require her to say something smart, witty, or alluring.

What did she want?

"I've been watching you," she said, in the absence of anything that fit under the headings smart, witty or alluring. To her surprise, Sian grinned.

"Aha," she said. "So I'm not the only creep around here. Good to know. I've been watching you too, or at least I think I have. It was you, wasn't it, at the portal?"

Trillin nodded. She concentrated on the gesture, creating it using an internal skeletal and muscular structure she formed just for the purpose, and then ruined it by sprouting the wings that would have been more useful when she was falling.

Sian stared at her. "Wow."

"I didn't mean to—"

"How can you do that? Everything here is so *changeable* and I've seen creatures separate from the landscape and melt back into it, and that big one was all about the teeth and eyeballs, but you can change your form and stay the same? The same person?"

"Changing is easy. It's staying the same that's so hard." She concentrated, and pulled the wings back in.

"Why would you want to stay the same?"

Trillin stared. New eyes opened on her forehead, the better to stare with, and she squeezed them shut and away. "Because I—"

She stopped.

She didn't *know* why.

Because Sian didn't change? Because the Endless was all-changing, all the time, and she was a fragment who didn't want to be a part of the Endless anymore?

No. Because humans didn't change, and the only humans she'd ever seen fall in love had fallen in love with other, unchanging humans. How could Sian ever like her if she was as changeable as the rest of the Endless?

"It had better not be on my account." Sian's grin widened. "I like the ways you change."

Heat rose all over Trillin's skin. Its colour changed, deepening, and fine opalescent feathers rose above the warmth.

Sian's eyes were starry again. "Like that," she breathed. She moved closer to Trillin. "Do you—" she began, more hesitantly than Trillin had heard her ever before, "I mean, you say you've been watching me – and you wanted to talk to me up by the portal, didn't you? And you saved my life, and – that was incredible, honestly, and you're – I mean, I've never heard of it happening before, but most of the records we have are more on the death and destruction side of things than anything … anything like…"

A ripple through the Endless interrupted her.

In her arms, the crumb squeaked.

"… or, on second thoughts, maybe this is a conversation that can wait until I'm standing on slightly more solid ground." Sian moved her feet uncertainly.

"Even if you find more solid ground, it won't stay that way. And … it won't help." Trillin's body had developed some new organs by itself, and one of them was twisting.

"Won't help?" Sian shivered and patted the crumb. "What *was* that? It felt like being in the middle of a muscle cramp. *In* the muscle."

"You're drawing attention." Trillin hadn't intended to change her voice, but the words came out in a whisper. Bristles poked up from her shoulders.

"Good attention?"

Trillin didn't think she'd done anything to her face but when Sian looked at her, her mouth flattened.

"Bad attention," Sian corrected herself. "Shame about my escape plan." She flicked the length of rope still attached to her harness, then flinched as the Endless squeezed around them again. "Was kinda counting on being able to find my way back to the one way out of here. Even before the bad attention, which … what?"

Trillin felt, undeniably, the eye of her former and future existence turning towards them both.

"The Endless. It can sense that something is here that doesn't belong here."

"The Endless? Is that – some sort of entity that this whole dimension is named after? And it's trying to squeeze me out?"

"Not … exactly."

Sian stared at her. "I'm going to need a bit more detail here."

"The Endless *is* this dimension. All of it. Any fragments you see, like me, or your…" She hunted through her memories for small, fluffy things. "… your pet, we're pieces of the Endless."

"Fragments. Pieces that broke off. But you mean that everything … *everything* here is the Endless?"

"Yes, and—"

"So it already knows where I am? There's no escaping it?"

"No, and no. And it's not only you it's after." Sian looked at her sharply and her spines quivered. "It's after me, too. Because I'm not meant to be *me*. Or if I want to be, there should be more of me. Enough that I can leave some of myself behind if I need to, to get away, and still have enough left to be me."

"God I wish I had time now to dig into this," Sian breathed, eyes shining. "Leave some of yourself behind? We always assumed the beings who came through to Earth were … but you're saying they're all part of one entity? One entity that wants them back? So it couldn't have—"

Water was sprouting from Sian's forehead. She glanced down

at something attached to her wrist, and wiped her face. The water smeared.

Trillin moved closer to her. "You said you wished you had time now, but you are talking about it, after all."

"I am, aren't I?" Sian's voice cracked. "Oh, hell. At least I'm not dissolving." She shot Trillin a look. "Or should that be, at least I'm not dissolving yet? Becoming a part of this place?"

Trillin shook her head slowly. "I don't ... I don't think that's how it happens," she said. "But we need to go. The Endless is very big, so it's difficult for it to sense exactly where we are. That's why it is—" Another ripple squeezed her edges. "—doing that."

"It's pinpointing our location."

"Finding the pieces of itself that don't move with it. That have our own edges."

"So dissolving might help in that case." Sian raised a hand before Trillin could disagree. "No, obviously not. But..." She twisted her neck to look up where she'd come. "My magic's still bust, but I might be able to – I don't know, freeze handholds into it, or..."

"I know another way out."

*

Another way out. Joy to her ears. In the current situation, at least.

Trillin was leading her through the Endless. Through the single organism that she was walking on and breathing in, and that kept squeezing itself around her, like an oyster trying to worm out a pearl, or whatever it was oysters did.

She couldn't tell how far they were moving. If her feet weren't stepping one in front of the other, she might have thought they weren't moving at all. The Endless kept changing around them and she had no way of locating herself within it.

She had to trust that Trillin was telling her the truth.

And somehow, she did.

"Another portal?" she asked as she leapt across a pit that turned out to be more solid than the 'ground' either side. "Aargh!"

"A small one."

Sian whistled. "That's – terrible news in the grand scheme of things, and great news right now. And it comes out…?"

Wings unfurled from Trillin's back and she hovered over the pit. "On Earth."

Sian got the idea she couldn't be any more specific than that. Well, that would just have to be good enough. It wasn't as though she'd be able to give directions to any particular spot of the Endless if the situation was reversed, anyway.

They kept running, and the pulses of attention grew stronger. Was it her imagination, that now that she knew they were the work of some massive consciousness, the pulses felt alive?

She shared her thoughts with Trillin. And her thoughts about oysters. Then explained what an oyster was.

"But instead of spitting us out it wants to make us part of it again," Trillin said.

She didn't like the sound again.

"Or not again," Trillin mused. "It would be making you a part of it anew. Everything you are, everything you remember, becoming part of it."

Her voice sounded nearer, and Sian turned her head to see – oh, how incredible – her mouth had actually moved around her head. No need to turn around or anything; just send your mouth a bit closer. Incredible. How much she could learn about this place, if she wasn't currently running for her life.

Unfortunately, being so intrigued by *how* Trillin was talking didn't distract her from what she was saying.

"*Everything?*" she asked.

"Memories, hopes, fears…" Trillin's eyes slid around to look at her as she ducked under a strange growth.

"So it would learn about you." Sian's jaw stiffened. From everything Trillin had said so far, that meant that her new friend would be in even more danger.

"It already knows I exist." Trillin's face twisted. *Actually* twisted. All her features spiralled angrily. Sian was so entranced she almost fell over her own feet. "That fragment I splatted back there will remember a bit of me, so it'll remember now, too. But it'll mostly remember … you."

Suddenly, Trillin spun around. She reached towards Sian, then stopped when her hands were a few inches from her shoulders. Except her fingertips stretched out further even then, as though they were, despite Trillin stopping herself, trying to touch her.

"I won't let it get you," she said. Her face was on the right side, now she'd turned her whole body around, and Sian got the impression that she was trying to look human again. "I promise. This is all my fault. If I'd managed to talk to you before you left the portal, maybe you wouldn't have—"

"Jumped headfirst into danger?" Sian snorted. "Not a chance. Best case, you would have realised I'm trouble earlier, and not jumped down after me."

"Not a chance." Trillin seemed to savour the words.

"Really?"

"Really."

"Well." A pleased warmth was spreading through Sian's body. Maybe this wasn't a total bust, after all. "We'd better keep, you know, not getting killed, then."

"Yes!" Trillin hesitated a moment longer, then flowed away. "It's close – just through here…"

Another pulse squeezed Sian's skull as she followed her new friend. Her new maybe more than a friend.

Nothing in the ethics approval about that. Not even her supervisor had thought anyone could get on *that* well with the residents of the Endless Void.

She wondered if –

"*Ow.*" Another pulse gripped her. It felt, unpleasantly, like being squeezed by a giant, damp, soft hand. More intense than the previous ones.

A horrible thought struck her.

"You have all of the Endless's memories?" she hissed to Trillin as they scrambled up a glutinous hill.

"That's right," Trillin said.

"Including the location of the – *ow* – the way back to Earth?"

Trillin's eyes spun onto the side of her head. She stared at Sian, horrified, then her hair twisted into tendrils that reminded Sian of anemones. "Yes," she whispered.

"So if it's seen me through the tooth monster, and seen that I'm human, it can probably guess—"

"We need to move quickly," Trillin gasped.

The pulses came stronger and closer together. They stopped squeezing, and started tugging, pulling at Sian's skin like they were trying to take her apart.

Her vision went fuzzy as Trillin pushed aside a fall of sea-weed-like growths.

"We're close," Trillin muttered. "It's – somewhere – there!"

A hole in the world.

If the Endless was everything, pressing close and changing and clinging, then the portal was nothing. It clawed at her eyes, but it was a relief from the Endless's clawing, too.

It was also approximately the size of a car window.

Well, she'd jumped out of her share of car windows in her time. This would be just like being sixteen again.

"I guess this is it," she said. Huddled into her side, the bunny monster squeaked. She scratched it under the chin – or what she was assuming was its chin – and Trillin made a small, protesting noise.

On impulse, she reached out and took Trillin's hand.

Her skin was cool. Not clammy, like the bits of Endless they'd been climbing over, but cool and smooth. Her fingers curved tentatively around Sian's. She could feel the bones, and thought, suddenly: she *made* those bones.

She made all of herself. She saw me, all those months ago, and wanted to get to know me better – and this is the body she made herself to do that.

A thrill of excitement went through her.

"You're coming with me, aren't you?"

She squeezed Trillin's hand tighter.

Trillin's lips parted. "I…" she began. "I said I would protect you. And I can do that better here. I can distract the Endless, so it loses track of you and where you went…"

"Until it *eats* you and remembers again!" Sian reminded her. "That's a terrible idea! And not just because it involves you *dying*!"

The world pulled at her. She bent over, clutching her forehead as though she could physically hold herself together.

Trillin's fingers tightened around hers, then twisted, turning into thin tentacles that wrapped possessively around her wrist.

"It's almost here," she said. "Quickly. You go through—"

"We'll *both* go through. Please. I'm not leaving you here! I—" Sian doubled over again as the Endless focused on her. Her skin felt raw, like an unholy combination of sunburn and road rash. The rabbit monster squeaked and she tucked herself around it protectively.

"Sian?" Trillin's voice sounded like it was coming from a long way away. The world pressed against her, sucking and clammy. She wanted to reply to Trillin, but she didn't dare open her mouth. Or her eyes.

Something clawed at her mind.

Hello, it said, and Sian screamed.

Strong arms wrapped around her. Something soft brushed against her cheek and she was lifted up. The Endless was still scraping at her, inside and out, but wherever Trillin touched her, it didn't hurt.

*

The Endless was *here*. There was no more time to argue, no more time to make up for not helping Sian when she could have made a difference. Trillin leapt through the portal.

There was a moment like the Endless had her, burning acid through every atom that made her *her*, and then Trillin hit the ground on the other side.

And the ground stayed *exactly where it was*.

"Aargh," she groaned as she discovered how unhelpful bones could be.

"What happened?" Sian gasped from beneath her.

Beneath her.

She propped herself up on her limbs, firming them up enough

to take her weight. Sian was sprawled beneath her, blinking as though she'd forgotten how her eyes were meant to work.

Her gaze focused on Trillin. Then flicked, ever so slightly, up and down, meeting all six of her eyes.

"Ow," Sian said softly. Then: "You came through?"

"The Endless had found you," Trillin explained.

"I felt it. It was like…" Sian shivered, and didn't elaborate. "Where are we?"

Trillin raised her head. They were in some sort of structure, with tall, vertical walls all around. The walls were a pale colour except for partway up, where they became thin and multi-coloured. The colours shimmered and for a moment Trillin thought they were still in the Endless, after all, and this was some sort of trap – the sort of trap previous fragments had set for the humans they were trying to ensnare – before she realised the shimmering was the result of something *behind* the colours.

"Stained glass, limestone … are we in a very small church, or what?" Sian pushed herself up as though she intended to look around, then flopped back down with a sigh. "Whatever. Earth. That's good enough for me."

"We're on Earth?"

Trillin gazed around. The walls were still in the same place. As she watched, they *stayed* there.

She looked down at herself and carefully tried to extend feelers from the tips of her fingers. They sprouted as easily as they could in the Endless.

"I'm still changing," she said.

"Good." Sian grinned up at her in a way that made her insides wriggle. Just in case she needed more reminders that she was a changing crumb of the Endless, and not an unchanging human.

"Is it going to follow us through the portal? Should we still be running?"

"No. It's too big, in all of itself. It would have to let fragments escape, and it couldn't guarantee that they would want what it wanted."

"Oh, good. We can just lie here, then." She was still smiling. "Shouldn't we…"

Trillin ran out of words. She'd run out of everything. None of her memories got this far. They'd always stopped as the humans escaped the Endless. She had no knowledge of what happened afterwards.

"What happens now?" she whispered.

"I think that's up to us. I should probably get in touch with Jonesy and the others and let them know I'm not dead. File a report. That sort of thing."

She didn't make any attempts to move.

"That sounds like a good plan," Trillin said. She didn't move, either.

Lying on top of someone meant being *very* close to them. Lying on top of Sian meant…

Trillin gulped.

She could see all the tiny movements Sian's body made. The ones she did on purpose, and the ones her body did by itself. The way her chest rose and fell as she breathed. The flicker of her eyelashes as a stray hair fell across her face. The lines that formed at the edge of her mouth, the warmth of her breath…

"What will you do now?" Sian asked.

Trillin had been thinking the same thing.

"I could go back," she said, even though that wasn't what she'd been thinking. Some of the energy fell out of Sian's face.

"Or I could stay here."

Sian's eyes narrowed. "Those would be your two options, yeah."

"You're not worried about me staying here? The other fragments that have made it to Earth…"

"Weren't exactly in the running for interdimensional friend of the year, sure. But I … get the feeling you're not here for the whole conquer and destroy deal."

Trillin's fingers curled, frond-like. "No…"

But what was she here for?

Something in Sian's expression told Trillin that she already knew what she was trying to say, what she was trying to find any words for at all. A teasing, tantalising lightness that made her want to find the words as quickly as possible and let it draw out, at the same time.

Before she could say anything, the crumb squeaked and wriggled out from between them.

"Oh God," Sian burst out, jerking. "I'd forgotten all about it! I'm the worst bunny monster mother ever."

The crumb jumped over to a wall, which it hit and bounced off. All its fur stood on end. Then it turned around and bounced off the next wall. Excitement radiated off it as it gave up on walls and started bouncing on the spot.

"Someone likes hard surfaces that stay surfaces," Sian muttered.

"Sweek!" the crumb squeaked.

"But…" Sian lifted her gaze to Trillin again, who felt warm. There was a speculating look in her eyes – and something tentative, too. As though for all Sian said she always threw herself head-first into trouble, right now, she was being careful. "I don't know how to look after a creature like that by myself. What does it eat? *Does* it eat? What if it forgets what shape it's meant to be?"

"I could help," Trillin said quickly. "I'll have to learn, too, but I'll tell you whatever I find out, and we can look after the crumb together."

"I'd like that."

They were lying so close together. Trillin was still holding herself up, but if she stopped…

But they were talking about the crumb. The happy little fragment of the Endless, which was as overjoyed to be in a world that didn't tug at its edges as Trillin herself was, even if it didn't have the mind to understand what had happened. They were talking about it, not … them … and even if there was a *them*…

Trillin didn't have any memories of how humans acted once they'd saved one another from the Endless. She could see one way her future rolled out: her and Sian, looking after the crumb as she learned more about the human world and Sian told her friends she wasn't dead. Maybe, slowly, Trillin could find out how humans said the things she wanted to say to Sian to each other. And practice. And figure out her body, properly, so that when Sian looked at her like … like…

Like she was looking at her now…

Forget memories. Forget what other people did. Forget getting her corporeal form right, and her words. She didn't need words.

Without thinking about it for even a second, Trillin leaned down and kissed Sian.

They touched. Together, but separate. Melding into one another and still staying each their own, edges burning with sensation, two bodies yearning towards one another.

She wasn't perfect. She couldn't help the tentacles that crept out from her form, to sweep that stray hair from Sian's face, and hold her close.

From the way Sian responded, she didn't mind.

Not perfect.

But definitely girlfriend material.

SALT WHITE, ROSE RED

EMILY BRILL-HOLLAND

Don't.

So, I did.

*

I hadn't come across green in so long.

The sea stretches for miles in every direction. Choppy grey, swelling to overwhelm the deep black rocks the lighthouse is built on. Everything is either black, white or grey. The mainland isn't visible and I—

I ached for green. It was the skipped beat in my heart, the lie caught in my teeth. I tossed and rolled awake at night, window open to the sea air, everything muted in its spray. Sprawled on her back and still smelling of kerosene from the lamp, she slept beside me, steady and oblivious.

*

The supply boat was late, and she went to the mainland to meet it. The revving of her boat over waves followed me as I hurried down the path.

It sat, waiting for me, panes frosted with salt.

Don't, she'd said.

I opened the glass door and slipped inside.

The walls swam with moisture and heat.

It was so green, it *hurt*. Leaves and vines and flowers spilled from pots. Everything burned with life.

I leaned on the door and cried. Heavy, thick, gulping.

*

My eyes adjusted gradually. By the time I eased myself off the door, sweat was dripping down the back of my neck.

It was deeper than I'd thought. The paths tangled, snarling with vines.

But the roses. Oh, the *roses*.

They bordered the greenhouse, a guard of honour soaking up the wet. White, pure white – a different kind of burn from the green.

This wasn't the white of salt or the white of the lighthouse tower. This was a new white. A white that breathed of snow and new beginnings and clean slates. All the things she'd promised.

I reached out and stroked a petal. Velvet, her cheek under my hand when I first kissed her.

I let out a breath.

They were living. Out here, on this rock, separated from salt by lightning and sand. Proof that something could root here. Survive.

Thrive.

A high-pitched whine *she's back* and I flinched—

Ow. The thorn dug in. Blood welled, a red tear. I sucked it away.

I met her at the dock, thumb tucked behind my back. If she

noticed my sweat-soaked hair and flushed cheeks, she didn't say anything.

*

Now I dream of red. Red running down glass. Of satiation. Of breathing for the first time in a century.

I break awake into heat and swimming walls. The sheets have twisted around my waist and the bedsheets on my side are drenched. My thighs throb.

When I lift my nightgown, I see dozens of tiny punctures.

And when I next visit the roses, they are a deep, deep red.

FLORENTINA

PAUL VEART

The Florentina climbing rose is renowned for its hardiness in cold climates. Frost will not delay it at all; snow, sleet and wind will encourage it so that by the time spring arrives, the rose will be covered in a layer of sharp green leaves and red flowers.

Despite this, the Rose Man preferred the hothouse. His favourite haunt was at the north end by the pool. The pool was the most popular spot in the entire gardens. It was wide and circular and constructed of old, crumbling concrete, with half a dozen lily pads across its surface. One of the first things you got told when you started work at the gardens was to keep an eye on the lily pads: children would stop at nothing to touch them, to run their hands over their fleshy surfaces, to put their toys on them, or even, apparently, a sibling.

That was where we found him, perched at the edge of the pool with his eyes closed. It was Tim who discovered him; I'd been weeding up at the high-country rockery. I can still remember the call over the radio, the request for assistance, the inability to explain what had happened. If it hadn't been for the wavering in Tim's voice I might've left it to someone else, but as it was I set off down the hill to help.

The first thing I remember seeing was the angle of the Rose Man's neck. If you've ever seen an infant's head flop back, that awkward, accidental snap, you'll know how it felt to look at him. There was something precarious about it, the way the skin pulled taut across his throat revealing a knot of flesh and cartilage. Later, when I was home before the mirror, I tried to mimic him, tilting my head back until I could feel the stretch in my oesophagus and the pinch at the base of my skull. I couldn't see my reflection; all I could do was gaze upward.

That was what the Rose Man was doing, too: staring up at the glass ceiling as if trying to catch sight of himself. The gardeners clustered about him. They squinted; they peered. But it wasn't his neck they were looking at: it was his rose. It was a Florentina climbing rose, with a trunk extending to a height of about thirty centimetres. Its bark was the usual pale brown you'd expect from a Florentina, branching off into a matted nest of limbs. Delicate thorns bristled amongst them; bright green leaves were beginning to emerge, along with a pair of deep red, many-petalled flowers. And all of it, trunk, leaves, petals and thorns were growing directly from his mouth.

The first request for the Rose Man to leave the hothouse came a few weeks later. During my time at the gardens we'd had three requests for specimens to be removed from the collection. The first was *Dionaea muscipula*, or the Venus flytrap. To be caught in a Venus flytrap is to have your body dissolved, processed and reborn as a pure white flower. While the end result is beautiful, watching it play out – even on a common housefly – can be a disturbing sight. The second specimen to draw criticism was the carrion flower. As the name suggests, the primary feature of the carrion flower is its smell. One visitor, on catching the scent at full strength, compared it to the time she'd discovered her great uncle after he'd died alone in his flat at the height of summer. Another had memories of his year as a private security guard in Iraq, but refused to give any details.

That made the Rose Man number three. The issue wasn't dissimilar. It wasn't that he smelt of death or rotting meat: his smell was different. The first time I noticed it was a couple of days after the initial meeting. I pushed through the hothouse doors, the sticky air hanging about me, and my nose filled with a scent. It was hard to describe. It was sort of woody and spicy and floral all at once, but there was something else to it as well, something that seemed somehow *inappropriate* in a room full of strangers. Something that made people blush.

I walked across the room until he came into sight. He was standing by the ferns, peering up at the fronds as if lost in thought. There were damp patches under his arms; a slick of sweat on his neck. Drops of water fell from his hair and onto the ground below.

*

It takes time to get the hang of pruning. It's not the risk of doing damage that's the tricky bit: the truth is that roses – like most plants – are quite hardy. An ill-judged snip or injudicious tug of the hacksaw is hardly ever fatal; if you cut a plant close to the soil's edge, more often than not it will re-emerge with more vigour than seems acceptable. Even so, there's something that not all gardeners develop, a sense not just of where a plant needs to be cut, but where it wants to grow.

The Rose Man had been moved out of the hothouse in October. There'd been a class visit; awkward questions; a formal complaint from the principal. Then there'd been confusion about everything else, from how to transport the Rose Man, to where he'd go, to whether the council even had a duty of care for him at all. Housing was in short supply across the city; queues stretched out doors at open homes and rows of cars held tired, anxious families. That was why they chose the zoo. There'd been a chimpanzee, a resident since the days of tea parties and fancy dresses, who'd finally succumbed. With a few hasty additions her cage was turned into a small, well-ventilated apartment and, without word of accent or complaint or any feedback at all, the Rose Man was moved in.

The call came not long after. It was from the senior primate keeper, a man used to dealing with pack hierarchies and prehensile tails. Foliage, however, was posing more of a problem. The Rose Man's Florentina had grown substantially since his arrival at the zoo, and he was struggling to enter or exit his new home.

"We're pretty sure there aren't any veins in it," the keeper said. "Try to think of it as feathers. Or toenails."

But some feathers do have veins. And so do some toenails.

The keeper led me to the Rose Man's cage, knocking on the door then walking in without waiting for a reply. I hesitated, but the silence went on until the keeper came back and brought me through.

Sheets had been hung over the cage's wire mesh. The concrete floor had been washed, rugs laid down. But already I could smell the familiar smell: the Rose Man's odour, mixed with a hint of the cage's former occupant. The Rose Man was sitting on a couch, a television in front of him.

"Morning, buddy," said the keeper. "The gardener's here, just like we promised. Going to give you a nice prune."

He nodded at me and was gone before I could ask any questions.

I didn't move for at least a minute. It was the first time I'd been alone with the Rose Man, the first time I'd been this close to him. I shuffled forward, keeping to one side as if I would somehow block his view of the television. Of course he wasn't actually looking at the television: he was looking at the ceiling.

"Hi," I said. The Rose Man didn't move; didn't fidget or dart his eyes about or do anything to show he'd heard me.

"Hello?" I tried again, but it sounded forced. So that was the last word I spoke to him. I took off my backpack and laid out my tools near his feet: the secateurs, the hacksaw, the hessian sack for the clippings. Then I picked up the hacksaw and walked around the couch until I was standing directly behind him.

Was it threatening, standing like that? I didn't consider it at the time. For another few seconds I stared at the saw, its teeth, its curved orange handle, before finally getting up the nerve to look – to actually, properly look – at the Rose Man and his condition.

Specifically, his mouth.

I had assumed he had one trunk emerging from between his lips, but on closer inspection I realised there were three separate branches, each as thick as a finger, entwined together to resemble a single trunk. The Rose Man had to hold his mouth open to accommodate them, and when I squinted I could see how his lips had become calloused where they rubbed against the wood. Was his throat calloused, too? Could an oesophagus callous?

I leaned further forward, so my face was directly above his. I could see his eyes, the blue irises and small, black pupils. I scanned them for a glimpse of recognition. Was there a person looking up at me? I glanced back down at his mouth. The trunk

85

disappeared into his throat, soft palate pressed against bark, uvula draped out of sight.

Did the trunk continue down into his stomach? His lungs? The roots of a rose bush run deep – how were they attached? I thought about asking him. If anyone would know he would. But I didn't want to face the silence again, the possibility that there was nothing in there beyond wood and bark and sap.

After a quick scan of the plant I took hold of one of the inner branches and moved the saw across it. The teeth bit quickly. I held the branch as tightly as I could, wary of what might happen if the rose came loose within. But with each cut I became more aware of how well it was embedded, as stable as anything grown in the thick mulch of a garden.

And then the branch was off. I examined it for nerves or blood or marrow. But apart from a small blob of sap, I couldn't see anything. I raised the branch to my nose, sniffed. There was a whiff of the same indecent smell I remembered from back at the hothouse, before it was lost in the general chimpanzee funk.

*

I didn't prick myself until the third pruning. It wasn't that bad, just a tiny impalement at the end of my middle finger. If it had happened a few weeks ago, before I got out of the habit of wearing gloves, I wouldn't have even bled. But I did. And it was seen. The keeper had taken to watching my progress, the angle of my cuts. Afterwards he'd backed away, was out the door before me. He was waiting in the staff room. I made my way to the sink and took down the first aid kit, fishing out the bandages.

"Put that down," the keeper said, but it was too late. I made to leave, but he held out a thick arm. I didn't say anything. I watched the stern expression on his face, the way he kept wiping his hands on his shorts. The zoo manager arrived about five minutes later. She wore a tidy suit, a lapel pin shaped like a tiger.

"Heard there was a bit of an incident," she said. "You're not to blame yourself. We should have foreseen it – should have taken precautions."

They took me to the hospital in a car, seated in the back even though there was no one in the front except the driver. He didn't speak the entire time. He cringed when I moved. The nurses met me at the carpark. I was led through a side-door, into a goods lift and up to the seventh floor. It was warm in the way all hospitals are warm, with drowsy light and an odour of instant coffee and bleach. Everyone apart from me used the hand sanitiser.

The room they had ready was actually four rooms, the curtain partitions pulled back to create one larger space. There was a walk-in toilet and shower; a single bed; a lock on the outside of the door.

"A little scratch like that, it's probably nothing," the doctor told me later. "We just want to be sure."

Up until that moment, I hadn't realised why I was there.

They thought I might have caught it. The Florentina. As if it was some kind of contagion, a bacteria or virus that could make the leap from thorn to bloodstream and nestle itself inside my body.

"Roses don't work like that," I explained. "They grow from seeds – from rose hips. And even if I did have a seed in me, it would never be able to germinate, it's too hot. Roses need cold weather before they'll do anything."

"Of course, of course," the doctor said. He left not long after, and locked the door. A few hours later I felt them tinker with the air conditioning.

And so I remained in hospital. At first I spent my time read-ing: books, magazines, whatever the nurses slid under the door. I spent hours looking out the window, memorising street names and counting cars. Eventually I managed to get my phone, and the hospital's Wi-Fi password. I read news, watched movies and TV shows. But then I gave up on that, too. I let the phone's battery go flat and spent my days lying on the bed. I began to wonder: what if, somehow, I had been infected? I tried to picture a seed in my lungs, because that, surely, is where it would aim for. It would be easy to survive there. It was warm, but there'd be plenty of crevices, and it wouldn't take much for a sprout to wheedle its way up towards daylight. It would be my own Florentina climbing rose, like the Rose Man's. I thought of him, too, alone in his cage. Would he have spoken to me if he didn't have the rose growing out his mouth? I didn't know for sure, but my guess was not. The silence had come before the rose; the rose had taken up the space where the words had been.

With that, I felt a shift. I realised that far from being afraid of having caught the Florentina, I wanted it. I wanted to have a rose nestled inside me. I wanted to smell right. I sniffed my skin, but couldn't tell if I did. I found a stethoscope and spent my time listening to my chest. I could hear my heartbeat clear enough, but was there another sound in there, the vegetative expansion I longed for?

There was not. Because, as the doctors and botanists and haematologists concluded after two months of observation, roses cannot be transferred to the human body via the bloodstream. And so I was allowed to go, my lungs empty except for the ebb and flow of air, my blood devoid of plant matter. The Rose Man's cage was empty as well. I went to see as soon as I got out. The sheets had been taken down, the television and couch were gone. I pressed my head against the bars and sniffed, but there was nothing.

*

Most people get their roses from nurseries and garden centres. They come pre-prepared in little tubs and black plastic wrappings, and all you have to do is slide them into freshly turned soil, give them some water and, more often than not, they'll thrive. If you want a rose that's a little more rare, or you just want a change, you can also buy them without soil or container or any other hindrance. You need to get them into the ground quickly if you do this, otherwise they'll die.

There's another way you can grow a rose, though. You can use a cutting. A cutting is a branch you've removed from another rose, maybe one you didn't even consider before, one you tossed in a sack and forgot about. There are some cuttings that are better than others: you want one that's not too old, with a few growth buds on it. You don't want your cutting to be too dry, either, but then, cuttings were transported halfway round the world on sailing ships and still grew at the end of it. The hardest part of using cuttings is the planting of them. They're sharp, which can be difficult. They require you to hold yourself just right. Lungs are not designed for this sort of thing, and the gag reflex is strong. Still, with enough cuttings, with enough practice, one is bound to find a home, to take root and grow and thrive.

OTTO HAHN SPEAKS TO THE DEAD

OCTAVIA CADE

A garden is a beautiful place to die. It was the only beautiful thing about Clara's death, which otherwise was a bullet and a broken chest, blood spilling over everything, the red scent of iron.

Had he been there, he might have vomited. Only might, because the revulsion he felt for death had lessened a little in the immediacy of the war, and he'd done so much to increase that death that it didn't do to be squeamish just because the dead in front of him now was a woman. One connected with him, and her death was a repudiation not directed at him – Otto wasn't the one married to her – but he had some responsibility nonetheless. He'd helped in the work she'd felt such revulsion for; she had seen the choice he'd made and refused her coexistence.

"Of course I did," she says after they took her body away. She'd been covered after it happened, the suicide kept from sight, but not all of the blood she'd shed had soaked into dress and dressings. The rest had soaked into earth, was scatter-droplets on petals, and in the moonlight no one could see it anyway, or was even out searching. Some things were too terrible to look at and her husband was inside, avoiding mirrors. The ghost of her stayed in the garden, with the closed-up blossoms, so she wouldn't have to look at him. "No decent person would be part of this."

Chemical warfare, and Clara a chemist herself. "There are some things I will not stoop to," she says, and it disgusted her that Otto had. That her husband had – that he'd covered his hands with burning, with suffocated blood, and brought them home to her afterwards, as if she were expected to touch them, to kiss them and be grateful for their presence.

She couldn't bear to be touched by him ever again. Hence the bullets, the garden death, and the house still in a mess from the party Haber had held to celebrate chlorine gas in trenches, and how he'd done it first.

"Better than the alternative," Otto argues. It's not exactly heroic, coming up with ways to slaughter at scale, but he'd rather cause others to choke and suffocate than do so himself. "There's nothing wrong with self-preservation," he says, because war is a terrible thing, yes, but sometimes scruples do nothing but extend it. Best to get it over with as quickly as possible, and with as little damage as possible. The rest he doesn't look at too closely.

"You should have the decency to look at what you've done," says Clara. She slips her arms out of her dress, lets the fabric fall to her waist. He doesn't want to look. It feels disrespectful, somehow, with her bare breasts slick with her own blood, and that gaping ruin between them. "Look," she says. "Look at what I think of you."

He'll go to his own grave swearing that he never got hard at the sight of her.

*

She's there every time he goes to sleep. A nightmare come to life. "You traffic in nightmares, don't you?" Clara asks him. "Well then. This is what you invited in."

She's a monster.

No, she isn't.

That's one accusation Otto will never have the right to make again. Monstrosity comes in many forms but Clara isn't it, and he thinks as long as he can hold to that then there's something in him human still, something the gas hasn't changed.

He has a gas mask of his own now. It was only a matter of time. There is argument out of Britain: "We cannot win this war unless we kill or incapacitate more of our enemies than they do of us, and if this can only be done by copying the enemy in his choice of weapons, we must not refuse to do so."

It is an escalation that was entirely foreseen.

His face in the mirror is masked and wheezing. Clara stands behind him, the front of her blood red and dripping, but her face is innocent of canvas and charcoal. "It suits you," she says. "But it won't make a difference."

She comes to him at night. He wakes to her kneeling on his chest, the breath being pressed out of him. Blood runs from her shattered chest, drips into his mouth, pools in the back of his throat. It's copper and iron and choking, the warm sweet scent of it. When she smiles down at him her teeth are rimmed with red, like they were in the garden when she coughed up the last of her own life.

"Poor baby," she says. "Did you have a bad dream?"

Her hair smells of flowers. That's always what sets him to weeping. If it were grave dirt, trench dirt, the scent surrounding him as he lay in his bed, he thinks he'd be able to treat her as revenant. To push her off him, to let horror take the place of bitterness and grief. That would be protection, of a sort, because the gas mask never is. He wears it to bed, when she's come too often for sleeping and sanity, but it smothers him regardless. It's too warm, too close, and he comes to gasping consciousness, slick with sweat, that same taste of salt.

Flowers are better. At least with flowers he can tell himself that what's waking him is external, the product of a grief he'd never admit to having, because what would that make of his life? His involvement is not peripheral. The responsibility for chemical warfare falls on him as much as anyone. Edith tells him not to worry, tells him he is doing his duty, and thank God his wife is not as dramatic as Haber's was, he does not think he could bear it. Flinches now when she goes into the garden. Pastes a smile on his face for her, makes of his features a smooth clean warmth, because she's never woken to ghosts in the bed and he doesn't want her to fathom what his work has brought them.

There are masks for horses, too, and dogs. All the innocent, useful beasts. Otto is useful but not innocent, and when he sees himself in surfaces, the canvas shifting with every breath, he wonders if this is what he looked like all along.

*

He's so sick of seeing her. "Why don't you haunt your own husband?" he snarls, an angry whisper because Edith is asleep beside him and he'd never admit it, never, but this night time atonement is nothing to do with her. Edith was never a chemist, she could never know what it was to have elements at her fingers, to be able to manipulate the very stuff of matter.

Clara's face freezes at him. Her red mouth, her red chest. Her red breath, because whenever she speaks small droplets spray out and smear the sheets, and he has to tell Edith he had a bloody nose in the night. "It will make no difference," she says. "Not to him."

Fritz Haber had left the day after the garden party, left to go back to the front. Left the garden still sticky with protest, left his young son still trembling with the feel of dead mother in his arms. Otto knows about necessity and the price of power, he's excused a lot for it, but he's not sure that this betrayal is ever one which could be excused. "Would you leave your son after such a grief?" Clara hisses at him, sibilant, with liquid in her chest.

He doesn't have a son. Is newly married, and children have not yet been gifted to him. "I'd never hurt a child like you did," he says, knowing it will hurt. He is good at hurting, has developed a proficiency for it. The thought of that child, alone, having found his mother in the garden, a garden he'll now have to look out onto every day … "Perhaps you *are* a monster," he says.

It's always so easy to condemn others.

"Do I look monstrous to you?" says Clara. In the moonlight the blood shimmers and fades, seems to seep back into skin, and the whole broken chest of her knits itself together, pale and gleaming. She's perfect, so perfect, and close enough to touch, and the entire bedroom smells of flowers now instead of iron, and the stars behind her give enough of a shine for halos and Edith is a pale thing in comparison, insipid, and part of him hates her for it because he's planning the murder of hundreds, of thousands, trying to make entire armies choke and suffocate and suffer, and this is something she can just skim over, like it's *nothing*. In their marriage bed, sleeping, peaceful, like it's nothing.

"Do you want her to open herself up for you?" says Clara,

smirking, and this is revenge, he thinks, for the cruelty of her son, for the way that Otto used him as reminder. "Do you want her to open herself up *because* of you?"

What a thing it would be to be so powerful.

(What a thing it is.)

*

Verdun, Zone Rouge.

A hundred years after World War One, the place is still un-inhabitable. 1200 square kilometres, saturated with ordinance, and with chemicals. The soldiers hit with chlorine gas, with all the gases that came after chlorine, they lived, some of them. Or died. Either way their stories were short ones. Packed off in stretchers, packed off in ambulances, buried not far from where the gas got them.

Not all the gas got sucked into lungs. Not nearly all of it. Most floated down, a gentle sinking. Soaked itself into soil, got sucked up again by plants, got eaten through plants by birds and mammals and gentle creeping things. Chlorine. Arsenic.

In some places 99% of the plants are dead. A hundred years later, they are still dead. Nothing can survive the contamination those shells left.

Chlorine. Phosgene. Mustard. Nausea, vomiting, headache. Blindness, asphyxiation, blisters. Lungs filled with fluid. Suffocation. Drowning.

Otto dreams himself awake to skin full of pustules and streaming eyes, irritation in his mouth and throat. Watery eyes, wheezing. The fluid in his lungs reacting to chlorine, forming hydrochloric acid. A burning, choking, agonising death, membranes leaking blood.

Clara takes her ghost-self through the undergrowth of Verdun.

There are dead trees there, dead skeletons. Nothing smells of flowers, but when the blood spills down her front – a smooth, endless gushing – it drops upon the earth like poppies, and for a moment the dead ground blooms. Then the soil gets them, drags them down, bleaches the petals to nothing and leaves them curled up and brown. Withered.

A ghost has light footsteps. They don't disturb the bombs, all the unexploded pieces, but sometimes when an animal wanders past, one too lost and mazed to be frightened by the dead, it sets off a small blast and dies, twitching, in soil that is anathema to it.

Little bones are everywhere. It's nothing like a garden, Clara thinks, but at the same time it's her own, left to go wild because no one can stand to go out in it anymore.

It's walking in a wasteland. Otto will never come here, so she scrapes the dirt up into her mouth, the dead dirt, whole horrible sterile handfuls of it. She is dead herself, so there's no danger of it. But when she goes to him at night, this man she never knew that well but can still see some worth in, worth that by the end she could never see in her husband, she breathes the scent of Verdun over him. The dusty, empty scent of it, crammed in her teeth, between canines and clogging up the hole in her chest.

There will be no escape. Not for either of them.

*

How to survive a chlorine gas attack:

1) Leave before it starts. Be somewhere else entirely.

Otto spends much of his time scouting for appropriate places for slaughter. Gas is a finicky thing. Climate and geography can make it less effective. Less lethal. This is war, after all, and it is best to be efficient. He is at Flanders before the second battle of

Ypres, but when men are being gassed there – with the prevailing wind – he is off looking at another site, and then another. Belgium, Poland, Italy … he gets to see them all. Clara is never with him, but whatever field he stands in smells of flowers.

2) Try not to run. Exercise exacerbates the effects of the gas.

He thinks the travel sees her off, that if Clara can't find his bed at night it's because she's no longer able. Hatred is a difficult thing to hold on to, perhaps. But he volunteers himself as human guinea-pig, standing with gas mask on – it's like a second skin, now – and waiting for the gas to take him. The one disadvantage to using chlorine on the other side is that it's harder to get hold of their bodies. He could get out of testing, if he wanted – there's not so many scientists of his calibre that they couldn't find someone as German and much more useless to take his place. But the responsibility nags at him, the sense of horror he feels at the sight of the gas clouds seeping towards him … this is what he has helped to inflict on others, and there is something in him that feels he must face the same. So he reports for testing, wears his mask and locks his knees together, hopes the protection he has is protection enough. If not, perhaps that is justice. When he forces his eyes open, Clara is standing with him, her face pressed against his gas mask, staring in. He can feel the chill breath of her through canvas. When he sees her watching, feels the strain in the legs that are not running, he understands that hatred finds a way.

3) Get to a high place. Do not lie down, not in the trenches. Chlorine gas is heavier than air, and it sinks.

Otto feels he is justified. He feels it over and over. The fit of the gas mask, the stink of chemical, of charcoal and urine … he has done his part. Self-respect staggers on, but it is nowhere near as close a justification as necessity. "We must break this deadlock," he says. "Better for everyone the sooner it's over. I'd not do this if I had the choice. No one would."

"Lots of people would," says Clara. "Don't tell me about choices." She made hers, in the garden, with her husband's service pistol, and everyone around her paid, is paying for it.

"Hard choices take strength," he says, but secretly, in himself, he wonders more and more if what made his choices for him is weakness.

*

Otto has a son. His only child, and when he wakes one night to screaming he decides to let his wife sleep, see to the boy himself. Clara is hanging over the crib, and cooing. Her breasts are leaking over him, a mixture of milk and blood, and the room smells of dead earth and dead flowers.

"Strange how their screaming affects you," she says. Little Hermann screamed when he found his mother, Otto is sure of it. He's spent more nights than he cares to collect picturing the young boy and the shot and the screaming, the small hands trying to stifle blood and flailing, frantic, as his mother dies in his arms.

"Even when they're old, you don't forget it," she says. Hermann must be nearly a man now, and later, much later, when Otto hears that he has killed himself, taken to suicide just as his mother did, he'll remember this conversation and wish ... for what? That he'd been kinder, to the creature overhanging his life? That he'd had sympathy for the devastation she'd caused? That he'd reached out, somehow, to another family's horror, and one he wasn't quite innocent of?

He isn't, and doesn't, and never does. She can't expect kindness, hovering as she does, like a ghoul. A hag. "You leave my boy alone," he says, snatching the child out from under and wiping his face clean with fingers that are smeared with old blood. "He's got nothing to do with this. With us." If her visits have waned somewhat there's an *us*, still. A relationship closer in death than it ever was in life, when she was the wife of his colleague and not much else. Why she's latched on to him he'll never guess, and refuses now to try.

Mostly he doesn't think of her at all. As time passes the trenches get further away. The nearness of death recedes, and it's easier to think well of himself. Easier to think on other things. Different things.

"There's a lot you don't think about any more," says Clara. "You made the world he'll live in. You think that's nothing to do with you?"

"He'll have a better world than Hermann," says Otto. A better mother. A better father.

"All those boys you killed had fathers too," Clara reminds him, and then she's gone, the nursery still as if she was never there, and the baby choking in his arms.

The little chest is heaving, the little cheeks red, at first, then redder and redder then paling down to blue, and if Otto's work has taught him anything it's taught him the signs of suffocation, of gasping for breath that won't come. Of lungs clogged up and drowning, of no strength left to cry and tears coming regardless.

It's croup, he tells himself, *only croup*, and the baby lives and it's a small alarm only, a common ailment or so the doctor tells him, but Otto could swear, he could *swear*, that with his head pressed closed to infant chest to detect the signs of life he could smell nothing but chlorine.

*

(Hanno Hahn does not die from croup. He does not die in World War Two, not from gas nor from bombs. He and his wife are killed in a car accident, leaving only a young son. The boy is the same age as Hermann was, when he found his mother dying in the garden and his father left him to go on alone while he arranged the murder of other men's sons.

Otto cries and cries where the boy cannot see, and wonders to himself if this loss is justice come at last.)

*

The War, the Great War, and he thought it was over. "The world we create is *never* over," says Clara, because there's another war coming, one bigger and more gaseous than the last, and now the responsibility is even more his because Otto has found something more dangerous than chlorine, and its name is fission. He and Lise Meitner discovered it, working together, and war will make of their work a wasteland worse than that ever seen in Ypres, or Verdun.

Lise is Jewish, and Germany is no longer a safe place for her. Otto helps her escape, because he has seen enough of blood saturating through the women of his acquaintance, and he was too proud, too stupid, too pleased with himself ever to help Clara. If he even could have. The only thing that could have saved Lise from the taint of her blood was the willingness to work, but work can only buy so much freedom and he has no belief in her ability to push through.

He knows she will abstain. Clara shot herself rather than

give the approval of her presence. Lise has removed herself as well, and she will not work on the bomb. Not ever. Not for the Germans and not for the Allies. Such things, she says, are too hideous.

Otto thinks he may have forgotten what hideous is.

He digs out his old gas mask, the first one. There are better ones since, he knows them and has them, but the first is impregnated with nightmares of suffocation, and when he wears it he can feel his throat closing. When he wears it to bed he wakes to find Clara crouched on his chest, the way she used to in the war gone by. It's been over twenty years and she's still wet with blood, still warm with it, and this time he licks it out of her mouth so he can remember what death is, what consequences it has. What his responsibilities are.

"I don't want to be that man again," he says. He can't tell when science stopped being a wonder to him and started being a horror, but in the back of his mind now is a fear that the chemical death he brought on so many is a small thing. A small and burning thing, and what is coming is holocaust. "I don't want to be that man again."

"Then don't," says Clara.

He does not work on the bomb. It's that easy.

The war drags on and on.

He cannot forgive himself for it.

THE WATERFALL

RENEE LIANG

I stand on the ledge, breathing hard. My boots tip the edge, the rock dropping sharply beyond. There used to be water here, cascading in delicate chandeliers, becoming a jewelled curtain in spring. People used to come and eat roast chicken on supermarket buns at the foot of the falls, back when supermarkets existed and chicken wasn't just for the ridiculously rich.

The river's long gone, but if I squint I can almost convince myself. Are there shoots winking among the boulders, tiny emerald fairies? Or is that just my hypoxia talking?

The timer vibrates and I pull the mask on just in time, taking a deep breath as I tighten the straps. The searing skin on my face throbs as the fan kicks in. I'm tempted to head downstream to investigate my green hallucinations, but the dust index is over 200 today and I have clinic starting in an hour.

"You're late again," the nurse grins. "You owe me a Q-bar."

"Shut up, Dave. I brought you beer instead." I throw him a jar.

"You might need it yourself at the end of the day," he says, not throwing it back. "You've got a long list."

The first record is a short one, as most of them are. The

people from the Outers don't seek medical care unless they have to. Actually, this free clinic is an anomaly in Aotea, but my boss is buddies with the Mayor. Call me cynical but it's good optics to sponsor Professor Rawene's projects, especially in an election year.

Mr Reyes, a 35-year-old man, has breathing issues. The crowded conditions in the Outers make that a fairly normal problem. But when I turn to the lung function graph, the pattern looks familiar. I flip the page to check his occupation and my stomach twists.

"Dave, does Mr Reyes have his family with him today? Could you tell them to wait please?" He nods.

Mr Reyes is stunted, not unusual for someone from his part of the City. I clasp his hand, feeling the clamminess of his skin, and sneak a quick feel of the pulse. It's weak and fast, with the occasional ectopic beat.

"My name is Dr An West. How are you today?"

"Fine." His smile warms me instantly. "I'm here now, you're going to make me better!" To be first in line for my clinic, he would have had to queue for hours, from long before the lights came on.

"You been working on the ventilation shafts?"

"Only for a few months. Ae but it's good to be outside!"

I agree, but don't mention it. Lots of people fear the outside because they haven't been there. But since I started sneaking out, I've developed a relationship with the sky. It's not as empty as one might think. I'm brought back by a hand on my wrist.

"I'm ok, aren't I doc? It's just a cough that will go away?"

I don't quite manage to make my eyes meet his. "Why don't I send you for an X-ray, then I can talk to you and your whole family." I try a terrible joke. "My room is big enough to fit a rugby team."

It works, and Mr Reyes grins as he follows Dave. My clinic room will be bigger than the whole of the cramped quarters he and his family share. Even the narrow tunnels of the Outers, originally dug for maintenance and sweltering from its proximity to the surface, is expensive real estate, rented out in small sections by predatory landlords.

I pull up the lung function reports I've saved. Mr Reyes' curve matches the others'. There's a catastrophic drop-off in total lung capacity. I already know that the X-ray will show fluffiness of his airways, as if he's inhaled a cloud. It's almost beautiful. But the fibrosis will slowly starve him of oxygen and in months or years, it will finish its job.

After Dave has ushered out the weeping family, I open the next case and work through the rest of my day mechanically. Normally I love the Workers' Clinic. It's much more varied than the uptight paying patients from the Mid-Levels and Core, and there's always some juicy pathology. But I can't get Mr Reye's face out of my mind. How he smiled, even when I told him what would happen.

"I trust you to look after me, Dr An."

I get home late, but Dad's awake and on his dialysis. He's been sleeping so much since Mum passed, I take every opportunity to chat with him, even if I have a pile of case notes to do.

"I went out to the waterfall again today, Dad."

He smiles, still distant. "How was she?"

I never know whether he means mum or something else. He and Mum used to hike out to the Fairy Falls as a date, and roast chicken featured regularly. Back then it still rained, and Mum would hold onto Dad's hand to steady herself as she clambered over rocks slippery with moss. One day he lost his grip and Mum had gone bumscooting over the rocks, laughing like crazy. He'd lost the ring he was going to propose with but she still said yes.

"I thought I saw some new shoots."

He almost returns to himself. "I wonder what species? Now that would have been something for your mother to figure."

My mother spent half her life working in a mushroom factory, but loved the colour green. Because of her I know lots of native plant names, scientific and traditional, even though I've only seen them in books. She never gave up dreaming that one day the lush bush of her childhood would return.

"An! Come in, have a chocolate. The mayor gave these to me after my speech last night."

Professor Rawene's office smells of her favourite scent, tea roses. She's a miracle worker, with the sexy backstory of having worked her way out of the Outers through sheer guts and sass. I couldn't believe my luck when she picked me out of the medical student line-up. I've spent my training years wanting to be her. Exactly like her, even down to her perfume.

"How's the clinic?"

I chew regretfully. Luxury items like chocolates should never be eaten quickly. "Busy. I didn't get home till after lights down."

She frowns. "I hope you didn't walk."

"I don't mind, it's perfectly—"

"The Outers isn't safe to walk through when it's late." She makes a note. "I'll get the Police to supply an escort."

I don't want one, but I can see there's no point arguing.

"Now what did you want to ask me about?"

"I've been seeing a trend." I pass her my screen. "There seems to be more and more of these cases."

She slides on her glasses. "That slide in FEV1."

"Yes, and the only thing they have in common is they've all worked on the Outside."

She frowns. "We know it's safe. The surface ozone levels have been stable for decades now."

Trust Prof to jump straight to the answer.

"Ah, ozone," I say, nodding wisely.

She's not fooled. "Go home and look it up, An. But that's not the reason. It's probably just a coincidence."

"But I've collected over seventy cases—"

"Focus on your real work, An." Prof passes me back the screen. "Your medical skills are good, but you need more practice or I can't sign off on your specialty registration."

I'm going to be a fully qualified general physician in two weeks. Mum would be so proud. Despite being Westernised, her Cantonese mama roots ran deep. My upcoming job comes with its own apartment in the Mid-levels. I suspect Prof's recommendation is why they picked me, a short half-Asian chick, out of tens of applicants. The apartment comes at the perfect time, when Dad needs access to running water for his dialysis.

Prof leans forward to offer me another chocolate and pats my knee. "Now go do your job."

Dad might have the best library in Aotea City – of real books, anyway. I have no idea how he and mum kept so many, over those years spent living in a tiny room with a vomity baby. Or what people made of a mushroom sorter and a pipe layer obsessed with stockpiling ancient local history. But if anyone asks me about bush loos of the Waitākere Ranges, I'm ready.

Their collection obsession even extended to Local Body

reports from the 2000s, showing rainfall and temperature records up to 2026, when the record abruptly stopped with the great Fire that destroyed most of the tree cover of Aotearoa. I guess it made them too sad to keep on documenting as the drought set in and the seasonal tornadoes blew away the soil. It's hard to imagine anything but lichen growing on the bare outcrops now.

"What are you looking for?" Dad asks. He's hooked up and can't move.

"Ozone." I slide my finger along the paper columns. "I remember seeing it once and wondering why they measured it."

"Ozone hole," Dad says. Even though he's so distant in the present, details in the past are focused. He goes on to explain. Apparently back then ozone was the good guy. No one even worried about surface ozone but the enthusiastic rangers of the Waitākeres measured it from the tree canopies anyway.

"Here it is." I've found it on the report. Fifty years ago, surface ozone was at 0.01 parts per million – well within the safe zone, from my reading. And these days – I look up the official City measurements online – it's at 0.09 ppm. Still safe. With its dampening effect on lung growth and promotion of inflammation and chronic lung disease, it would have been the perfect explanation for what I was seeing in my patients. But nothing is ever perfect.

Dad's fumbling through his work chest, the one that holds all his treasures. Finally he sighs, flicks a switch and holds something out to me. "It still works, after all these years."

"Wow. A retro digital display." I weigh the solid block in my hand.

"It was state of the art once," says Dad. "An ozone meter."

"It was hers?" I'd forgotten that, long before my time, Mum was a local ranger.

"Take it," says Dad. "Maybe she'd like it if you gave it a whirl by the waterfall."

The sky is bluer than I've ever seen, but still potentially deadly. In spring, storms can arrive without warning. But taking off my mask will allow me to see better. Right?

The dry hot air burns at my face and upper chest as I take Mum's meter out and flick it on. The numbers blink for a seemingly long time before settling. *6.2 ppm.*

That must be wrong. A ten times increase from what the official website showed? I press the button to go again. *6.3 ppm.* The meter must be stuffed, because if it were right, I would be breathing in highly toxic levels right now. I pull out the official numbers to compare and then I notice something.

There's no natural variation in the numbers. They cycle evenly: 0.6, 0.7, 0.8. 0.6, 0.7, 0.8. As if churned out by a computer, far too perfect to be real.

Prof is at her desk, staring at the graphs I've just brought her. "Where did you get these numbers?"

"I – found a portal that was unlocked."

"An! You went outside? You collected these illegally?"

"Aren't you the one who taught me to always double check my evidence?"

"But not at the risk of your own life!" She's standing up now, her face a picture of concern.

"You said it was safe to go out."

"It is, with a mask –"

"I wear a mask," I lie.

"You still shouldn't go out. You have no idea what might happen."

I think of standing at the top of that waterfall, looking at rocks tumbled by a long-extinct river and feeling at peace. I want to tell her but I know how busy she is, even though she makes time for me. "Do you know why the official numbers are ten times less?"

She frowns, then smiles. "Why do you doubt the official numbers?"

"I don't know, I—"

"An. Let it go. Leave it to others to keep the records, your job is with the sick."

I remember the touch of Mr Reye's hand, cool and clammy, and his warm smile. "Shouldn't my job be to work out what's making them sick?"

Prof sighs and rolls her eyes very slightly. "An, are you really ready to be a Specialist? I'm beginning to wonder."

The next time I go to the portal, it's been protected by a key-code. So have all the other portals. So I find a crowd of workers, ready to slip out behind them.

Hanging back, I see a familiar face coughing and wheezing his way towards the doors.

"Mr Reyes! You won't remem—"

"Dr An! Of course I remember you! The one who is going to save my life!" He clutches my hand delightedly.

"You shouldn't be going—"

"My wife is pregnant again. Yes, yes, it is wonderful news, we accept God's gift. But now I have to work even harder."

I look at him and the other workers. "Where are your masks?"

"The city doesn't supply them to us any more. We have to buy our own if we want one. But it is no matter, it is safe to work. Masks will only get in the way."

"Why don't you take mine?"

"No, I cannot. It is so expensive." He hands it back firmly. "Don't you worry, dear doctor. Look after yourself."

When I finally get home, Dad is asleep. I carefully place the meter on the table beside him. This afternoon, I took it to Biomedical, who said it was still perfectly calibrated and the best-preserved old tech they had seen.

I sit down at my desk, and open the records I got from the city archives.

"Your mother would have wanted to find the truth too," Dad says. The click of the meter must have woken him.

"How did you know—"

"You're not eating. And you're muttering a lot."

I groan. It's no wonder I drive away boyfriends if even my dad thinks I'm weird.

"You've always cared too much about your patients," Dad says gently. "But if you don't want to get too deep, I'd stop right now."

I suddenly stop scrolling and stare at the line of numbers on the screen. My mouth drops open.

"I'm too late, aren't I?" Dad says, smiling.

The Commons is where the great and good of the City gather. It's protected by lines of guards to keep out the riff-raff, but no one's ever commented on the irony of the name.

Today, it's also where I'm meeting Prof for lunch in a fancy café. She's promised to buy me real coffee in celebration of my attainment of Specialist status. From now on, I'll be one of the elite, like Prof, just not as famous.

"I've got something to show you." I've spent all night imagining how excited and worried she'll be.

Prof takes my screen. She frowns, reading, as I gabble.

"That first graph shows that surface ozone levels had been gradually rising since the 1990s, when global warming was first raised as an issue. But the great Fire of 2026 is when there was a huge jump in ozone, brought about by the perfect storm of hydrocarbon release and intense heat. In fact surface ozone was one of the reasons construction of an underground city became so urgent."

"I can't see why this is news," Prof says.

I nearly burst with anticipation. "I plotted the second graph from the measures the City engineers have been taking ever since the City was founded, in 2027. It shows that Outside ozone levels have stayed high since the Fire, though with seasonal variations. In summer, the levels routinely go as high as 7 or 8 parts per million. It could explain all the cases we've been seeing."

"That's quite a big leap to make."

"I've run the data controlling for all confoundables. Can't you see? If those workers are outside in those high levels, after just a few weeks their lungs will start to show changes. I talked to them and none of them have masks, it's a major health and safety issue."

"So what do you propose?"

"We need to tell the Works Department urgently. I know it's more money but it's worth it for the lives saved."

Prof closes her eyes and holds them shut for a few seconds. When she opens them again, her expression is blank.

"Maybe you could talk to the Mayor," I say, hoping for more enthusiasm.

"An. You're a good doctor but you really are naïve, aren't you? What do you think will happen if the Mayor announces that masks are now needed, after all this time? She'll be sued by every Worker family in the City. There'll be demonstrations. An uprising."

"But—"

"We need to do our job without getting involved in politics."

"But this isn't politics! What about the workers who die and leave their families without an income? You know what happens! Children disappear—"

"An, I'm starting to seriously question your fitness to practise. The City needs Specialists who will serve the needs of its population, not chase false rumours. The ozone levels on the City website are correct, they're measured by automated sensors, so not subject to the human error of the past. You need to stop worrying."

She smiles and for the first time I see that it's a tiger smile.

*

My bare feet clutch the edge of the burning rock as my mouth inhales heavy, warm air. My breath comes faster as I dig my toes into the final foothold and drop into the valley. The boulders stretch out in front. I focus on stepping one by one, making slow, steady progress towards the tiny glint of green. My mask timer has gone off long before, but it seems futile to use it now. I don't have long, but I have all the time in the world.

Finally I reach it. A tiny plant, three delicate shoots extended, and a single heart-shaped leaf. Kawakawa. My mother would have been pleased it was this one that I found. She used to talk about the healing balm and how she itched to pluck its leaves one more time. But this little leaf is safe, at least from me.

I turn back to look at the waterfall. Maybe my parents used to look from this spot too, in a time long ago when this world was still green and flowing with abundant water.

By now, my report will be flowing into the inbox of every doctor and public servant in Aotea City. A summary sent to all the news reporters, with a link to where I found the data. My father will be dozing on his chair, waiting for the lifesaving fluid to drain from his abdomen. We'll lose the apartment once they tell me I no longer have a job, but it doesn't matter. Dad's disease was already progressing. "I'll tell Mum what you did when I see her," he said.

There is all the time in the world. I might retrain: journalism seems like a good option now. I slide on my mask and walk towards the waterfall. Gripping the rock, I begin to climb.

THE DOUBLE-CAB CLUB

TIM JONES

Mike nosed his electric van into the garage. Amy and Oliver were already home, he saw, their bikes next to each other. Mike's SUV stood in the other parking bay, waiting for tomorrow night.

The van, with its ladders in the back, its pipes and guttering, its toolbox, its battery that needed to be charged every night, was work. The SUV was freedom.

Today had been a long, hot day, lots of people trying to cope with the effects of the last downpour, lots of people trying to get ahead of the next one. He wanted to grab some food, knock the invoicing off, and head for bed. But he'd promised Amy he'd be there for the start of her meeting instead.

Amy was buzzing around in the high-tension way he recognised so well, the way that made him want to find a quiet corner till the air was less electric. But she'd spotted him.

"There you are! Get a shower quick, and then see if you can get that boy of ours moving."

"He's old enough to get himself moving."

"Just talk to him."

Three-minute showers? No problem. Mike emerged twenty seconds under the limit, changed into his second-best clothes, and went to roust out his son.

Who'd fallen asleep on his bed again. That boy could sleep for his country. He was sure as hell going to get a rude awakening next year – lots of rude awakenings.

"Whaaaa—oh. It's you."

"It's me. Your mother needs you to get up and get moving. Have you forgotten you promised to open up the hall and get the zip on and the kettles ready? What with yesterday's announcement, the place will be full of people falling over each other to complain."

"It's not enough," said Oliver.

"Not enough?"

"An 8% cut in carbon allocation next year is nowhere near enough. We need a 12% reduction per year, minimum, worldwide. And richer countries like us—"

Richer countries? Jeez. Everyone else must be in pretty bad shape, then. His son was off on one, banging on about contraction and convergence.

Mike's gaze swept around Oliver's room. So many books: books were back, now streaming used up too many carbon credits. *The New Colonialism. The Great Burning. Silent Summer.*

"You read too much," Mike said. "Come on, get moving."

Amy had already eaten and was off getting her papers together. Mike made dinner for himself and Oliver, then shooed the boy out the door in the direction of the school hall.

"What do you think?" asked Amy, coming back into the room and giving a little twirl.

"I think you look beautiful."

"You know that's not what I mean," she smiled.

"I think – yeah, I think it works. Maybe the dark grey jacket, though, not the blue?"

Amy's face sobered. "This is where they're going to start hating me, isn't it? Last week at the marae was the good part. Now comes the part where I have to convince people to make do with less. No wonder Kahu was so keen for me to take over."

"It's not like you'll be up on the stage by yourself," Mike pointed out. "Kahu will be there too, and she won't let you come to any harm."

"I wish you'd stay for the whole meeting."

"But you know I—"

"Have got to get your invoices done. But you could do those tomorrow night if you weren't taking that bloody credit-guzzler out to meet up with the boys."

"Do we really have to get into this tonight?" asked Mike. "Really?" He was aware his voice was rising. He hated moments like this, when he started to echo his father.

Amy crossed her arms, looked at him, and sighed.

"We don't," she said. "But it can't wait forever. Now I'm neighbourhood captain, whatever you do is going to reflect on me. Anything from Emily?"

Mike shook his head. "Bit early yet. Hey—" He crossed the room and reached out his arms. She snuggled against him. "I'm proud of you. You're going to be great at this. And if it gets really nasty tonight, I'll stay."

*

The school hall was an oasis of light in the night-time darkness. Inside, adults stood in couples and clusters while kids ran around. Mike nodded to Prakash Kumar, who was arguing with Dave Bruce, as usual – you'd never know they'd been friends for twenty years. He chatted for a while with Zhang Liao – just as Oliver was facing the prospect of service in the Climate Corps next year, so was Mr Zhang's daughter.

"I'm after a coffee," said Mike, and excused himself. He studied his son for a moment before crossing the room. Oliver was seventeen now, a young man. He inhabited his body as if it was an ill-fitting suit.

He had so nearly not made it. From the incubator to his early teens, Oliver's life had been a battle for air. Four years ago, when a salbutamol shortage had coincided with the start of fire season, Oliver had spent three terrifying nights in hospital. He'd never been as bad again, but next year, he would be assigned to some collapsing corner of the country and expected to plant trees or shore up seawalls or rewild wetlands. With his asthma, he could have applied for a medical exemption and got a desk job, but Oliver had refused. Mike didn't know whether to admire him or tell him he was an idiot. "You talk to him," Mike had said to Amy. "He listens to you." But so far, Oliver hadn't budged.

Fathers and sons, a continuing story.

Mike's own Dad had been massive on sport. When Mike was young, the Bathurst 1000 had been their appointment viewing. He remembered curling up in the crook of his father's arm on the couch as the Holdens and Fords roared round the Mount Panorama circuit, the gums in the background hazed by heat and exhaust fumes.

But that had been before the big fires came, when Kiwis still thought Australia was the land of opportunity.

Oliver noticed Mike staring at him, and stared back. "Want something?"

"A coffee?"

"Oh," said Oliver. "Sure."

A hush rippled outwards from the stage: it was time for the karakia.

Mike took a seat in the third row, between Dave Bruce and an elderly woman he didn't know, and followed the formalities as best he could. His reo was very much a work in progress: he was confident enough with his pepeha, but soon got lost after that. Now Amy had risen to the heights of neighbourhood captain, it was another way he was going to have to step up. She could move smoothly in two worlds, while he could barely avoid tripping over himself in one.

"Thank you," Amy said in English. "Thank you for putting your trust in me. If I didn't already know I have big shoes to fill, Kahu's example makes that very clear."

Amy paused for a moment. Here comes the hard part, thought Mike.

"Now the citizens' assembly has decided the base carbon credit allocation will be reduced by a further 8% next year, we need to decide what we're going to do as a community to make sure we can meet that target and help those who find it hardest."

Someone down the back shouted "We've cut to the bone already! What else are we supposed to do? Stop eating?"

"Quiet!" called Kahu, and the audience piped down. Amy would have to learn to command a crowd like that.

"We all knew this was going to be tough," Amy said. "The key is that we share the burden, share the pain. Common effort for the common good, right?"

"Unless you've got mates in the black market!"

"Which is why the Government is also announcing an expanded tribunal system for dealing with black marketeers."

"So you want us to dob in our neighbours, is that it?"

On it went. Mike was in two minds. He cheered as loud as anyone when they announced black marketeers had been put on trial, but at the same time, he knew people who knew people who could get you things, and once or twice, when he was desperate for parts, he'd made use of them. All at arm's length, of course, nothing that could be traced back to him … he hoped.

But that would have to stop. Now Amy was neighbourhood captain, that would have to stop. All eyes would be on them.

The crowd simmered down. All across the city, all across the country, meetings like this would be happening, knitting communities together even as the climate emergency tried to tear them apart.

Mike loved Amy and admired her skill with people, the way she could read them, the way she could talk them round. But all he really wanted was a couple of beers and a chance to de-stress with the boys.

He stayed till the tea break then caught Amy's eye. Heading towards the door, he navigated little eddies of conversation:

"Of course I agree it's an emergency, Prakash. But what I want to know is, how long will it last?"

"Some Government of National Unity – they spend all their time arguing with each other!"

"…then she told me she was hapū. I said, Julia, you know we can't… "

"Those billionaires have just hunkered down. They haven't gone away."

No message from Emily. What the heck, he thought, and called her as soon as he got home. She answered right away.

"We're just getting dinner, Dad. Hey, I'll head out on the

verandah. Did you know this used to be a milking shed?"

"You look tired," he said.

"I'm working hard, Dad. Humans aren't as good at pollinating fruit trees as bees were. I saw some, though!"

"Saw some what?"

"Bees! Large as life. One nearly stung me. But that's a good sign, isn't it?"

Mike remembered a day when no one was excited to see a bee. What a world.

"How's that girlfriend of yours?"

"She's good. Hey, Camila!"

Camila was full of words, as usual. How two people could stand to be so bubbly together was beyond Mike, but he was glad Emily had found her, especially after that horrible thing with Emily's team leader last year. Finally Camila handed the phone back.

"How was Mum's meeting?"

"She's in her element. I came back early. Got to get the invoicing done."

"It's your night with the boys tomorrow, isn't it? The Double-Cab Club?"

"Sure is. I'm going to enjoy it while I still can. Are they giving you any breaks?"

"Day off on Saturday. We're off to a barn dance!"

"Where do you get the energy?"

"Good genes, Dad. Love you!"

His daughter's face, smiling, an orange sky behind. Was that just the fabled Southern twilight, or had fire season already started in the Catlins?

With luck, Oliver would get posted to the West Coast. Down

there, they had what everybody else wanted: more water than they could use themselves, and no long droughts to endure before it arrived.

*

Late Friday afternoon. Mike was tired and hot and sweaty. He'd passed a couple of late jobs on to a mate so he could get home in good time to hit the road. Amy was deep in admin, Oliver was – wherever Oliver was.

Mike gave his SUV an unnecessary polish before setting out. God, she was beautiful. They made things to last in those days.

Rush hour wasn't what it used to be. Suburbanites made their way home by bike, bus and foot. Mike passed a painter on a cargo bike, his cans and brushes in the cargo compartment, his ladders on a spindly trailer behind. That must save a bunch on carbon credits, thought Mike.

It was getting to the point where he was starting to feel conspicuous in an SUV. Kids were giving him the gimlet eye.

As he waited at the crossing for the packed intercity train to crawl through, Mike could see the thunderheads forming again. He was heading straight into the weather. When the rain fell these days, it really fell.

The air conditioning hummed. The tracklist from one of his Dad's old driving compilations filled the cab. He sat back, one hand on the wheel, and drove like there was no tomorrow, his mind already on pulling up to the roadhouse, on blowing the rest of his month's personal carbon budget on a succulent, miraculous steak. Beers and bros, a long evening of bullshit and banter before he had to face the journey home.

The road was wet now: his lights showed pools of water

forming. A crack of thunder drowned out Cold Chisel. Hail hammered the windscreen. Bugger, thought Mike, and switched his full attention to the road. The roadhouse was another thirty minutes away through bumpy hills and steep-sided valleys.

Not so many people came this way any more. The road was beginning to fall into disrepair, potholes eating away at the edges of the tarmac. Mike gunned the engine and climbed up a switchback hill cloaked with regenerating bush, then coasted down into the next valley. The streams and little rivers were filling rapidly. Some farmer's crop, too dark to make out in the twilight, was in a lot of danger.

The rain grew heavier, Mike's wipers barely keeping pace. He turned up his music to drown out the deluge: Chisel had never sounded better.

Sometimes, he wished the world had just ignored the terrible events of the early 20s, fire, flood and pestilence, and put up two fingers to the future. Eat lots of meat, drink lots of milk, burn hydrocarbons and be merry, for tomorrow we die: a short life, but an exciting one.

Even with all these cuts, all this drawing in of belts, there was no guarantee they would succeed. The world was still getting warmer year by year, and it would be a long time before the blanket of carbon started to thin. A very long time.

Mike shook his head to clear it of the gloom. Ten more minutes and he'd be pulling in for food and beers.

If he'd been paying closer attention, he might have seen the washout. Mike negotiated a sharp left-hander and discovered the bridge ahead of him, probably weakened by storm after storm, had disappeared downriver. He jammed on the brakes, but it wasn't enough. His SUV slid on the wet road, went over the edge, and nosedived into the rapidly rising water, barely remaining upright. The torrent swept the vehicle downstream, only Mike's seatbelt saving him from being smashed against dashboard and windscreen and steering wheel. He braced himself and hoped, prayed, for the battering to stop.

It did. With a shuddering thump, the vehicle hit the bank: not hard enough to trigger the airbags, but hard enough to shake Mike up. As the driver's side began to sink into the deeper flow of water that was scouring out the bank, Mike scrambled to the passenger side, opened the door as the weight of water lifted, and managed to scramble out. He tried to balance on the tilting vehicle, but it was no use: his legs went from under him and he fell into the muddy, swirling torrent, banging his head on the vehicle as he went down. For a sickening moment, he thought he was going to drown right there – then the current washed him up against a tree that had fallen from the bank. He clung on, managed to lever himself up.

Light dazzled him. Upstream, his SUV had broken free of its resting place. Now it was floating towards him, picking up speed as it went. If it hit him, he would be either crushed or drowned.

Amy. Emily. Oliver.

With a final effort, he heaved himself along the trunk. Trailing roots still clung to the soil. He jammed his hands and feet into any gaps he could find and hauled himself to the relative safety of the bank above.

He lay and watched his taillights disappear downstream. As they cut out, he heard a chunk of the bank fall in the water. He dragged himself further away. God, he was cold.

"Move," he told himself. "Move." He climbed to his feet, pain beginning to cut through the adrenaline.

Across the fields, barely visible in the driving rain, he could see a shed. It offered the possibility of shelter. Mike trudged across the sodden field. Dark sky above, drowning world below.

The shed was locked, but when he rounded it, he saw a farmhouse ahead, a welcome glimmer of light in one window. It was going to be embarrassing to admit what a careless fool he'd been, but there was no time to delay: he was shivering. Mike knocked loudly on the farmhouse door.

*

As summer drew to a close, they saw Oliver off at the train station. Their son had been assigned up north, where things were getting really desperate. He was equal parts elated and scared stiff. It would be the making, or the breaking, of him.

An empty nest, at least for now.

"Emily's got leave in a month," Mike said. "Let's make it easy for her and invite Camila as well."

Amy nodded.

"OK," she said. "Back into it. The Karaitiana whānau have invited me over, and then we're all meeting with the community gardens crew to see if we can get yields up again. The trouble is, the individual allotments…"

Mike listened with half an ear. He was catching up with the boys again tomorrow, for the first time since the accident. Finally, they'd decided to let him live down the loss of his SUV.

Beers and a barbeque, he'd promised them, though the beers would be low-alcohol and the steaks vegan. He thought they'd cope with that. The real worry would be what they'd say about the new trailer he was constructing for his cargo bike.

WILD HORSES

ANTHONY LAPWOOD

You couldn't hear a sound or see anything moving. It was another world. The houses on the shore didn't belong. Nor the people either.
— From "A Great Day" by Frank Sargeson

The sunlight stung Adam's eyes and the world kept falling out of focus. His visual field, his root feeling for the world—everything was disrupted. Things were easier when he closed his eyes. The darkness was comforting—relatively—though incomplete. Amoebic patterns of pale white and orange blinked and slid across the darkly shuttered view.

The car shook with their speed. They were travelling with frightening urgency towards or away from something. Hands on the wheel, Jeremy had tried to explain, but his words had been hard to make sense of, and for a while Adam had been lapsing in and out of a heavy blackness. He knew he had to think carefully, now that he was conscious again, but it was difficult through the expansive pain in his head.

Hey, Adam. Knock-knock.

… Uh-huh?

Come on. Knock-knock.

… Who's there?

Server request. Knock-knock.

… Who's there?

Server request server request server request. Knock-knock.

…

Knock-knock, man.

Okay. Who's there?

Server request server request server request server request server request server request server request server request server request server request server request server request—

Okay! Stop. Please.

You see how that works?

No. It just hurts.

Now imagine a thousand other people knocking and yelling at you, all at the same time: server request server request server request server request server request—

Okay! It fucking hurts.

Overwhelmed computer servers go down for a bit, then they come back up. But people, they get pushed too far, it can be game over. Psyches entirely screwed. They stumble around, pissing and shitting and groaning, nothing more than dumb brain stems on legs.

… But not us?

Not us, bud.

Adam opened his eyes. Jeremy was smiling wide. Then he looked at Adam, frowned, and turned back to face the road, hunching over the wheel. Adam looked too, at the noon-lit wasteland of dirt and scrub stretching out all around them, the Desert Road one long black line splitting the landscape in two.

It looked uglier and more barren than Adam remembered it ever being.

Jeremy looked like how Adam remembered. Except of course for the shaved head, stippled and stubbly, indentations catching the light, showing the subtle ways all heads are misshapen.

Not us, buddy. The question is, are we the only ones who aren't fucked?

Adam touched the bandage at his ear. It was wrapped tight under his jaw, and angled up to the back of his skull where the central throbbing was, where Jeremy said to be very careful. Jeremy looked at him touching the bandage and Adam brought his hand back down.

I'm glad I could get you out.

… Yeah.

It's a bit of a procedure and it's not fun. It was a challenge but I did it for you, buddy. Lucky I had some practice first. Jeremy tapped the top of his own head with the points of two fingers like testing a soft-boiled egg. He checked his wristwatch, an antique analogue with large hands, Roman numerals, a cracked face. You can have more oxycodone in half an hour. Try to chill. You can rest against the pillows, don't worry about getting blood on them.

Adam nestled his head gently back. Pillows all thin and ratty but collectively they provided cushioning, piled up between his neck and shoulder and the door. His head ached with a strong, steady pressure, as if the fused seams of the bones of his skull might buckle and break open.

They hit a bump in the road and Adam felt his brain smack against the inside of his head. He screamed, and his vision went white, then black, and hot automatic tears streamed down his face. He heard himself whimpering.

*

Last time Adam had seen Jeremy, they'd both been drunk and got kicked out of a bar because Jeremy tried to pick a fight. On the street he kept going, shouting at people around them, and the bouncer shoved him off the pavement, into the gutter. Jeremy called the man ignorant scum, and Adam apologised and dragged Jeremy away by the arm. Adam was furious. Had Jeremy lost his stupid mind? There was no chance of just having fun anymore, because all Jeremy did was start shit. Jeremy was unhinged. Jeremy was an arsehole. Adam didn't care what was up with Jeremy, he just wanted him to stop wrecking everything. Jeremy spat and took off. He left Adam a voicemail the next morning. He knew where Adam was coming from, knew he was difficult to be around. He was taking charge of the situation, so Adam didn't need to worry; he wouldn't see him again. Adam said thank fuck, not sure if he truly was thankful to see the back of Jeremy, but guessing he probably was. He deleted the message, and with the larger problem of a savage hangover to be reckoned with, he fried up a big greasy breakfast...

Something in the memory was missing. Five, six, seven, eight. Eight years ago, and a lot of memories of nights like that final one, the memories all stacked up, overlaid, none especially distinguishable from all the others like it...

What apart from being the last time was different about that night?

What was different—what was different was—

There was a moment when Jeremy stood triumphant in the gutter. And Adam hadn't grabbed him by the arm, not that night. He'd tried but Jeremy tugged free, his fist closed tight around something. Jeremy stood eyeballing the bouncer for what felt like a long time, but must've been a few seconds, tops. Adam told Jeremy to move on but Jeremy was impassive, smirking. Jeremy called the bouncer some name (ignorant scum? something like that) then let something drop from his hand. It was small and black with a tiny glowing light. Adam didn't know what it was until he turned and saw the bouncer reach up to his head, feeling for the missing earpiece. When Adam looked back to Jeremy he was grinding his foot down into the gutter, breaking the small black thing into pieces, before running off into the darkness where a string of streetlights had failed, with the bouncer shouting after him, and Adam was running too, as fast as he could, though he never caught up.

*

We're not digital. We're animal.

Adam opened his eyes and groaned, a small, wounded sound.

We conceive of things very differently to a computer. We remember things differently. We process things differently. Simple facts.

I need to get out.

Bud, no. I'm sorry.

I'm going to be sick.

Here. Go ahead if you need to. Jeremy reached across and unlatched the glove box. He pulled out a plastic bag and handed it to Adam.

Adam fumbled the bag open, let the bitter vomit rise up and out. It dribbled down his chin and the front of his T-shirt, and then he saw that part of the bag had stuck back on itself and hadn't properly opened.

Shit. Well, don't worry. We can wash that up.

Huh?

But Jeremy was already slowing down, angling the car towards the side of the road. They stopped, then Jeremy was outside, opening Adam's door. Vomit slid off the surface of the bag as Adam stumbled out. The bag fell and caught in the gravel behind the front tyre. The lower half of Adam's T-shirt was soaked and Jeremy said to take it off. Adam raised his arms and Jeremy lifted the T-shirt up, slow and cautious around Adam's head.

I feel dizzy.

Just a sec.

Jeremy dragged the T-shirt off the ends of Adam's outstretched hands. He balled the T-shirt up and Adam sat on the edge of the passenger seat, feeling the warm air across his naked torso and scalp. The air tingled his skin and it felt good, like the gentle tug of a tether, reminding him he was bound to the world. The world was still there for him outside Jeremy's car. He watched Jeremy collect the bag and hold it out with one hand, allowing the breeze to fill the bag with air. Jeremy stuffed the T-shirt into the bag and sent the unpleasant package, with a gentle underarm toss, into the scrubland.

We're not taking it?

Why? It's just stinking rubbish.

Won't someone find it?

Who, Adam?

Adam had spent stretches of time phasing in and out, but as far as he knew, as far as anything he'd seen, little as that was, it was true. They hadn't seen any other vehicles, any other people. Jeremy moved to the back of the car and opened the boot.

Why didn't you stop before?

Because we have to keep moving.

Jeremy slammed the boot shut and came around and handed Adam a bottle of water and a fresh T-shirt.

Wash your face before you put this on.

Adam rinsed his mouth out and ran a wet hand across his lips and chin then splashed some water over his hand.

Careful with that. We have a limited supply.

Okay. Adam capped the bottle and slipped the T-shirt on without Jeremy's help this time. Easing his head slowly through the hole, he felt like a turtle emerging from its shell to see what the world had to offer. The thought made him smile, a little kid's game. He stifled a stupid laugh – a sudden partial uncoiling of the tension that had been twisting through his body. He took a long, uneven breath, in and out, then turned and sat back in the seat, buckled the belt, began rebuilding the pile of pillows, as Jeremy climbed in the driver's side.

Adam closed his eyes and watched the pale patterns shift.

When he was twelve, Jeremy had tried to kill himself. He and Adam weren't friends then, weren't even in the same city. Their friendship happened a couple of years later, in their first year of high school together. Jeremy told Adam about it after another boy, sneering, said to Jeremy at lunch break, I thought you were long dead, ghostdick. Jeremy said to Adam, I'll tell you so you don't have to ask, and he told Adam how his dad had found him, how the hospital pumped his stomach and locked him in a psych ward for six months. Word spread quickly, though most kids didn't bother saying much to Jeremy's face. When they did, Jeremy snapped back, Haunt your dreams forever motherfucker, and Adam would draw a finger across his own neck as if that made more sense of the threat. One morning, the school counsellor—a stocky woman with sharp grey eyes behind thick glasses, and the rasping voice of a committed smoker—pulled Adam aside after biology class and told him it was a very fortunate thing Jeremy had a friend like him to rely on. Adam hadn't suspected until then that Jeremy and the counsellor perhaps spoke regularly. But something caught on and the general responsibility he had felt towards Jeremy became absolute from that point, like an invisible cage had coalesced in the air, encapsulating the two of them however far apart their bodies ever were in space.

*

Show it to me.

Show you what, bud?

The thing you took out. The chip.

I can't.

Show me.

… You don't believe me?

I just want to see it.

You think I'd lie about this?

… No. I just want to see it. See what it's like.

It's nothing special. Anyway, you can't.

… Why not?

I attached it to a rat … Caught it and kept it for just this purpose.

What … purpose?

Anybody who wants to trace that chip, assuming there's anybody left who can trace it, they're going to think you're lost in the Kaimai Ranges.

…

I let it go while you were still bleary as hell. Check out the cage on the floor back there.

Adam looked behind Jeremy's seat and saw the construction of wire bars half-concealed by a stained towel. The bottom of the bars were attached to a grey plastic tray lined with wood chips.

I'm not a liar, Adam.

I know.

The world's gotten all fucked up. I saw it coming and I did my best to get us prepared.

… Thanks.

This is a rescue operation. You can't kidnap your best mate, right? Jeremy laughed. We're still friends, yeah? That's not going to change.

Jeremy looked thinner but not older than he had eight years earlier.

Adam had no recollection of meeting Jeremy again—Why?—Only the time afterwards—Last night, wasn't it?—In the Milky Way room—

I'm not paranoid, Jeremy said. I can see why you might think that. Paranoia should have been more normal.

I had a normal life. An ordinary life.

Appearances, eh!

Talking about the end of the world excited Jeremy. He was enthusiastic about it—he felt vindicated. But he was volatile, too. Easily riled if his motivations were questioned. And he wasn't afraid to wield a weapon against a friend. If the story could run wild, if Adam could let Jeremy run wild with the story, would something open up? A clue, a way of understanding this senseless situation? This—Whatever Jeremy was doing————Hoping to do————Test the tale but not the teller——

Augtech's banned. Dad always said he never saw any.

Banned? Kind of.

... So they?

They shut down the commercial enterprises. But I think they were already transferring the technology to the military by then, or soon after.

The military?

... Your head okay, bud?

Sore. But I'm fine. I want to know ... what we're dealing with.

Well ... augmented realities are a great way to create smoke-screens. Hide all sorts of shit and control populations and basically just fuck with people.

The advantages are ... obvious, I guess.

Evil's the word. I mean, working things in the other direction, there's direct psychic espionage—sucking your thoughts right out of your head. And you know, our brains are hugely powerful machines. If you could find a way to network them and harness that animal processing power, then maybe you could drastically improve your chances against all kinds of unpredictable chaos. Calculate the future to some greater extent. Forecast weather months in advance. Out-manoeuvre enemies every time. All for the sake of maintaining a self-managing population of protein-based processors.

... Until they go down.

Right. Until the animals go down.

Was it an attack?

Perhaps, but there's been no follow-through. Not yet. Just this mass disabling. I think it spreads region by region.

Spreads?

However it's working. It could all be a monumental acci-dent... You're going pale again. Try to relax. I know it's a lot to take in.

… Where else, apart from here?

Must be loads of countries. Just another arms race. But whether or not they've been scrubbed out too … What're you looking at?

… The mountains.

In the distance to the west, the mountains were bare and brown.

Where's the snow?

There hasn't been snow for a long time. This is good. You're beginning to notice things. What else is different?

Adam looked around. Heading south on holiday when he was a kid, his mum and dad would challenge him and his older brother to spot wild horses. They're out there somewhere, his dad would say. If you look hard enough, his mum would chime in. If they found one, then everyone would get an ice cream when they reached the end of the Desert Road. Adam never spied a wild horse, but one time his brother said he did. Fleeting, barely there for a second. Dad acted surprised, but they all got their ice creams.

When Adam was thirteen, his dad admitted that the last wild horse had died a long time before he was even born, and Adam had laughed with appalled appreciation at his parents' commitment to the joke.

But it wasn't only horses. Spotting other things, real things, had been worth an ice cream, too.

Isn't this an army training ground?

No way. Jeremy laughed again, chirpy and light. I mean, yes, in the sense that it was once. And in the illusion they maintained for you and everyone else. But no, I don't think so. Not in reality. Not anymore.

*

It was like the Milky Way on the darkest nights, a thick smattering of lights, but every star was blood red and wet, dripping across the sky. The pain had been immediate and severe upon waking. Then the shock of seeing the spray of red, the abrupt crinkling of plastic when he tried to move. He wasn't looking up at the sky. No. He was propped up in one corner of a room. Red stars superimposed upon the nearest wall ... The room that contained him, seen through sheets of milky plastic covering every surface, looked like a curdled dream.

I had to. I had to, a voice said, and Adam recognised the voice of his old friend Jeremy, back from the dead again.

Then there were feet and legs, the knees bending as the body crouched. The plastic crinkling with each movement. Arms and torso, then Jeremy's serious face, close enough to Adam's that it filled the whole space.

They get them in through the fontanelle, his face said, mouth moving out of sync with the words, which had a long droning tail to their sound. When we're still babies with soft baby heads. Before our cranial bones harden into place. They do it like that so we can never get them out again.

Jeremy's face lifted out of view, followed by the torso, then the legs. Crunch of plastic underfoot. Adam turned his neck, slowly, slowly, and saw on the ground a blood-slicked power drill.

In through the fontanelle means out through the fontanelle. I'm sorry, bud. I had to.

The blood stars had blurred then, their colour deepening into black as they sank back into the heavy night falling down over Adam.

*

There's probably no going back.

Jeremy had slowed the car, approaching a gap in the low bank to the right, the ghost of a dirt road clear in the early afternoon light.

I mean, there's definitely no going back. So we should check things out. Stay cautious.

Jeremy reached across and rummaged in the elasticated pouch at the rear of Adam's seat. He leaned back in the driver's seat, lifting the black binoculars to his eyes.

There's a rise in the way. Can't see shit beyond a hundred metres.

Jeremy opened his door and got out of the car and Adam sat there saying nothing. Jeremy stuck his head back inside.

You coming?

They walked twenty metres to the top of a hillock. Unfiltered sunlight heated Adam's newly shaven scalp. The effect was entirely different to the earlier breeze, that tingling reminder of his place in the immediate world. Sunlight came from a great distance, it didn't at all care what it touched. The sweat beading all over his head and soaking into the bandage aggravated his sense of corporeal violation, his awareness of his mutilation.

Jeremy peered through the binoculars.

Look, he said after a minute, handing the binoculars to Adam.

Adam squinted ahead, ignoring Jeremy, watching with his own two eyes. He could see a row of objects like tree stumps halfway out to the horizon where the air shimmered above the earth and made everything within a certain band look as though it was moving in some direction——on towards the horizon or——towards him and Jeremy——

Take them and look.

Adam accepted the binoculars and raised them to his eyes. He found the line of tree stumps and saw that they were box-shaped rocks. Beside him, Jeremy began to huff and pace. Adam kept scanning, scrutinising the rocks.

Well? You see them? I guess you were right about this being an active army base.

Ah-huh.

They're fucked though. See the way they move? If our military's scuppered … Well, they're a mid-level power, they don't run the show. But…

Adam gave back Jeremy the binoculars and Jeremy looked again.

Twenty, maybe twenty-five.

Was Jeremy really seeing soldiers? Adam stared at the back of Jeremy's head, trying to occupy his friend's mind. Jeremy's head was shaved but Adam got the idea he'd just kept it that way after operating on himself. How long ago had he done that? There was nothing to indicate a fresh infliction. There was no pink scarring, no older pearled scarring.

Jeremy lowered the binoculars, turned and slapped Adam on the arm, a cheap gesture of camaraderie.

Let's get back to the car. We'll be safe to drive through, but I'd like to get a good look at them. We can follow the road a bit longer then walk inland.

At the foot of the hillock Adam spotted what he needed.

I think I can see something, he said.

Yeah?

Adam pointed ahead and to the right where a formation rose from the ground. It looked to Adam like a thicket of bushes, a thicket of nothing.

Jeremy raised the binoculars and looked out.

See anything?

… Not sure.

I thought I saw movement.

Adam picked up the rock and with one quick step forwards he swung it down on Jeremy's pale head with a resounding crack. Jeremy made a gulping sound and fell, the arm with the binoculars twisting under him. Adam dropped the rock onto the dirt and rolled Jeremy over to check. Jeremy's mouth and chin were covered with blood where he must have bitten down hard on his tongue. The blood bubbled between his lips. Adam held his hand under Jeremy's nose. He felt the ragged, warm breath. He turned Jeremy onto his side and positioned his limbs to keep him that way, in case his friend vomited. Adam took the keys from Jeremy's pocket then went to the car and popped the boot. He saw packets of dried food and trays of bottled water. A pup tent. A khaki tarp and a shovel. He grabbed bottles of water and muesli bars, walked back, placed them in the shade of a shrub within Jeremy's line of sight.

He returned and found paper and a pen in the glove box. Scratched down in childlike letterforms: I'LL SEND HELP.

A soft exhaustion was beginning to wrap all around——Don't let it take you over———over———

He drank water then walked again and put the note beside the supplies under the shrub, weighing it down with a stone, then went back to the car, sat in Jeremy's seat, legs shaking, turned the engine on. He turned the engine off and returned to the note, one glance at Jeremy to see he was still out. He lifted the stone and picked up the note and read it over, and read it over again, the square of paper trembling in his dusty hands, then stuffed it into his pocket. Jeremy's interpretation would only be a dangerous one. It was the only way of seeing he'd left for himself.

Now Jeremy was knocked out in the dirt and Adam back in the car had to—through the pressure in his head——he had to think.

The road is empty because it is closed.

(The road only closes in bad weather. It's warm outside. No snow on——)

Whatever the reason for the road's closure.

(Patrols would be stationed up and down————)

There's a township not too far away. A café and a military museum. The army base itself, somewhere off————Drills or————

Jeremy had halluci————————

(Jeremy had been filled with conviction, you saw that———— You hadn't seen————————)

(And aren't things different from the way *you* remember, from the——————Gone————)

The road is empty because——

Move————Just—Start driving——Just————

(Why are things different from how you both remember. Different from what each other sees.)

(Jeremy had no scar, no————————————)

But all heads are misshapen.

Adam found the oxycodone, swallowed four with water.

The fuel indicator, anyway.

Too low on petrol to turn around, to make it home.

Adam swung the car's shuddering metal body out onto the road, pointed it in the direction they'd been going, the only direction left to go. Don't look————Keep——Eyes dead ahead———Focus on the road out front———Eyes off the rear-view———Don't look even half a second. Jeremy stumbling onto the black bitumen, one hand raised to his head and the other in the air. That's all you'll see and then you'll have to choose.

Head throbbing, applying erratic pressure on the pedal, grip on the steering wheel unsteady, Adam sped on through the wild emptiness, never looking back—————Never——— —————Never looking———————————————

———————————————————————————————

———————————————————————————————

——————

YOU AND ME AT THE END OF THE WORLD

DAVE AGNEW

Nobody really noticed the day the world began to end. The sun rose as usual, though its warmth seemed to not quite reach the world's surface. No gods came for the faithful, no slumbering dragons rose from beneath the oceans to consume the unlucky.

I got out of bed, made a coffee, went to work. You did the same, and kissed me on the cheek as I left. You hadn't shaved. Somewhere deep behind the scenes, something started to wind down towards zero.

The first sign anyone took notice of came a few days later, when Matariki didn't rise one evening. We'd gone up the hill so we could watch the seven stars come over the horizon, bundled up against the cold midwinter. We laughed and leaned into each other, and pretended to worry that somehow we'd gone to the wrong hemisphere, while fighting down our growing unease.

We drank our travel mugs full of cocoa and drove home. On the radio, an astronomer was intrigued, confused, but not worried. A crazy called in to claim it was a sign God had left without telling anyone. Another blamed gay marriage. We laughed at that, and joked we'd take the moon next.

The next week, ash started falling like snow. People could ignore the other signs, write them off as coincidences, or hoaxes, or viral marketing. But when a blanket of ash began to inexplicably fall from the sky all across the world, people quickly accepted something was wrong. You said it was from an underwater supervolcano, shoving its way out of the depths to remind humanity that this planet didn't belong to us, no matter what we might think. I thought it was a meteor, disintegrating in low orbit.

We both hoped it would stop soon.

But the ash kept falling, suffocating cities and choking rivers. Weeks passed. People didn't know what to do. I stopped going to work. I couldn't see the point in it anymore. But you kept working, until you were the only person left at the clinic – patient or doctor. You stopped going a few days after that. It's what I've always admired about you. You hold on until the last minute, and then keep holding on just a bit longer.

Some people gathered in churches to pray for deliverance. Others opened their wrists in the bath. You and I stayed at home, watching our emergency supplies dwindle. We'd stocked up in case of an earthquake. You told me the bigger disaster would be when we ran out of gingernuts.

People started seeing angels doing battle on high. Flaming swords, wheels within wheels, asymmetrical wings covered with dozens of eyes. We heard that one crashed into the Waitematā, boiling the harbour away and setting fire to half of Auckland. By then, lines of communication had started breaking down. Television stations ceased broadcasting, the internet just stopped working one day. We had radio, sometimes. So there was rumour and hearsay, stories heard by a friend of a friend and broadcast over unsecured AM channels. You said you liked it better this way. At least gossip was honest about the confusion.

I lost track of the days. Eventually we lost all power and the radio fell silent. Proclamations in dead languages burned across the sky in letters of black flame. We couldn't understand what they were trying to tell us, so we made our own meanings. You decided that they were telling us to leave.

We got in your car and drove to the coast. The roads were eerily quiet. You guessed everyone had gone north, but I thought that most people just wanted to wait for the end in their own beds. The falling ash quickly covered our tracks, erasing all signs of our passage. On the edge of town, we drove past a burnt church, the fallen steeple lying in ruins in the graveyard surrounded by broken headstones.

When we got to the beach, it was covered in ash like everywhere else. We found the seas had turned to blood. Crimson waves swept up and down the shoreline, staining the ash not washed away by the tide.

We cleared up a patch of sand and tried to build a fire, frail flames struggling against the chill in the air. There were no more angels now. The words of black flame had stopped burning, and looked like an infected wound decaying across the sky. Everything was falling silent. We huddled by the fire to watch the sun sink beneath the viscous red ocean, and we ate the last of the now-stale gingernuts. There were no more stars left. The moon looked forlorn, all alone as she rose above the horizon.

That night we lay down next to the flickering fire and tried to sleep. The fronts of your knees pressed into the backs of mine, the way they used to in our tiny apartment when you were a student. I was glad you were there with me. I didn't want to be alone. I felt the steady rhythm of your breath, barely audible over the howl of the wind.

The next morning the sun didn't rise. The sky lightened and the moon bled away, and that was that. The wind had died, and it wasn't cold anymore. If cold is the absence of heat, then this was an absence of temperature. We just sat in the half light of that false and final dawn, and held on to each other as we waited. Minutes stretched out into hours, into days. I don't know how long we sat on that beach. We might as well have been the only people left on earth. By that stage, maybe we were.

The roar of the ocean faded to nothing. Ashes finally stopped falling from the sky. The fire flickered out. Colour leached from everything. The world steadily faded away, until everything was gone but you. There was absolute silence.

Hand in hand, we floated into the abyss. You held on until the very last moment.

Then everything ended, and you finally let go.

Alone in the darkness, I heard the first notes of a song ring out.

THE SECRETS SHE EATS

NIKKY LEE

Not all secrets are given willingly. Sometimes I have to hunt them from street to street, town to town. They run, scramble, try to weasel their way out of my grip, slippery things that they are. Often they beg, sometimes they cry. And sometimes, once they're cornered and at a dead end, they simply stand there, resigned and waiting for my final reckoning.

I blow into town like a tumbleweed on the wind. A woman in black, cloaked and hooded. Knife in my belt, pistol on my hip and boots crusted with mud. The villagers don't see my face, not straight away, but they are not fooled.

"Eater." The whisper announces my arrival, rushing ahead of me in undertones. Along the dusty main street it goes, passing through blacksmiths and tailors' shops, into the saloon. In an hour it will have reached the plains; a day later, the plateau beyond.

They know what I am. And yet, there's something in my step that makes them turn; in the 'swish-click' of my boots that mesmerises. Something in my scent that draws the villagers in, like moths to a flame.

The first one staggers out of the saloon and finds me there in the street. There's distilled spirits on his breath and a pink flush on his dusty cheeks. He's young, pretty-like; soft brown curls grace his brow.

"I love Josie Fisher," he tells me.

The words roll over me like a sprinkling of sweet bread crumbs. I lick them up, savouring each one. Barely a snack, but I'll take it. I nod and he turns away, his shoulders relaxing, an ecstasy of relief on his face.

"I love Josie Fisher," he says again, walking away in a daze.

An innocent secret. A smile twitches my lips. They're not particularly filling, but they are sweet. A footstep crunches at my back and I turn. An older woman is there, a hessian bag of groceries abandoned in the dirt. She trembles as she approaches. Her blue eyes dart to my hood, then away again, even as her mouth opens, revealing yellowed teeth. "I stole my husband's best horse to buy milk of the poppy," she murmurs.

Ah, a secret with a little more meat. The weight of it eases into my belly, a tasty morsel. But there's more, I can smell it as sure as I smell the horse shit swept into the gutters. I peel back my hood and the woman's eyes lock with mine. She quivers like a marmot caught in the glare of a snake.

"And?" I prompt.

She hugs her arms about herself. "I told him vagabonds did it. He went out searching for them and came back with fever. It's bad this year, you know? Real bad. Young Sally it took. And the Miller's wife."

Her words are like tiny steaks on my tongue. Juicy. Succulent. I breathe them in, relishing their taste. I nod again and a gasp whistles out of her. She sinks to her knees and releases a sob: her burden suddenly dissolved. I step away and she frowns as she finds herself slumped in the middle of the street. She picks herself up. With deft strokes, she beats the dust out of her skirts, picks up her shopping and walks off.

Perhaps now she'll have the courage to make it right. If not, well, I'll get another meal later.

I set up shop in the saloon. Soon they come, sweet and tender alike. They can't help themselves. A line forms out the door. Clearly it's been many a year since one of us has come through these parts. One by one, they sit down at my table and lean in to whisper their guilt.

"I stole a drunkard's shoes last winter." This from a girl in a woollen sweater patched over and over at the elbows.

"I put salt on Mary Cole's cake at the last town cake competition," a busty woman admits, wringing her gloves.

A sheepish grin from a grey-haired man. "I have a mistress. Every Thursday." That one barely touches the sides as it goes down. He'll come back later for sure.

"I wagered my father's fortune in cards and lost." From a gaunt young man in a fine cloak and polished shoes.

"I hate my children."

"When customers piss me off, I spit in their soup."

"I fucked a cow once." That one made me blink twice.

On and on. Bit by bit, their secrets fill me. Albeit briefly. When the afternoon shadows lengthen, Vander the barkeep lights the hearth and a slow heat creeps into the emptying saloon. The line waiting on me thins and clears with the coming of night. Fear of the dark overrides their instinct to spill their burdens. I curse under my breath. My mouth craves that big something I'd followed into town. Big and thick and heavy. Like wild bison roasting on a spit. It's here somewhere. I know it. Something I could sink my teeth into one hundred times over.

A throat clears next to me. My gaze swings back to the thin, dark-haired man – a boy really – sat in the opposite chair, waiting. I'd scarcely noticed him.

"Yes, yes," I say absently, and I reach for my drink. It won't sate me the way a good secret might, but it dampens the craving. Then I get a whiff of him; of his secret. I freeze, scenting the air between us. Not quite the same *big* I'd been hunting, but there's a kinship there. Something … important.

The boy shifts uncomfortably in the seat, straightens his too-big, probably hand-me-down, vest. His nails are bitten to the quick.

"I'm listening," I say.

"I, um …" His fingers twist and writhe, nimble-like, a tailor's apprentice perhaps or a jeweller's. They clench together as he swallows. "I saw something the other night." A gulp. "Something strange."

The magic rises in my belly, but I hold it at bay. The boy is twitchy, like a rabbit ready to duck back into his burrow if I push him too hard. This is a secret that needs teasing out. I sip my drink, trying not to let my interest show too much. "Go on."

"I was coming home late two nights ago," the boy begins. "Closed up shop like Mr. Cole asked and cut across Roper's field. I know I shouldn't but it was late, you know, and Da was waiting at home; he gets anxious when I'm out past tea. Roper's field is just grazing for his horses, and they're all trained gentle-like, wouldn't kick a gnat if it landed on them wrong, so I figured no harm done. I've taken that way plenty of times before."

He pauses as Vander arrives and places an ale on the table before him – and lingers. "Any dinner, ma'am?"

"No, thank you."

Vander is still for a long moment, before slowly turning for the kitchens. I sigh. I know his type; clever like a vulture and ready to wring every coin he can.

The boy furrows his brow at the drink, then reaches for his pocket.

"It's on me," I say and wave my hand. "Continue."

"Well, two nights ago, I took the shortcut, like always. But halfway through I heard a grinding sound." His lips purse, evidently trying to think of a way to describe it. "A pestle on mortar sound. Then cracking a few steps later, like sticks breaking. I froze, thinking it was perhaps a horse having a roll in the grass, or rubbing his back on a fence post, but then I saw sparks from a flint—" He shifts back in his seat as I lean in. Then realises what he's done and flushes.

"And?" I ask, unperturbed.

"I rushed at it. Think I even shouted, 'Hey, what're you doing?' Or maybe I thought it. Either way, lighting a fire in a grass field was asking for it to go up like a tinderbox. I wasn't raised a farmer, but even I know that." His eyes go distant, and he shivers, then takes a pull of his ale. "What I found, well. It was a fire, trapped in a stone circle, but the … *thing* next to it. I don't know what it was. But it wasn't human – I'm sure of that."

"What did it look like?"

The boy stares into his mug. "Ugly. Wrinkles all about the face." He traces a finger along his cheeks and jowls. "Snout for a nose. And small, squat. Like someone sat on it."

"And what did it say?" I ask.

The boy is silent for a long moment. "Nothing," he says at last into his ale. A deeper flush creeps up his throat and into his ears.

"I screamed and ran away."

I nod, running a light finger over my empty glass. "Wise move," I muse, wishing he'd paid more attention to its appearance; I can name a hundred fey clans the creature might belong to. But a lead is a lead, and I yearn for something juicy. I stand. "Show me."

*

Aben, for I've learned that is his name, rests a hand on the fence paling. "In there," he says, pointing into the dark field. And it is truly dark, no kerosene lamps this part of town and there's little light beyond what our lantern provides – even to my eyes. Not that my eyes are much to brag about. I'm not fae-sighted like my father. I have my mother's eyes. Mortal eyes.

And a fae's hunger.

I set the oil lamp down on the post and listen. Grass stalks chitter in the breeze. The fence creaks ever so slight. I frown.

"What is it?" Aben asks.

"No insects."

"Tucked in for the night?" he suggests, the edge of a coy smile quirking his mouth. When I don't respond, he coughs and looks down at his shoes. They're well made, shiny iron buckles polished to a gleam. A shoemaker's apprentice then.

I sigh, set a foot on the bottom rung of the fence and swing a leg over.

Aben swings his leg over too.

"What are you doing?"

He stares at me dumbly, as if the answer is obvious. "Coming with you, of course."

I snort. "No, you're not."

His eyebrows bunch. "I can't let a lady go out there on her own."

"Do I look like I need your protection?" I raise an eyebrow in return.

He considers me a moment there, straddled on the fence, gaze travelling to my calloused hands, the knife on my hip and the pistol holstered under my cloak. "No," he admits and shrinks into himself, looking more boyish than ever. "I want to show people I'm not a coward. I can do more than run away."

The words hit me like a sucker punch. A memory rises up: my mother dabbing a rag on my torn lip and me, ten years old, saying, *"I'm not a monster. I want to show them."*

"You will," my mother says in the same, tired tone of a parent listening to a conversation so old it's worn holes in its sleeves. *"Give them time."*

My fists clench. *"I want to show them now!"*

And mother's patient words, *"Give them time."*

Atop the fence, I roll my eyes. "Stay behind me."

Aben beams and scrambles over the pilings.

We creep through the field, lantern held high, dry grass scratching our legs. Halfway in, we stumble into a clearing where the grass is flattened – not trampled but carefully squashed down so that in another day or two it might spring back. A small stone circle lies in the middle, ashes cold.

"This was it," Aben says. There's an edge to his voice as he turns in a circle and squints into the dark. He stands so close his back brushes mine. The lantern in his hand quivers and the sphere of light around us wobbles.

"Relax," I tell him. Taking the lantern, I bend down to examine the ashes. "There's nothing here." I crunch a piece of charcoal in my hand and sniff. And there, underneath the smoke and soot, birch, lavender and rosemary.

"Were you always a secret eater?" Aben asks from over my shoulder. His voice is stronger now, more confident.

"Always."

Aben's forehead rumples into a frown. "And you've been doing this all your life? Journeying from town to town, relieving people of their secrets." He pauses. "Why don't I feel your coercion anymore?"

"What's to say you're not?" I dust my hands off, catch a glimpse of his face and laugh. As a rule, I don't prey on people's insecurities when they fess whatever is on their mind – that's a sure way to get run out of town, but his shock catches me off guard. "It doesn't work like that."

"It doesn't?"

"I can't force you to tell your secrets. Deep down you've got to be willing. If you have a secret you'd never tell anyone, I can't force it out of you." Those are the ones I hunt, when they have the right scent; rich and with full copper notes. I make a show of leaning close to him and taking a whiff. "You don't have the smell, you're all leather and pomegranates since I took your secret. At most, you'll have a slight inclination to tell the truth for a few days" – I cock a grin at him – "depending how headstrong you are. I've had married men fess their adultery then walk straight back into a brothel."

Aben doesn't answer, but his eyes follow me as I pick my way across the clearing, pausing at two rocks nestled in the flattened grass. Both are smooth, one wide and flat, the other round and about the same size as my head. Residue cakes one side of each. I run a finger down the head-sized rock, hold it to my nose. Lavender and rosemary. "You were right about the mortar and pestle," I say, wiping my hand on my cloak.

My companion squeaks a response. Actually squeaks, like his voice has been caught on a hook and yanked out of water. I turn to find him standing rigid, the tip of a rusted knife jutting up at his throat. At the other end of the knife is a squat figure wearing old children's clothes, patched and threadbare.

"What you want?" the creature hisses through a frog-like mouth and its perfectly round eyes narrow into slits. Hair hangs limp and straggled from its brow, like it has been out in the weather too long. Behind it, a mound of sticks and firewood lay scattered on the grass.

I hold my hands out for peace. "Easy, we mean no harm. What's your name, friend?"

"Dalziel."

"And what are you, a boggart?"

"Broonie," the fae spits. "No boggart here."

My gaze wanders those ragged clothes again, then to the rows of scars on the back of his exposed forearms. Layers upon layers of them, turning his skin to knots of puckered scar tissue. He might have been a broonie once, but not anymore. Bad luck or perhaps a bad contract has transformed him from household hearth spirit to homeless sprite. Either way, he's old fae, from across the sea. My nose twitches, catching a lingering whiff of a copper secret. As if he senses it too, Dalziel's knife presses under Aben's jaw, all he has to do is stab up.

"What are you?" Dalziel snarls. "You look human, but you don't smell like one."

I open my palms to him and slowly crouch so we're closer to eye level. "I am a Secret Eater."

"Pah, lies. Eaters aren't real. Just stories."

"I assure you we're not. Not on this continent, anyway."

"Eater," Aben's voice squeezes out. He makes eyes at me, casting a meaningful look at my pistol.

Dalziel's grip tightens on his knife.

"It's fine," I assure them both. "Aben, broonies like Dalziel are harmless fae. A few pranks, nothing sinister. Dalziel, Aben is a harmless human, he wants to be friends."

Dalziel's knife eases off Aben's jawline, but still hovers close to Aben's throat.

"He'll trade you his shoes, in a show of good faith," I add.

Dalziel's eyes light up. "Oh, why didn't you say sooner?" It's impossible to miss the excitement in Dalziel's voice. He kicks off his worn boots, all cracked leather and flapping soles, and holds them out to Aben.

Aben shoots me a glare. "I will not—"

I cut him off with a glare of my own, until he sighs and reaches for his polished shoes.

"No buckles," Dalziel says.

Aben frowns a beat, then, "Oh right, iron." Even out here, everyone knows fae can't abide it. He loosens the buckles off, puts them in his pocket, and reluctantly holds his shoes out.

The knife drops away, sheathing back into Dalziel's belt. "My thanks, friend Aben." The boggart drops to his bottom and pulls Aben's shoes on with obvious glee. His feet, I notice, are scarred too – thin white strikes across each arch. The shoes are too big, but Dalziel's up and strutting around in them like Aben has handed him gold clogs. Then he turns on Aben, blinking his round eyes expectantly.

"Put on his shoes," I whisper to Aben, motioning to the discarded items on the grass. "It'll seal our concord."

Aben's face twitches like he wants to object, but under Dalziel's watch he bends down and slides his feet into the old shoes. His toes poke through the holes at the tip like they're a pair of sandals.

"Wonderful! Our friendship is set." Dalziel claps his hands and admires his new feet again. "Very nice gift," he says. "A nice gift indeed. Our friendship will be grand!"

"How long do I have to wear these?" Aben murmurs to me.

"Until we leave his domain." I gesture to the field.

Aben sighs, resigned to his fate. "What about you? Don't you need to trade?"

"I'm getting to it." I raise my voice, catching Dalziel by the shoulder as he hops about. Again, that copper whiff. Very faint. But it's there. I focus my attention on him. It's harder to work my power on fae, but I can if the secret is strong enough. And with the right kind of probing. "Friend Dalziel, why are you out in this field burning lavender and rosemary?"

Dalziel's eyes turn glassy, his face relaxes. Tranced. I grimace: I've pushed too hard. I ease off, releasing my hand from his grubby coat and coaxing him to sit at the edge of the pit. Dalziel blinks, shakes himself and starts building a fire, a house for the flame from his sticks and wood.

"What's with the lavender and rosemary?" I ask again, motioning to the two stones and the fresh bundles of herbs waiting to be pulped.

"To ease the bones," Dalziel says simply, as if the answer is obvious.

Aben and I share a confused look. "Your bones?"

Dalziel snorts. "Dead bones." He thumps his chest. "Not these. These still have plenty of life left in them. The bones under here." He stomps one foot, indicating the earth below.

Copper fills my nostrils. I'm getting close. I lean in, eager. "There are bodies buried here?"

Aben's face drains of colour. "Bodies?" he squeaks and he crosses himself. Funny how humans get all squeamish about these things.

Dalziel busies himself with the fire, lighting it with a practised strike from a knife and flint. He's been out here a while it seems.

"How many bodies?" I ask.

Dalziel considers. "Many. Dozens. Maybe more."

Another wick up my nose. My magic prowls in, hungry. *Closer, closer.* I press him a tiny bit more. "Who puts them there?"

Dalziel stiffens, back turning rigid, his hands clamp tight around his flint stone. *He knows.* Gods and spirits sure. He knows. Dalziel's eyes find mine, bathwater grey and glistening in the firelight. "Don't make me say," he begs. The hand around the flint quivers, and what I'd mistook for tense caution reveals itself: blind fear. It's so strong I could poke out my tongue and lick it off the air.

"Please," I say. "It's important." I gesture to the field. "And don't they deserve justice?"

Dalziel stares after my finger, eyes glazing over.

Damn, I've pressed too close again. For a fae as susceptible as this, he must have human ancestry in him, like me. Maybe not half-half like me, but it's there. Inside my chest, something I thought tough and hardened squeezes. It's not easy straddling two worlds. You never fully step into one or the other, it's always a balancing act between the two.

"My apologies," I say and shuffle back, my stomach giving a disappointed gurgle.

Dalziel opens his mouth, tries to speak, fails, then works his lips as if trying to chew through a particularly tough bit of bread.

Aben eases down on Dalziel's other side. His face is still pale, but his gaze is tender. He pats the boggart's back. "We're here," he assures. "One word at a time."

"I … c-can't!" Dalziel manages, spittle flying, straining to get the words out. It takes all his willpower.

Understanding clicks. I curse under my breath. "He's been Compulsed."

Aben lifts his head, concern rippling across his brow. "He's been what?"

"Compulsed. A spell. Stops him talking to anyone about this. Nasty stuff." Before I can think, I am up and pacing. Nervous habit. I swear again and cast my sights nightward. I would have been perfectly happy with a simple serial killer, but no. "We're dealing with wicked magic." I glance at Dalziel. "Nod if I'm right."

He nods.

"Shit."

There goes my easy meal.

*

"Anyone can use wicked magic," I explain to Aben. "You just need the know." *And a spell book.* But the less people who know that the better.

Around us, leathers and needlework of his shoemaker's shop line the walls. It was the easiest place for us to confer out of the way of prying eyes. Next to Aben, Dalziel looks miserable. The lamplight shows his limp grey hair, owl-eyes dim and cheeks sallow from exhaustion. That's what a secret like this does to a person – fae or man. In this we're all the same.

Aben grips Dalziel's forearm and gives it a reassuring shake. "We'll find a way to remove the Compulsion, I promise."

A tick of annoyance twitches in my jaw. He is right. I'll grant him that. No one deserves to live with a copper secret eating them up from the inside. But Aben makes his promise with the conviction of one who has never dealt with wicked magic before.

Dalziel swallows and nods. "My thanks, friend Aben."

We sink into a stony silence. "So many people," Aben murmurs. We'd questioned Dalziel best we could on the way to the shop, keeping to the backstreets. The total count before Dalziel managed a nod: thirteen.

And those are the ones he knows about, I think but don't say.

Aben rubs his eyes. "How did no one notice?"

To this, at least, I have an answer. "Easy. Disguise their deaths as something else. Who in town has died recently? And what did they die of?"

Aben falls still, his fingers pinching his chin as he considers. "Sally Barton, fever. Bobby Ruthford—" his eyes dart up to mine "—fever. Frederick Sawyers—" he swallows "—fever. Those were all in the last month."

My gut knots. "All unrelated? No contact? They weren't family or neighbours? Or lovers?"

Aben shakes his head. "Not that I know."

I curse. "Then it's not a normal fever."

"But I *went* to Bobby's funeral, he was buried in the church cemetery," Aben objects.

My eyebrow cocks. "And did you see the body?"

Aben pauses, then shakes his head, uncertainty dawning on his face. "It was a closed casket."

An empty casket more like. No need to say it, it's clear from the horror on Aben's face that it's occurred to him too.

"But why bury them in the field?" Aben asks.

"Hiding—" Dalziel manages before the compulsion cuts his words short and reduces him to a coughing fit.

"It's all right Dalziel, I know," I assure him, patting the boggart's arm. With a glance to Aben, I add, "They're snatching the bodies before anyone gets too good a look and hiding them in Roper's field." My mind darts back to the woman who'd given up her secret on the town road; who'd sold her husband's horse to buy milk of the poppy. What had she said? *He went out searching for his horse and came back with fever.*

Where, then, had he gone? And what had he seen that he shouldn't have? I come to my feet. "The woman with the poppy addiction, where does she live? I need to talk to her husband."

Aben scowls, his hands clenching into fists on the table. "There's more than one woman with poppy addiction here. In case you hadn't noticed."

Curious. A sore point I hadn't expected. I raise an eyebrow at him and he sighs.

"My brother got mixed up in the trade. Didn't end well. Swore I'd stay the hell away from it."

Dalziel places a hand on Aben's forearm and pats it gently. "Please friend, this is important," the broonie croaks out, skirting around the edge of his secret. I suck in a breath, scenting the air on my tongue. I'm on to something. When Dalziel glances up at me and gives the faintest of nods, I know I'm right.

Aben sees it too. He closes his eyes, takes a moment, then releases his fists. "Describe her."

I do, and his brow wrinkles. "Sounds like Macey Gruber."

"And her husband is ill?"

Aben nods.

"Take me there."

*

We find the grave in Macey Gruber's front garden. Its earth is freshly turned and stinks of copper, the scent lies on the mound thick as a snowdrift. My hunger stirs with a faint gurgle. *Soon,* I promise it. From inside the farmer's cottage, a woman wails.

"We're too late," Aben says.

"Not necessarily."

When we knock, a bloodshot, tear-streaked face greets us. She's barely coherent enough to talk, but she opens the door and starts making tea. I sigh and take the teapot away and sit her down at the table. Her clothes are dirty, gravel soil still stuck to them. Five mile from town and on her own, she'd had to do the deed herself. My heart twists, thinking of another grave far from here and the mother I'd buried in it. That hurt never truly leaves you. It fades into the background, scabs over and scars, but never goes away. Not completely.

"It's my fault," Macey Gruber says, staring at her hands. There's dirt under her ragged nails. She fidgets, anxious in her own skin.

I rest my hands on hers and flex my magic. "Where did he go, when he went looking for his horse?"

Macey Gruber stills, her pupils dilating. I don't like using my power like this, smothering people with it. I can't force people to talk, but I can make their tongues loose; fill their heads with haze until the world turns so dream-like the secret just slips out.

Macey sways, her head rolls to one side. "All the way to the plateau." She closes her eyes and relaxes into my magic like it's a warm bath. "That feels nice."

"Up to the fae kingdom?" Aben whispers. "I knew it! They did something – ow!"

Dalziel stamps on his foot. "Fae don't work wicked magic!" Dalziel protests, and he wants to say more, but the Compulsion chokes the words in his throat. He works his jaw for a moment, a vein pops in his head, cheeks flushing with anger, then gives up with a "humph!"

"It's outlawed," I explain to Aben. "Work wicked magic and you're cast out. Magic sealed. No longer fae. Few dare risk it. Is that what we're looking for Dalziel? An outcast?"

Dalziel shakes his head.

"Human then." At this, a copper scent curls off my words, strong and delicious. I'm closing in. I take Macey's hands again, give her a little shake.

Her eyelids flutter open. "Let me sleep," she groans. "It's all my fault. Let me sleep forever."

"Why is it your fault, Macey?"

A long pause and her red eyes, too red to be just from crying, study my face. "I sold his horse. His favourite." The smell of the old secret fills my nose like stale bread. Dry and ordinary. I've not asked the right question. "Who did you sell it to?"

"Vander."

The name drops into my belly like a bite of marinated pork. Full bodied flavour rolls over my tongue. Copper fills my nose. I breathe it in, chest swelling, my mind revelling in it. It's *here*. The trail's *here*.

"Vander, the *barkeep*?" Aben interrupts, incredulous. "What would he want with a farm hor—" but I hold up a hand for quiet.

"Why Vander? Why did you go to him?"

Macey swallows, sensing she's on the edge of spilling it all. "Because he has the poppy," she whispers. "He runs it all."

Got you.

Copper hooks my nose, pulling my head around. A trail flares to life in my mind's eye, burning a path to my quarry like a line of gunpowder. It points straight back to town.

Dalziel grunts. Aben and I glance over to find him twitching on the floor, nodding furiously between his spasms. Once Dalziel sees we've noticed, he slumps, utterly spent. Aben hurries over, sits him up.

"Easy. Breathe," he says.

"Water," Dalziel croaks. "Please, friend Aben." Aben fetches a cup and the cold kettle from Macey's stove and Dalziel gulps it down.

"Stay here," I tell them, striding for the door. My trail beckons.

Aben's hand closes around my elbow. "I'm coming."

For a heartbeat I consider telling him no, that it's dangerous. Human my quarry might be, but he's got wicked magic at his disposal, and I can't protect Aben from it.

"Please."

His request turns to a bitter taste in my mouth. Not quite a secret – at least not the kind I like. It mingles with the copper, defiling it with its guilt. A secret blame then. That he'd turned his back when he should have helped. Of all times to grow a conscience. My gaze roves the room as I try to find the right words to explain why coming with me is a bad idea; the worst idea actually. My eyes light on the corner of a small envelope poking out of the pocket in Macey's dress. When I bend down to pull it loose, her hand catches my sleeve.

"Stay," she begs, rousing from her dream-state. In hindsight, working my magic on a poppy addict might not have been such a wise play. "Don't go." She claws at my clothes.

I detach her fingers one by one and slip the envelope into the fire at the hearth. It goes up in a heady whiff of burned poppy powder. "I have to," I tell her. The trail calls. But I don't like the idea of leaving her here alone. She needs more help than I can give.

Dalziel stands up with a grimace and dusts off his coat. "I will look after her," he says.

Aben casts me a doubtful look. "I thought you said he was a prankster."

"Broonies are not pranksters," Dalziel huffs. "We help." He pauses and the flicker of a grin crosses his wide mouth. "If the trade is right."

I study the squat fae. Maybe I read him wrong, perhaps there was more of the broonie left in him that I'd thought. After all, he'd been trying to appease the dead in Roper's field. If I gave him this chance, might he return to the fireside spirit he'd once been?

I crouch before him so we're eye level. "You would do this for me?"

Dalziel nods, then holds up one finger. "On one condition."

"Here we go," Aben mutters, attention dropping to his second-hand shoes. He's not had a chance to change them.

"Name it."

Dalziel motions me close, "Stop the bastard." His eyes snare me with their intensity and there's something pleading in them. Something he cannot say. "*Please.*"

*

"I suppose it makes sense," Aben says through a yawn as we watch the saloon from across the street, waiting for the last of its patrons to stagger out. Our alley stinks of horse shit, cat piss and garbage, but it's the best we've got. Now that I've found the trail, the scent of copper hangs over the place, thick as soup. Coats the saloon like sticky paint. In my pockets, my fingers itch something chronic, begging for release.

"All those shipments from the coast. I thought it was just ale," Aben says. He rubs his face and slaps his cheeks to keep himself awake. "He has them bring it right up Main Street, you know. I can't count the number of times I've seen a cart full of kegs and the like parked out front with men unloading it – all of it in broad daylight! I never thought to question. No one has."

"No one alive," I correct him. If I had to guess, more than one corpse in Roper's field was there simply because they'd gotten too curious. A bit of wicked magic and they fell sick and died. Some in their beds. Some on Vander's floor, depending on how potent he made the spell.

Only it wasn't that simple. Wicked magic *always* had a cost.

My hands curl into fists as I think of Dalziel. Compelled to aid a murderer and not tell a soul. I can imagine how it happened. A contract of servitude to a smuggler in exchange for conveyance across the sea. Ten years, maybe twenty; a small price for a long-lived fae. Worth the risk for new life on a new continent, far away from the feuding and bloodshed of the old world. Only, his contract had been sold on to the likes of Vander once the ship arrived at port. It's a sad and all too common story.

At last, the final patron sways out the double doors and the lamp-lit windows turn dark. I glance at the moon; three, perhaps four o'clock in the morning.

I flex my fingers, feeling the prick of claws under my nails. Time to move, before this secret has a chance to escape.

We slink out from the alleyway. The moon's out and high, casting long drifts of shadow across the street. Aben follows doggedly behind. I'd tried to talk him out of coming, but he wouldn't hear of it. And from the stubborn set of his jaw, I'd known better than to argue, else he follow and give the hunt away. No, best he see this through to its end where I can keep an eye on him. With any luck, I won't give him nightmares.

Across the street and into the saloon. Aben catches the double doors so they don't swing behind us.

And there he is.

Waiting. The cold barrel of a '76 Winchester pointed our way.

"You picked the wrong night to be nosey, Eater."

Like I said. Some secrets beg. Some cry. Some do nothing at all. And some, when cornered with no way to run, turn around and bite.

Vander levels the shotgun at us.

The world sinks into fragments of time. A slick, copper-laden breath filling my lungs. I dive for Aben; pushing him to the floor.

Vander's rifle cracks. One saloon door erupts into shards of wood.

The next beat I'm up and running, leaving Aben reeling on the floor.

Vander aims his gun again. Too slow. Much too slow for my fae blood all frenzied with the hunt.

I dodge, my vision turning to a blur of hunger and lamplight. A bullet whisks past my shoulder, snags a hole in the wall.

Vander's growl fills my ears, anger turning desperate. I close in, ten paces between us. He cocks the rifle again, aims for my chest.

Before I can think, before reason or judgement sets in, my body twists.

Jumps.

The bullet finds my gut. Buries deep and gnaws with a gusto that brings me to my knees. I stagger, clutching my belly.

"Ha, got you, fairy bitch," Vander snarls. He glances up to the balustrade where a small squat figure is waiting. "Another one for the field, Freda." The figure's perfectly round eyes fix on the scene below, frog mouth pinched shut. Another broonie. This one is softer than Dalziel, younger too, her hair thick and swamp green. But there are features I recognise. Dalziel's ears. Dalziel's nose. His kin through and through.

No wonder he was so insistent I end this.

She doesn't move.

"Freda!" Vander barks.

The broonie juts her jaw, squares her shoulders and stays still. Below, blood oozes from between my fingers. I'm too far gone to feel pain, but soon the weakness will seep in. I lurch to my feet.

Vander curses, snatches a switch-knife from the bar and scores it down his forearm. He utters something unintelligible under his breath. The blood oozing from the gash evaporates, exposing the open rent of flesh. Pressure washes over the room. I feel it wrap around my limbs and squeeze me still, right down to my itching fingers. *Wicked magic.* Damn, I'd gotten sloppy. I search for Aben but can't find him. *Double damn.*

"Freda," Vander growls.

Above, the broonie's legs jerk, pulling her down the stairs.

"Why all this?" I ask. My seized jaw slurs the words together. It's not much of a question but it's all I can think of to buy time.

Some secrets can't resist bragging when they're exposed. I hope Vander's is one of them.

Vander pauses, a slight curl in his lip. "What does it matter?"

"Matters ... to me." I say, forcing the words through my teeth. "To the people left ... behind."

Vander shrugs and nonchalantly flicks his knife open and shut. Open and shut. "Truth be I've forgotten why."

His words slide down my throat and into my belly in juicy morsels. But I want more. "Why use sickness then?"

Vander pauses, considering me. "Some couldn't pay, some wouldn't, some threatened to expose my operations. Bad business leaving them to talk." He comes closer, flicks his switch-knife out again under my jaw. "You really should have bought dinner."

It comes together in a heartbeat.

"You feed them cursed food." I swallow and fight to raise my voice. "An easy thing, I imagine, to cut yourself and work a spell behind a kitchen door instead of behind a bar." I still can't see Aben, but I hope he's listening.

Vander studies me, curious, as if I'm a puzzle he hasn't figured out yet. "It is."

"Why not poison?" It would be easier. I eye the gash on his forearm. If it took that much blood to work a binding, how much more to work a spell of killing? I think of Dalziel's scars; those hundreds of white lines scoured into his skin and probably Freda's too. Rage boils inside me.

"Poison's too expensive. No money in it." Vander's tone is dry, matter of fact.

All about the money, eh? That's the thing with wicked magic, it can get you what you want, but it turns you cold inside. Once, he might have been an honest merchant, but the magic sunk in, twisted it all up, turned his morals inside out. It's one cost few recognise until it's too late.

Vander's switch-blade wanders along my chin and my jaw relaxes at its touch. I work my mouth open, testing this sliver of freedom he's granted. It's not much. He flicks his wrist, and the tip of his knife burns a line across my cheek.

"Ow!"

His eyes fixate on that first red line. Then the knife quivers close again, pauses above my other cheek, then shifts to my forehead, as if he's debating where to cut next. "To think of the spells I might cast with your fae blood," he whispers. And there's excitement there. A man enthralled in the power of magic. He presses closer and the scent of his sweat and blood fills my nose. Rich and coppery.

My mouth salivates. I bite down on my hunger. "You've fucked up."

He frowns, steps back, suddenly unsure. I suppose he's used to his victims begging – at least the victims he finished like this.

"You stopped counting us," I say, and grin.

Vander's eyes search me, then dart to Freda still standing at the bottom of the staircase. Realisation dawns on him in a slackening of his face, a strickening in his eyes. He whirls – just in time to see Aben plunge a meat cleaver into a leather-bound book.

Just like we planned.

It's no light cut, Aben throws his whole body behind the blow. The blade sinks through the cover as if it's made of butter, slices through the marrow of pages and thuds into the wood of the bar underneath. It sticks there like an axe in a tree stump.

His spell book is the source of his power. I'll distract him while you find it. That had been our agreement going in. I almost thought it hadn't worked.

"NO!" Vander's shriek turns my hairs on end. He lunges for Aben, even though it's too late. Far, far too late. His spell sloughs away, releasing my limbs.

Time to feed.

My fae blood boils. A burn building in my gut around Vander's gunshot. Copper swims up my nose, into my lungs, driving the hunger deeper. In a heartbeat, my *chelae* extend from my fingers, long flexible claws, strong as steel, sharp as swords. One set catches Vander in the boot, piercing through leather and sole to the floor beneath. He howls and buckles to cradle his trapped leg. My second set locks around his ribs in a cage, thumb and fingers pincering him still then drags him down in a sprawl.

I'm on him in a blur, straddling his chest. Pain flares in my belly. *Soon.* I tell it. *Just a little more.* Anticipation pulls my lips into a grin.

"Don't touch me!" Vander snarls, just once, before I lean close and brush my mouth over his. His lips are rough and scaled, with a hint of an old poppy on them. I kiss him.

Vander relaxes in my hold, eyes rolling into his head. *Lustitia*, my mother named this. *Judgement's Kiss.* Reserved for the worst and most delicious secrets. I open my mouth around his and suck out the blood-tangled untold. It slips from him to me, gliding down my gullet and into my stomach heavy-like, healing and filling me in a blink. Whole and delicious.

Sated at last.

My chelae retract. I release Vander; his head thunks to the floor. Limp.

"You killed him?" Aben asks into the silence.

I wipe my mouth with the back of a sleeve. "See for yourself."

Aben eases out from behind the bar, still holding the meat cleaver at the ready. His eyes don't leave me as he bends to check for a pulse. When he finds it, he blinks and his gaze breaks away as he runs a hand over the smuggler's chest, feeling the rise and fall there. "He's alive."

I snort. "I'm not a murderer."

Aben's cleaver drops to his side, forgotten. "What did you do?" He stares at me, searching. I smirk, it's not often I'm met with wonder. But I suppose Aben has seen enough this night to look beyond fear.

"I ate him."

"*Ate* him?"

"Him and his secret, everything that made Vander who he was." And come morning he'll wake as a blank slate. He'll never regain those memories. They're in my gut now, slowly digesting. A fresh start for a feed.

There's a humph from the stairs and a pad of feet crossing the saloon. Freda leans over Vander's sleeping form, pursing her lips. "Good as dead," she says at last. Then she lifts one foot and swings it hard into Vander's side. I wince at the crack of ribs breaking. Freda spits, straightens her tunic and turns to us. "My thanks."

*

I finger the bullet hole in the gut of my robe, frowning at the dried blood there. I'll have to get new clothes in the next town.

"You really can't stay?" Aben asks.

We're back in Roper's field. Dalziel and Freda are building a bonfire of herbs and bracken to calm the bones once and for all now that their murderer is gone. Dalziel practically dances as he does it. He is free, his daughter is returned and, if my hunch is right, they've found a new hearth to share at Macey's farm.

The widow watches Dalziel and Freda work, holding a bunch of lavender to throw on the blaze. A faint smile plays over her lips.

"No," I tell Aben. "Secrets to find, souls to eat and all that." More wicked magic to hunt. It's never ending.

As if sensing my thoughts, Aben produces the two halves of the spell book and gestures it at the fire. "Can I?" He asks. "I mean, is it safe to? I'm not going to get cursed, or jinxed for all eternity?"

A snort escapes me. "You won't." I assure him. "Without a wielder it's just a book. A dangerous book." *As for how Vander got his hands on it, that's a secret I'd like very much to know.*

That's the frustrating thing about secrets. They might nourish me, but they don't reveal the inner workings of their creators. The same way a person will never know the mind of the cow that became a steak on their dinner plate.

We sit together, watching the pages curl into ash until the bonfire burns low and the sun breaks over the grass.

Aben stands, still in his toe-holed sandals from Dalziel, and holds out a hand. "If you must go, know that my door's always open," he says. "Don't be a stranger."

I take it. His grip is firm, yet warm, and a pang echoes through my gut. Emptiness of a different kind. Funny as it may seem, I've come to like this rag-tag crew tonight. "You know," I say, slowly. "I might just hold you to that." A grin creeps across my lips. "You better have some good secrets to spill when I come back."

Aben grins. "Count on it."

HOW TO BUILD A UNICORN

AJ FITZWATER

Step One.

Visit all the butcher shops with your purse jingling a pretty tune.

They'll try to sell you the tender cuts perfect for sizzling on the grill or for cooking slow over the fires of the eternal damned. The cuts grass fed, grain fed, blood fed. See the marbling here, exquisite. See how the blood shines there, like rubies.

You don't want those.

You want the tough, the gristle, the fat, the offcuts, and sweetmeats. The pieces well aged on the bone rather than in the butcher's enormous cool store where hocks and heads are strung on hooks, their eyes glazed with *What did I do to deserve this?*, rumps quivering under a good slap.

You want the bones that can be ground up for bread.

The butcher shrugs and takes your coin. He doesn't mind making bank off the waste.

Step Two.

Sneak into the glue factory under the splinters of two dark new moons.

Barrels of hooves and vats of unctuous paste in various stages of aging fill the great hall. From the high scaffold, you choke, sniff, hock, and spit into the vats too far gone for you to salvage, taking delight in tainting the pot with long, thick, bitter gobs.

Separate the unicorn hooves from the centaur, satyr, and minotaur, muttering under your breath how anyone can get them confused, you don't know.

Take the perfect, the split, the ones filed to nubs, and the ones that could slice a man's throat. Put the ones riddled with nails and shoes into special silken sacks; soon you will shred your fingertips removing the unnatural iron.

Step Three.

When the moons are full of themselves and whispering dark nonsense, hie thee to a cemetery.

No, not one of those burial sites with straight rows and broken teeth.

Offer a bow from the waist to the upright boughs who hold the girls safe until they're ready to spit vengeance upon the world: the Madonnas; the sex workers; the trans girls; the black, brown, and bruised girls.

You'll find them stuffed between the roots of the greatest queens, forming the O horizon. There's one, left in the shape of the snake they thought her to be. Another bent at a right angle to fit the space. Another bent in half, her curve gentle and neat. Yet another laid out cruciform.

Once you've cleared the mud from their mouths, the ejaculate from between their legs, and the bullshit from their ears, tell them there is no magic wand in this world or the next that can turn their blood from clean to dirty.

Let them rage it out and work that salt, acid, and heat back into their fat so that their blood runs cold.

Sit with them as they plunge needles into their veins and let it all run rose red into neat plastic bags. Offer them hot tea and chocolate biscuits to bring their sugar up to socially-acceptable levels.

Make sure they don't keep giving until all the iron is pulled from their bodies. Their voices are enough to be the scythe that reaps what is sown.

Sit with them as they weep and the night feeds them morsels of tasteless dreams.

Step Four.

Try not to cry.

Cry a lot.

Collect your tears, as they are the perfect solution with which to refill the venom sacs behind the unicorn's teeth – a reminder to those who don't check a gift horse that their bark *is* as bad as their bite.

Step Five.

When the sky has been ruined and they blame you for it, steal back the rainbow.

You'll need a sledgehammer to break through the glass.

By the time you're finished, you'll be an expert at cutting rainbows to the perfect second in the arc, so that the flow of mane and tale will ripple and shine.

This is not vanity. Like a cat, the tail is for balance. Like a warrior, the mane is for armour.

While time is haunting you – you've been here before, you'll do it again – precision is key. Inventory carefully every bottle of sunlight you captured before it disappeared behind the grey-brown halitosis.

Then break them.

Weave the rainbows with this shattered crystal while it's still warm. Have plenty of bandages available. You will cut yourself.

Don't clean the blood from your weaving. It is an excellent binding agent.

Marinate for a millennium.

Step Six.

Say his name three times.

Then, without hesitation, walk into his office and scrape the gold off his maggoty, white walls.

Strip it from skin and buildings and statues. Sneak into morgues and pull it from the teeth of the dead. Slip it from their fingers and wrists as you shake hands in bored meetings and charity events. Wander into forts and reserves, invisible as air, and break economies by taking what you fancy. It's what you're owed.

But don't bother removing it from toilets. You don't need that shit.

Teach the girls who want to how to slip through high society, where their pale or ashy skin and haunted eyes are always the life of the party. Show them how to breathe undeath upon stretched necks and empty ears and corpulent offshore accounts until the gold simply falls into their cold hands.

Become the spinster you've always been. Ignore the tales that say you don't have the skill.

Spin that gold into fine and tough thread. Then make more. You're going to need it.

Step Seven.

When the moons hide their shameful expressions from you, pluck the stars from the sky and fashion them into eyeballs.

Polish the eyeballs with water distilled from the seas of change and cloth cut from the velvet power of a righteous scream.

Step Eight.

Dive into the hay and find the needles fashioned from the recycled nose points of nuclear warheads.

By the light from the eyes of the girls gathered in a circle, puzzle the pieces of meat and hoof back together with neat, tight gold stitches. Attach sparkling mane and tail, pop in the eyeballs, inject the girls' blood, and stuff any saggy corners with straw.

Don't bother with a hide; it will grow back of its own accord. Let them see how the machinery really works, blood and guts and all.

Step Nine.

When that asshole tooth fairy is too busy counting his money, wander into his lair and take his horde.

Feed them to your unicorns and allow them to chew it over.

History is happy to forget a unicorn's horn is an evolution of teeth. Those molars you grind together as you attempt to hold your anger in check fuse and twist, tunnelling up through the skull until they erupt triumphant as a beacon of prismatic light, a weapon of caste eruption.

Step Ten.

Bake at a fury hot as ten thousand suns.

Step Eleven.

Let your unicorn army stand for three days at the enemy's gates while the enemy scrambles to wash the best porcelain, polish the silverware, and hide the crystal.

Break all their carving knives while they secretly calculate the profits from the aphrodisiac they think will come from ground-down horn.

On the dawn of the fourth day, when they finally open the gates with a painted-on smile, leave.

You're not there to fight their wars for them. You've got better things to do. Like saving god from themself.

Step Twelve.

Best served ice cold.

EVEN THE CLEAREST WATER

ANDI C. BUCHANAN

From water, white-capped, rushing over pebbles and stones, chasing round rocks, my flesh emerges; limbs stick-thin and translucent like the freshwater they came from, wings glinting in the late-summer sun. I perch on the river edge, soft grass and slipping mud, listening for footsteps.

There's water in the ground, even after summer brightness, and through it I can hear the child before she comes into view. I hear soft footsteps on the grass and bare toes curling round the damp soil, soaking in the grainy texture as if it were a sensation she'd been deprived of all her life and yet was as essential to her as breathing.

She wanders over the hill towards the stream, where she has been headed all along even if she doesn't know it. Her pigtails are pulled so tight they must hurt and yet she shows no sign of distress. Her clothes are all green; her t-shirt and patchwork skirt, and likely her socks and shoes before she lost them, far behind her. She walks in small steps, her feet spread apart, her eyes wide as if this is a new world waiting for her. It's not magic, just observation; paying attention to these things about her tells me instantly she's autistic. Many humans would give her less understanding labels.

She sees me. I hold still, careful not to scare her. I pull my wings back, feeling them tremble in the breeze. Like many children, she moves forward with wonderment and curiosity rather than fear. I flutter a little way into the grass to entice her away from the water.

It works for a few moments, but then the pull of the water is too strong. She falls and the undercurrent pulls her down. I fly down, slipping into water, becoming water, and I speak to her.

"Do you want me to save you?" I ask. It's the beginning of a negotiation. A bargain. Many humans would criticise me, but I am here and they are not.

This child is face-down in the water and does not respond. This is a child who does not speak, perhaps not ever or perhaps not now. I need her agreement if I'm going to save her. I look at her more closely.

I see a child who wants to live. A child who loves her family and the soil beneath her feet and, yes, the water. The fact that she can't say any of that doesn't make it any less clear. It does not mean she is not communicating.

Her will to live is a bargain with me, and I will be back one day to claim my part of it. I pull her choking, spluttering, from the river, turn her over, and let her vomit into the grass. There are other footsteps approaching, quick and frantic. I hear the child's name on the softly-moving summer air, and it sounds like bird-call: *Cora, Cora.*

Then there's a woman running, then kneeling beside the child, checking her for breath, for a heartbeat, sobbing with relief or sobbing with fear. Normally I would disappear back into the stream, letting myself flow into it. But this time is different.

I look up at the woman holding her daughter tightly, and realise that I recognise her. I know her name.

Rosalind. The woman who paid me a debt before I came to collect.

*

The first time I saw Rosalind, she was fourteen years old. I'd known she was on her way, sensed her trudging, determined steps through the river to the waterfall. I pulled myself out of the pool below, crashing water refracting rainbows into the winter air. The water was bone cold and the ground cracked with ice, but neither would stop her.

Like so many children, Rosalind had always been drawn to the water, but she grew up playing in parks without fountains and swam in chlorinated pools under the watchful eye of an instructor, learning to keep a panicked child's head above water or to tow a patient in a rescue tube. But this was later, and she was older. She wasn't making her way through the river because she loved water. Her face was calligraphed with thick eyeliner, because Rosalind had always liked to make a statement, but the barely-clotted blood on her arms was not art.

Rosalind had her reasons, even if I didn't know them. She was here to die.

She continued towards the waterfall, clothes heavy-laden with water. I didn't think she'd do it, thought she'd back out just in time, but she crashed down through the water, bouncing against the rocks, and I swooped down and caught her from the waterfall before she hit the pool below.

"Do you want me to save you?" I asked over and over.

"No," she said, thrashing against my hold. "Let me die. Let

me die."

I pulled her from the water anyway, carried her all the way to the tourist car park, and left her for others to find.

That was my mistake. She still owed me but, because she had not consented to the bargain, she could fulfil it any way she chose.

*

"Her debt is mine," Rosalind says. "But you will not take her. You will not take my daughter." It's a bold statement, especially to one of the fair folk. But she's right. We don't ask for firstborn these days; when we did, it was almost a blessing. Better to lose a child to us than to the factories that wrench skin from bone, to the blistering wars of imperialism, to illness, or to starvation.

"You?" I say, edging scepticism onto my tongue. "What do you have to offer?"

But the woman gazing back at me could be my equal – one who can play at my own games. She's in her thirties now, a lawyer, tying knots with a clever turn of phrase as well as I ever could. Cover-up tattoos on her arms have twisted her scars into swaying strands of seaweed, fish swimming between them. Those are arms that have pulled her daughter from water before. At work they are always beneath a blazer, but now it is summer and she has a daughter within them, tapping out a rhythm on her mother's shoulder.

Rosalind has not been one to cheat me. She could have chosen so many ways to fulfil her debt, but she did not choose the easy ones, the perfunctory ones. She copied out poems on pages torn from her school books, wrapped them in plastic, and dropped them into rivers or off wharfs. She collected coins when she travelled and threw them into the sea as if she were skimming stones. When her grandmother died, Rosalind gave me a necklace she inherited of blue-green stones that glint even through water.

"Time," she says. She's gazing just to the right of my face and into the distance, a trick she's learned to give the impression of eye contact. I don't mind. "I can give you time."

I let the silence hang between us and wait for her to continue. I have saved so many from the water – mostly children, some older. I once stayed away from all humans, but those I saved were those who fascinated me. I have emerged in rips at beaches, in lakes and rivers and waterfalls, to drag them from drowning. None have ever been like Rosalind. None have ever bargained like she does.

It is not that I have no feelings for them. But I understand, as so few of them do, that to exist among others is a series of exchanges, of bargains, and I am making another one. It is true that I would prefer these mortals to not drown, not so young, but so many mortals are lost already. Death is simply part of their existence.

"I am told," she says, when she's realised I'm not going to respond. "I am told that your kind sometimes want us to give up something of value more than you want to receive it. Your years are long; ours are short, and they are all we have."

Her voice softens as I listen. She continues.

"Come and spend some time with us. Come and be with us, with me, in the places we go. Let me give you these few short years. They will barely register for you, but for me they are everything."

I smile despite myself. She's doing well at making it sound like she's doing me a favour, and yet I am oddly pleased. I remember that I have kept everything she gave me, hidden behind rocks in a waterfall. I did not know why I kept it until now.

I look up at her and she's smiling back, standing now. She has no powers of glamour, and yet it's hard to look away.

The years of mortals are so short. But they can be so beautiful.

I pull myself out from the river and take her hand, feeling the flow of water in the soil below and the summer breeze upon my wings as Cora, now recovered, runs rings around us as we walk.

YOU CAN'T BEAT WELLINGTON ON A GOOD DAY

ANNA KIRTLAN

"Give those back, you bastard, bastard, bastard wind!" The man's suit jacket flapped behind him like a superhero cape as he chased his papers down the street. I giggled slightly to myself as I ran to help him gather them up. He grinned sheepishly when I passed over a handful of documents. "Wellington!" he sighed in exasperation and we shared a knowing look.

Most Wellingtonians have a love/hate relationship with our signature element. The scourge of washing lines, terror of trampolines and reason we can't have nice outdoor furniture, or umbrellas – the twisted skeletons of which are often seen poking up from rubbish bins. I've seen an open umbrella haring down the street by itself, no owner chasing after it. A friend of mine once spotted a pair of pants walking down the waterfront with no human inside.

When all that's said and done though, we are fiercely proud of our city – wind and all. "You can't beat Wellington on a good day," we say to anyone who will listen. If you can tolerate the occasional gale force tantrum, the city will reward you with a single, perfect, jewel-like day which makes it all worthwhile. It's part of living in and loving this city. Or at least it used to be. Somewhere along the line, things changed.

The first murder of that summer was at a bus stop. An argument over a delayed arrival got out of hand. The perpetrator was a policy analyst, who pled guilty immediately. He had a completely clean record. His family, friends and colleagues were shocked and he himself had no real explanation for his behaviour. One minute, he was in the midst of a heated discussion and the next, the red mist descended and he had his hands around another man's throat.

This was the beginning of a flood of unlikely killers – policy wonks and politicians, teachers and florists. A particularly nasty brawl that broke out in a rest home between the residents and the girl guides who were there to sing for them had to be broken up by the police riot squad. News reports about Wellington grew increasingly grim. Domestic violence rates were up, road rage incidents were on the rise. It was as if the entire city woke up one morning in an unfathomable, unnatural rage.

Nobody mentioned the good days anymore.

I was more careful when I went into town and stopped making eye contact with strangers, but for a long time, it was only on the periphery for me. I felt a sort of sadness for the state of our once vibrant city, but it wasn't until I was paying one of my regular visits to my Great Aunt Polly that things really hit home.

Polly's cottage was just a block away from our old family home in Island Bay. As a kid, I was obsessed with my great aunt. As far as I was concerned, she was the fount of all knowledge. I was one of those precocious kids who needed to know everything about everything immediately. I'm certain Polly's presence was a huge relief for my Mum, who would often send me down for visits.

I suspect to get a break from the incessant "What's that? What for? Why?"

"Why don't you ask Aunt Polly?" was a common phrase in our household. She was technically my great aunt, but that was a bit of a mouthful for a toddler, and 'Aunt Polly' stuck.

Luckily for Mum, Polly was more than happy to answer my questions and fill my head with knowledge of her own. "Did you know?" followed by whatever I had learned from Polly that day replaced the whys and what fors. I don't know which was more annoying actually. I must ask Mum one day.

Polly taught me all about Wellington. About its storms and its shipwrecks and where the shoreline used to be. She showed me which local plants were poisonous and which could fix a tummy ache when brewed into a tea. We would go for walks along the beach and she would tell me which shells belonged to which critters. Most importantly though, she taught me about the wind.

It was on one of our beach walks that Polly first told me about listening to the wind. I had found a shell on the seashore and excitedly pressed it to my ear to see if I could hear the ocean like I'd heard about from some kids at school.

"That's not actually the ocean you hear, dear," Polly said to me softly. "It's the sound of the air around you made bigger because it is echoing inside the shell."

Seeing my look of disappointment, she knelt down to my level and whispered conspiratorially, "Don't be upset. I can show you something much better."

Instead of listening for an ocean that wasn't really there, Aunt Polly taught me to listen for something that most definitely was. I know it sounds rather obvious. I mean everyone can hear the wind, especially around here. It whistles and it howls and it knocks things about. It's not exactly subtle. But there's a layer underneath that, and that's what Polly showed me.

If you try hard, and at first it is really hard, you can hear more than just air rushing past. It sounds silly but it's almost like words. People talk about the wind whistling and howling, and that's exactly right. It does all of those things. But on a good day, you can hear it sing.

Aunt Polly and I would go for walks up into Wellington's hills on windy days. Mum would fuss and wrap me up in jackets and mutter about why we couldn't do it on a nicer day. Polly showed me the wind's emotions. When it whistled, it was happy. Those were the kind of windy days where there was a sort of a spark in the air, when you were full of energy and excitement but you weren't entirely sure why. When it howled, it was angry. Those times could be scary but also strangely cleansing, like it was blowing all the anger and rage of the earth somewhere far away.

It was on one of those howling days that Polly taught me that I could talk back. I'd had a rough day at school. I would sometimes get picked on for being a little different from the other kids. Most of the time, I could handle it, but that day had been particularly wretched. Mum was working late that afternoon, so I went straight to Polly.

She took one look at my tear-stained face and grabbed her jacket. "We're going for a walk," she said.

It was an absolute belter that day. Polly and I were forced to cling to each other as we clambered through bush and over rocks. Once we reached the peak of one of the hills, we looked over the bay down to Polly's cottage.

"Okay, tell me about it," she said.

I blurted the whole miserable episode out. "Normally, I can ignore them," I sputtered, the wind ripping the words from my mouth. "But it just got to me today. They were being such bitches!" I glanced over at Polly, expecting a reprimand. I'd never said the B-word in front of her before. But she said nothing. In fact, I could have sworn I'd seen a little smile.

"I know I should be better than them but I just can't be that all the time!" I sobbed.

"You don't have to be perfect all the time," Polly said. "It's not healthy. It was a crappy situation and you're allowed to feel angry about it."

My eyebrows just about rose right off my head.

"Especially when they are being such …" she paused, a wicked grin spreading across her face as she waited for me to finish.

"Bitches," I said, quietly but firmly.

"Say it again," she said. "Louder this time."

"Bitches!" I said, raising my voice.

"That's it!" she said, joining me. "BITCHES! BITCHES! BITCHES!" she yelled savagely into the wind.

The wind swirled around us, ripping away our words as we danced and swore and howled like a couple of crazed banshees. I could have sworn the wind's own howls were forming words.

"Be angry. It's allowed. I am too. Be angry. It's allowed. I'll take it away."

Utterly spent, Polly and I collapsed on the hillside, the wind still crashing around us.

"Thank you," I whispered. To Polly and the wind.

It was on that day that I became BFFs with the scourge of brollies city-wide. I loved nothing more than to go for a walk on a day when the wind was singing, listen to it tell its stories and sometimes, when I was on my own, sing back.

When I had bad days that coincided with stormy days, I would climb up to the highest point I could access and scream my troubles into the void. It was a dance of joy and rage and power.

At 102, Polly is still going strong – a little frail but a lot tough. I visit her as often as possible and it was on one of those visits that Wellington's new insanity came crashing into my life.

Before I even managed to get a third knock in, the door was wrenched inwards and there was Polly, brandishing a carving knife, her eyes burning and her slight frame trembling with rage. Instinctively, I jumped back, just in time, as she lunged towards me with a surprising amount of speed and power.

"Aunt Polly!" I said, trying to calm her – and myself. "It's me!"

It was no use. Her glazed eyes barely registered me as she swung around, stabbing in my direction.

"You won't take me! I'm not going! I'm coming out of here feet first, you motherfuckers!" she screamed.

My legs were trembling and tears sprung to my eyes, an involuntary sob wrenched from my lips. Whoever this was, it was not my aunt.

"No one is taking you anywhere, Polly," I said, hands up in surrender as I tried to lead her back towards the house. "Let's sit down and talk this over."

It must have been my tears that snapped her out of it. She dropped the knife and collapsed to the ground. "Oh, oh! I'm so sorry!" she said, tears pouring down her cheeks. "I don't know…"

"It's okay, Polly," I said, gently helping her up. "Let's just get you inside."

Both in shock, I steered her towards her favourite armchair and busied myself in the kitchen, where I could still keep an eye on her, making us both a cup of tea. I was scared and confused. As far as I was aware, there had only ever been one conversation between my mother and Polly about her going into care, and it ended the way we all thought it would. Mum really only suggested it because she felt obliged to point out there could be an easier way of life, but we all knew the old woman would never willingly leave that cottage. I had no idea what had put it in her head now.

I passed Polly her mug and sat in the chair opposite. Her eyes had cleared, and all I saw was confusion and contrition.

"I don't know where that came from. I really don't," she said. "Everything's just got so ... heavy. Sometimes I feel like everyone is out to get me. I get so scared I can't breathe. Would you mind opening the window, dear? Let a little air in?"

I squeezed her hand and got up to open the window, but I knew it would be in vain. There would be no fresh air. Wellington had been uncharacteristically still for a long time. "How long have you been feeling like this, Aunt Polly?" I asked. "Be honest."

"Probably about three months," she said sheepishly. "I didn't want to worry you or your mother."

"Three months is a long time to feel out of sorts," I chided gently, not wanting to upset her more than she already was. I settled myself back into my chair, now sticky with humidity. To be honest, I was a bit on edge, too. I hadn't slept for a long time. The nights had been so muggy. It felt like Wellington had been like this forever, heavy and still and sullen. How long had it been? I wondered, an idea formulating in the back of my mind.

I pulled out my phone and checked the latest 'Why is there

no wind?' story in the media. 'Record drought continues … no wind and rain for three months.'

For three months, our city had been hot, muggy and listless. Crops were drying out, yachts stayed put in the marina and nobody slept.

I did another search, heart pounding. Three months ago, almost to the day, Wellington's first unexplained murder. The man at the bus stop. We'd had three months of darkness, violence and rage.

It sounded crazy but, in a way, it made perfect sense. For three months, we had been without our identity. We complain, but the wind is Wellington's fierce beating heart. Without it, we don't know who we are. It's our lungs. It blows away our anger, pain and sadness – and for three months, it had been holding its breath.

I cast my mind back to before I stopped hearing the wind sing. We'd had a few decent blows in quick succession. Power lines downed, seawalls breached, one man tragically killed when his car was crushed by a falling tree branch.

Mostly, it was frustration though. Our language around the wind had changed. People were busy and didn't have time for its shenanigans. Knowing smiles had been replaced by curses. We hated it. We wanted it to stop. When I thought about it, the vitriol against the wind had been the worst I'd ever heard.

I showed Polly what I had found. Her eyes widened.

"I think it's on strike," I whispered incredulously.

She just looked at me.

I was certain now, and what's more, I was angry. "The wind has been sulking for the last three months and it's destroying our city."

"The selfish shit!" Polly, the old Polly – my Polly, was grinning at me, eyes sparkling. I stood up and grabbed my jacket, heading for the door.

"I think it's time someone told it to pull its head in," I snapped. Polly pulled herself up to come with me. I took one look at her 102-year-old frame and shook my head. "Not this time, Polly. You've taught me everything I need to know. I'll sort this one out myself. Don't get into any trouble before I get back," I finished sternly, closing the door behind me before she could talk her way into the expedition.

Sweating, panting and cursing the fact I hadn't had the fore-thought to bring a water bottle, I clawed my way to the highest point of the hills behind Polly's cottage. I stood for a moment, catching my breath and surveying the bay and the city, all the tiny people in their tiny houses. I thought of the anger and the pain and the death. I thought of Polly in her cottage, alone and angry and not knowing why, and I screamed at the top of my lungs.

It was a ragged, raw, painful scream that echoed across the hills. I was angry too, but I knew exactly what I was angry at.

"WHAT. THE. FUCK?" I screamed, not caring if anyone could hear.

"WHAT DO YOU THINK YOU'RE DOING?" I screamed again, a burning, guttural cry of rage. I spat and snarled; a woman possessed.

"WHY?"

Nothing.

I collapsed to the ground sobbing, laying on my back with my eyes squinted closed against the sun. Exhausted, my breathing finally slowed, and as it did, I felt something prickling at the back of my mind.

It was pain. Pain and then anger. It was a barrage of constant curses and snide remarks. It was hearing it was hated thousands upon thousands of times. I lay there, not even trying to wipe away the tears streaming down my face.

Sitting up, I looked around. Not a whisper. Everything was achingly still. "It's not true," I rasped, my throat raw from screaming. "We need you. Yes, people can be arseholes, but they're just people. You're the wind!"

Still nothing.

"Have you seen what this city has become without you? People are dying!" A flash of an old man, dead in his crushed car.

"That's different!" I yelled, my energy creeping back. "That sort of thing happens. That's nature. You're nature! What is happening now is the opposite of natural!"

I thought of Polly and the men at the bus stop. The man who was murdered and the one who might as well have been.

"Alright!" I yelled. "You've made your point! Do you want us to beg? Watch the news, we fucking are! Are you really going to let a bunch of bipedal bullies win? You're the fucking wind!"

I could have sworn I felt a tiny gust. It only stirred my rage.

"Blow, you coward!" I screamed.

The prickle in the back of my head turned into an angry surge. 'Good!' I thought. 'Let it get mad. I'm mad.' The pain became intense. I ignored it.

"Are you mad?" I screamed, heaving myself up from the ground and flinging my arms wide. "Come on then. Knock me down. Come on, you coward. Fight me!"

A stabbing pain behind my eyes. I doubled over but stood firm. I thought back to the first time Polly took me up into the hills in a gale. How upset I was, how the wind blew away my pain and rage. I thought of the words I heard in the wind's howls and I shouted them into the air, spinning around and around.

"Be angry. It's allowed. I am too. Be angry. It's allowed. I'll take it away." I felt a strength grow in me as I recited the words like a mantra.

"Be angry. It's allowed ..."

I thought of the silly schoolgirl fight and of all the bullies in the world, of the people cursing and hating.

"BITCHES, BITCHES, BITCHES!" I screamed, electricity crackling around me as I turned faster and faster.

I didn't notice at first that the rage building up inside me had burst outwards. It wasn't until I slowed my spinning to catch my breath that I saw the sky had begun to darken, that the branches around me were beginning to sway. It had been so long, I had almost forgotten what the sound was.

I felt the wind's rage building up around me.

"Come on then!" I taunted. "If you're so pissed off, knock me down! Do it!"

It did.

One minute, I was shouting at the sky and the next, I was on my arse gasping for breath and grinning like an idiot.

"Yes!" I howled wildly. "Harder! Stir us up! Blow all the shit away!"

The wind finally obliged. I heard an almighty crack as the limb from a tree behind me crashed to the ground. Leaves spun through the air as I braced myself against a rock on the hillside. I let go, stumbling blindly down the hill, spinning in erratic circles.

"Be angry. It's allowed. I am too."

Grasping at tree trunks as I made my way back down to Polly's cottage, I pushed myself against the gale. I looked up at the clouds racing across the sky and smiled.

You can't beat Wellington on a good day, and today was a good day.

THE MOAMANCER
(A MUSOMANCER SHORT STORY)

BING TURKBY

I made up this whole story. Or, did I…?

Yep. I did. It's fiction.

Any resemblance to anybody, living, dead, undead or reanimated is unintentional.

Written with huge respect for Te Āpiti – Manawatū Gorge, and its past and present inhabitants.

I wanted to share the natural wonder of the place with everybody, and hope I haven't caused offence to anyone in doing so.

Please visit teapiti.co.nz to find out more about this special area.

*

ONE

I was soldering a new pickup into my Telecaster when Alex dropped round. She eyed up my sloppy work on her way to the fridge to blag one of my fancy beers.

"I see the Gorge is still closed," she said, as she offered me one of my own brews. I nodded to her to put the beer bottle on the coffee table for me. I'd learned the hard way not to gesticulate while holding a soldering iron. Took me weeks to grow back my eyebrow and the fingerprint on my left pinkie.

"Well," I said with a sigh, "I can't talk about that."

"What do you mean?" said Alex.

I shifted my position to get a better angle on the ground wire. "Just that I'm sworn to secrecy on the Gorge closure. No speaky, sorry, buddy."

Alex slumped onto the couch and popped the cap off her bottle. "Sworn to secrecy about the Gorge? About the fact that slips on the hillside have caused the road to be closed for ages now? What's the big secret?"

I put the soldering iron down carefully and eyed the joint I'd been working on. It actually looked like it might hold this time.

"Listen," I said, "You've got to stop pestering me about this. I've signed paperwork with the government and everything."

Alex blew a raspberry in my general direction. "Sounds like another one of your cock-and-bull stories to me. So, are we still on for the gig this evening?"

"I'm serious, you have to stop asking me about the Gorge closure."

"Pretty sure I already did."

"I can't say another word or I'll go to jail."

"Cool – about this gig…"

"Okay, okay, I'll tell you! They closed it off to traffic to allow time for the moa population to rebuild." I threw my hands in the air. "Are you happy now? They've probably got my house bugged, you know."

"The moa have your house bugged?" said Alex. "I think it unlikely. Also, for the gazillionth time: what the hell are you talking about? Moa have been extinct for hundreds of years."

I rocked back on my heels and gave her a resigned look. "Well, now you've pried it out of me I might as well tell you the whole story."

"Um," she fiddled with her beer bottle, "I only came over to ask if you're still going to the gig tonight…"

I stood up, popped open my beer and went over to gaze pensively out the window. "In school they'll tell you that the giant flightless bird, the majestic moa, was hunted to extinction well before the arrival of Europeans on these shores."

"I think I already covered that."

"Hush! Feel the gravity of the situation. You'll tell your grandkids one day."

Alex nodded. "Yep: 'hey kids, did I ever tell you about the day I had to drop my friend Jareth off at a special-care facility?'"

"For reals, girl." I turned to fix her with a steely gaze. "Seriously. There are still a few moa left, and they've been hiding in the Manawatū Gorge all this time." I plomped down on the couch next to her. "A few people knew about it, and they resolved to keep it secret, and pledged to look after the birds."

"Wait up," said Alex. "A few people managed to keep secret the fact that giant birds, bigger than emu, have been living twenty minutes away from Palmerston North?"

"You start to believe now, don't you, youngling?" I said in my best Jedi voice.

"No, I start to disbelieve," she replied, with a touch of the Sith about her. "My disbelief is strong, and growing stronger with each statement you utter. How could people possibly keep something that big from getting noticed?"

I gave it a good theatrical pause, raised an eyebrow, and then:

"With the help of the musomancers, my friend. Musomancers have saved the moa. And I am but the latest in a long line of moa-helpers." I couldn't keep the proud grin from my face at that point.

"Now," stated Alex, "You've mentioned that you're a musomancer before." I nodded. "You say," she said, "that you can make magic through musical means." Another nod from me. "You say," she continued, "that you have already thwarted an evil mage who was about to cause the destruction of the world." A third nod from my noggin.

"And yet," said Alex, "there is absolutely no evidence of any of that. Anywhere. Ever."

"Exactly," I replied. "That's how good I am." I took a smug sip of amber ale. "Anyway, the government asked me to use my musomancy to cause the slips that cut off the road through the Gorge, and also to cast a spell that would keep the moa from being spotted."

"You!" and here Alex pointed her finger at me like an accusatory blame-stick. "You caused the slips in the Gorge."

"Yep." I took another self-congratulatory sip.

"The slips, which cut people off from their easy access to employment and trade."

"Um…" I gulped the beer, which had somehow got a bit stuck on the way down my throat. "Yep. Yeah, I guess so."

"By using music-magic."

"Musomancy." I corrected her. "And you're missing the bigger point here: I'm helping to save the moa!"

"Riiiight…" Alex drained her beer and stood up. "Anyway, text me later when you decide if you're going to the gig or not."

"No," I exclaimed.

She turned back to me. "No to the gig?"

"No, there is absolutely no way I can take you out to the Gorge and show you the moa. I've signed papers. I could go to jail!"

Twenty minutes later we were at the turnoff to the Gorge.

*

TWO

Alex kicked bits of loose plastic off the dashboard of my old MkIII Cortina wagon. "Sigh…" she said. (Yes, she literally said the word "sigh".) "This is bullshit, man. Let's just go to a cafe."

"Nah, nah … wait a minute, this is going to blow your mind," I assured her as we swept like a dilapidated yet vigorous broom into the carpark that marks the start of the Gorge walking track. "You'll see."

I grabbed my backpack, leapt out of the car and crunched across the gravel. Alex reluctantly slouched along behind me.

As I passed under the arch with the walkway information, I paused and looked back at Alex.

"This right here is where my work starts." I spread my arms wide and spun around in a slow arc, taking in the natural beauty that surrounded us.

"What do you mean? Is this where you pick up rubbish when you're on Diversion?"

"No, you fool," I grumped, deflated. "You're starting to try my patience. First you insist that I reveal my secrets, then you act all bored now that we're here."

Alex rolled her eyes, as she knew this conversation was an unwinnable game. (Literally – I was keeping score, and it was already 6–2 to me.)

"This is where my bubble starts," I said, gesturing to the completely invisible bubble that sprang up behind me. It covered roughly a gigabyte of hectares worth of ruggedly beautiful native bush; a boisterous river that could only be stepped in once according to Heraclitus; and a sizeable chunk of air, which came in very handy for the flying creatures residing therein.

"Let me guess," said Alex. "This is a magic bubble, which protects all those moa that can't possibly live here due to them being extinct?"

"Correct, my fledgling apprentice."

She pointed to herself. "I'm not your apprentice." She pointed at me. "And you're non compos mentis."

I got out my phone and emailed that line to myself so I could use it in a song. (Don't worry – if the song does really well, I will definitely pay Alex a portion of the royalties. For sure.)

"You'll see," I said, stuffing my phone inside an ethically-woven hemp bag and then tucking it into an internal pocket of my jacket. Alex raised an eyebrow in silent query. "Oh, the bag? Yeah, you got to keep phones away from the moa." I started along the track into the Gorge.

"Why? Does the radiation fry their toenails or something?"

"Nah, if they get hold of your phone you'll never get it back. They love phones, those moa."

Tramp, tramp, tramp, we went, like a couple of trampers tramping along a track. It's very similar to walking, but comes with more kudos.

We saw a kererū, a couple of pīwakawaka and an empty potato chip packet, which made me mad. (The bag, not the birds.) I picked it up and virtue-signalled the shit out of the place for a few minutes, just in case the perpetrator was lurking nearby.

I can't say Alex was enjoying the day too much so far.

As we trudged along, I pulled a mandolin out of my backpack and strummed a few gentle yet very specific chords.

"I can do without that racket, for a start," said Alex.

"No, I need to do it so you can see the moa." I waved my picking hand to encompass the greenery that surrounded us. "My musomancy is currently hiding them from sight, but if I play just the right chords, you and I will be able to see them. You and I…" I turned and fixed her with a meaningful gaze, "…and nobody else."

"So," she said, "if you play the wrong chords … everybody will be able to see them?"

I gulped. "I don't really need that kind of pressure right now, thanks Alex." I let out a long shaky breath. "My fallback chord is always just a nice straightforward G major. Works for a lot of spells, because it's confident and supportive, but also calming and restorative. If you're ever in a tight spot, musomancy-wise, hit 'em with a G, I say. Now, let me concentrate."

Alex thought for a minute. "How long have musomancers been hiding the moa here then?"

"Oooh, for at least five hundred years, I should say. As soon as someone noticed they were on the verge of extinction. Why do you ask?"

"Just wondering where the old musomancers got their mandolins from, that's all."

"Oh, right. Good question. So, it doesn't have to be a mandolin. In fact, traditional Māori instruments work better with the moa, since they're native birds. They're more attuned to things like pūtōrino and kōauau. But only experts in taonga pūoro have been trained to play those with the correct physical, mental and spiritual technique. I can only use what I know. I'm strongest on guitar, but I can get the job done with mandolin, Irish tenor banjo … heck, I can even muster a reasonably powerful invocation with an accordion if I have to."

"True," said Alex. "I've seen you clear a room with an accordion on more than one occasion." She smiled. "Quick as a flash, you did it."

On we trudged.

"Hey, Alex." I pointed to a mossy tree. "Old man's beard must go. Huh? Amirite?"

"That is sooooo last century," she said as she brushed past me.

"Hey, you're from last century, too, pantsface."

"Yeah, but not the boring part of it," she threw back at me. "Anyway, where's these damn moa? Let's get me moa-vated. I wanted moa out of this tramp."

"That is all really good banter, actually, Alex. I'm very proud of you."

"You rub off on me like a chalky deposit. It's not a good look for either of us, really."

I chuckled. "Chalky deposit … nice one."

A few minutes later we crested the rise of a rising cresty bit. A ridge, I guess. Through an opening in the trees we could see across to the other side of the Gorge, where a railway track twisted and turned through the bush. Below us, the water of the Manawatū River made like Geoffrey and rushed. With the force of a thousand washing machines, the river punched its way through the ranges, keeping the Ruahines away from the Tararuas as if they were squabbling siblings being given a watery time-out.

"Hey, Alex."

Sigh. "Whaaaaat now?"

"Did you know this is the only place in New Zealand where a river starts on the other side of the main divide to where it finishes at the sea?"

"If you're just going to look up stuff online and then parrot it back to me, you know we could have done this back at your place, right?"

"Wait," I said, "think about it. That means this is a place of coming together. Even though the river separates the ranges, it also unites the opposite sides of the island."

"So you're thinking it would be a good place to host a music festival, like Woodstock? Or you could open a refuelling station for crystals or something?"

"You're getting close," I replied. "I think the place has a healing, preserving magic all of its own. And that's probably why the last moa are here. Even before musomancers came along to help, the moa were already finding sanctuary in this special area."

As if in reply, an eerie call echoed through the Gorge. The hairs on my arms stood up. All the other sounds of the bush fell silent, as if the forest creatures were in awe of the primordial sound. It was like a cross between a goat bleat and a parrot squawk, but much deeper, like it had been put through a glitchy old octave guitar effect pedal. If you put a stethoscope to the stomach of a giant with intestinal troubles, it might have sounded something like that.

I turned to Alex, mouth open in wonder.

"Did you hear that?"

Alex shifted her weight from one foot to the other. "OK, yeah, that sounded weird. Could have been…" she trailed off, and then weakly ended with: "A rooster fighting a ram, maybe?"

"Alex," I whispered.

"What?"

I patted the air with my hands. "Be very quiet."

She froze, staring at me. "Why?"

"Turn around. Very … slowly."

*

THREE

Alex raised an eyebrow. She did not look amused. But she humoured me anyway, by turning around in a slow fashion which managed to cover her long-suffering frustration with a thin veneer of compliance.

She turned to look straight at a mossy brown tree trunk that had inexplicably materialised behind her. Then, as her brain allowed her to slowly comprehend it, she realised the tree trunk wasn't mossy, it was feathery. And it swayed gently. And it … swallowed.

She looked down and saw the tree trunk get wider and wider, until it was rather obviously a body, with two huge – and I mean huge – powerful legs.

Finally, she looked up. And up. And up. Until she saw, looking down at her, two eyes and beak, like a duck crossed with a diplodocus.

The animal's head was about a metre above her. It was looking at her with mild curiosity and some wariness.

"Oh. My. God," she breathed. "Jareth. It's a moa!"

"I feel I should remind you," I hissed back, "that's exactly why I brought you here. Do you believe me now?"

Alex tentatively put her hand out towards the gigantic beast. "Okay," she said. "I'll give you this one. Can I touch it?"

"They don't usually like being petted, but for a special person they have been known to allow it," I whispered. "Just be aware, it might…"

SKROOOOOONK!

Alex's legs gave out and she collapsed backwards, cowering in front of the gigantic animal. The moa let rip with another mighty call, dipped its head as if in farewell, then strode past us into the dense bush.

"…It might let out an incredibly loud, growly rumbling sound," I finished. "They don't mean you any harm, that's just them saying hello." I gave her a hand up.

"Right," I said, as she brushed dirt and leaves off her trousers. "Time to go to a cafe, is it?"

"Are you kidding?" said Alex. "I want to see more! Are there more of them? How many?"

"Okay, okay, yes there are more moa. Many more moa. If we're lucky we might see a few making a nest in a tree."

"What? How the hell does a huge bird like that nest in a tree?"

"I don't know, I think it would be very difficult. That's why I said we'd have to be lucky. I've only ever seen them on the ground."

She punched me on the shoulder.

"Hey! What was that for?"

"That was for everything! Including that lame joke you just crapped out. That was for making me think there weren't any moa, and then standing me right in front of one."

"Um," I said, "point of order. I've been telling you there were moa here for, like, the whole day."

"Yes, but you made it seem like you were just talking bullshit."

"That's just the way I talk. That's what my voice sounds like. I'll take the rap for the bad joke, and let's simply chalk the rest up to the excitement of the situation."

"Screw you, you liar," she said, and stalked off.

For the first, and perhaps only, time in recorded history, I was at a loss for words. I tagged along behind Alex, my mouth opening and closing soundlessly.

*

FOUR

Eventually I caught up with Alex. By that time she had rid herself of some of the antihistamines – no, what's the word I'm looking for? – adrenaline.

"Sorry for punching you," she said.

"No problem, I'm a tough book nerd. If I had a dollar for every time I've been punched on the shoulder I'd have enough money for a very cheap, second-hand phaser guitar effect pedal."

She fidgeted with the zipper on her coat. "I'm sorry for calling you a liar, too. I honestly thought you were pulling my leg earlier."

I shrugged. "I do have a bit of a rep for that kind of thing, to be fair."

She perked up at that. "Yeah! Like when you told everyone you battled a musical dragon in a lair underneath the clock tower." She snorted. "You doofus."

"But that's…" I waved it away. Not the time to get into that again. Maybe once Alex had time to reflect on the moa situation, she might start to see some of my other stories in a different light.

Because now we could hear the distinctive low, rumbling calls of several moa up ahead. It sounded like a dozen big motorcycles singing while they cooked dinner.

I strummed a few more chords on my mandolin, tweaking the muso-magical field that protected them from human perception, to make sure we got a good sighting of them.

The sound grew louder. It seemed like we were rapidly getting closer to them. Much faster than the speed we were walking. They were obviously coming towards us. In a hurry. The thunder of twenty or thirty massive moa feet pounding the earth set our teeth chattering. Their groaning roars grew more frantic.

"We need to move," I said. "Now!"

"Are they charging us?" cried Alex.

"They don't usually do stuff like that," I yelled as we raced off to the left. I was heading for a dense stand of kahikatea, hoping that the moa wouldn't be able to penetrate it. "Something must have riled them up. Run!"

The treetops in the distance were swaying. We could hear the moa growls getting louder and louder. I pelted towards the trees, looking for a gap to sneak into. I risked a quick look backward to check on Alex. She was right on my heels, thank goodness.

We were only twenty metres away, but now we could see bushes being uprooted and smaller trees pushed aside, as the first of a large group of rampaging moa came crashing towards us. One of them roared, and leapt over my head as I ducked down just in time. Alex jerked to a stop as another moa raced in front of her, its bulky body only centimetres from crushing her into the fecund mulch layer. It was so close to her that it would have whipped the hat off her head, had she been chapeaued. (She wasn't, so that was lucky, I guess.)

As soon as it sped past, she kicked herself into motion again, racing along behind me. We were almost there.

I spotted a gap in the stand of trees – it was skinny but so were my jeans. We might just make it. I put on an extra burst of speed that I didn't know I had in me.

"Alex!" I yelled, and turned to point the way. That's when my foot hit a tree root, I fell face-first into a rock, and everything went black.

*

FIVE

I woke sometime later. Well, I could hardly wake up earlier, could I? I was lying in the recovery position, and my mouth tasted like dirt and kererū droppings.

I moaned and put my hands to my head. This was worse than the time I drank a two-litre bottle of Bloke-a-cola at a recording session.

I opened my eyes a little, and the sun speared into them like it was trying to interrogate me in an old-fashioned cop show. As my vision cleared I could see I was in the middle of a stand of stumpy trees, and I could hear soft chords coming from … maybe a harp? Was I in heaven? Seemed unlikely, and frankly it would be quite embarrassing, as I didn't think heaven existed.

"Jareth, are you awake?" Alex's voice came from nearby. "Are you okay? You hit your head pretty hard."

"Mmrrrpphhh," I mumbled. "I mean, pah!" I spat out some dirt and various bits of foliage. "I think I'll be okay. Looks like the rock I fell onto had a good covering of moss, so it was spongy."

I tried to rise but the tree trunks wavered in front of me and I fell back down.

"You got us to safety, Alex," I said. "How did you evade the rampaging moa?"

"Well … I didn't exactly get us away from them," she said.

"How do you mean?"

"Look around you, buddy."

I finally raised my sore head, and as I did, the stumpy trees that surrounded us resolved into feathery stumpy legs, and then I realised they had wrinkly clawed feet, and they were shifting this way and that.

"Um, Alex?"

"Yes, Jareth?"

"Are we surrounded by several large flightless birds of the ratite family, perchance?"

"That's what I'm telling you, mate. Also," she added wearily, "I'm running out of chords to play on this mandolin, and my fretting hand is getting tired. Would you mind taking over for a minute, please?"

I dragged myself up to my feet, still a bit wobbly.

Now that I could see properly, I took a second to drink in the astounding sight of a couple dozen full-grown moa encircling us, swaying slightly in time to the sound of Alex's mandolin playing. It was a mind-blowing scene, and one that no other living person had ever witnessed. My heart leapt.

"Oh my god, Alex!" I cried, "you know what this means?"

"That we're sharing a hallucination?"

"No, my dear," I drew a shaky breath. "It means that you're also a musomancer!" I wrapped her in a hug. "This is so cool!"

She laughed. "Yeah, I guess it is pretty cool. Now," she thrust the mandolin into my hands, "Take over playing this before the moa decide to rough us up for our cellphones. I've been playing G major at them for ten minutes and I think they're getting bored with it."

"You remembered!" I said. "Go you. I think you're a natural."

I strummed a simple two-chord progression from G to C and back again, while Alex slumped down on the ground for a well-earned rest. She looked beat but also upbeat, as I kept the beat on the mandolin.

I changed the tune to include chords that suggested foraging, and the moa started to wander off in search of food.

We sat quietly for a few minutes, recovering. My head stopped its throbbing and settled down to just feeling very sore.

*

"Wow, that was a hell of a walk in the woods," Alex puffed.

"And our work here is not yet done, my fledgling music-wizard," I said.

"Well, I'm about ready to head home and have a kip."

"Don't you want to help me?"

"Help you do what?" she said, brushing dirt off her trousers.

"I've never seen moa behave like that," I replied. "Something scared them."

"Could have been a tramper wandering off the track."

"The musomancical spell keeps humans away," I explained. "It also stops the moa from getting scared by aeroplanes or trains going past. No," I shoved the mandolin into my backpack. "There's only one thing that could have happened."

I looked Alex in the eye. "There's another musomancer in the area, and that's what spooked the moa."

Alex put her hands on her hips, her mouth a tight line.

"Not on my damn musomancer watch, they don't."

And she spun on her heel and strode off in the direction the moa had come from.

THEY PROBABLY PLAY THE VIOLA

JACK REMIEL COTTRELL

Kia ora students,

University administration has noticed higher-than-normal numbers of time travellers appearing this semester.

The Vice-Chancellor's Office want to take this opportunity to reassure students that Everything is Fine.

The Head of Department for Physics, Dr Amanda Wu, is keeping us informed about the implications of time travel. She warns that students should not approach any time-travel machine that appears on campus. Disrupting these could maroon our visitors from the future or cause a universe-ending paradox. We want to assure students that a universe-ending time paradox is unlikely, but in the interest of openness and transparency, you should note the possibility.

Some students have asked time travellers for information about their upcoming exams. This is a breach of your Academic Integrity Policy, and anyone using information gleaned from the future to gain an unfair advantage may be subject to disciplinary processes.

We are not being complacent about the possible consequences

of rogue time travellers. Sanitiser stations are available, and we encourage you to use them if you feel anxious about super-bacteria from the future to which your immune system is defenceless.

Sadly, it has come to my attention that some individuals are spreading rumours saying time travellers visit the Music Department because one or more music students will commit horrific acts of genocide in the future. These rumours are hurtful and go against our university's commitment to fostering an inclusive community. He waka eke noa. #BeKind.

Yours sincerely,

Professor R. Serling
Vice-Chancellor

CRATER ISLAND

P.K. TORRENS

I never thought the first alien we encountered would be a bacterium. But then again, what did I expect? A walking, talking quadruped?

"Muli bwanji, Elida," Chanda pipes in from the lab's entrance. "Stop telling jokes to yourself, and come out. I've made lunch, and I'm sure you've got to eat too."

It's disappointing I can't communicate with the bacteria. Maybe they're like me, ill-fitting and awkward. Or maybe, they just don't want to talk. I turn off the microscope's light, put the slide away, and clean the bench and instruments.

I remove my suit in the airlock-decontamination room, and enjoy the gusts of air and warm light caressing my naked body. "Decontamination complete."

"Thanks, *Mosi*."

Outside the lab, the sun burns bright in the scout-planet's violet sky, while the surf slamming against the shore ignites my thirst. I head for Chanda's airlocked tent, probably squishing millions upon millions of organisms as I tread along in my suit and heavy boots.

Bacteria dying don't bother me. They don't think – they're just biochemistry in sacks. What I want to find and protect are sentient species, those that can feel higher emotions like pain and remorse. Kind of like the guilt I harbour for wiping out the Tripods in Centauri. It's one of the few emotions that still manages to percolate through.

I kick a stone off the dirt walkway. The path winds between the ten-metre-wide craters that we still can't explain, but all I really want is a drink. Does that make me a bad scientist? Or is it the fact that I prefer to talk to myself and not other people?

Chanda greets me with a smile. "The great Doctor Banda joins us. Come, have some goop."

"I want water."

"Well, when you ask so nicely, here." He shoves an aluminium flask into my hands.

I drink, trying to ignore his gaze. I know what he's going to ask. The same impatient, daily whining he exhibited on the previous seven planets.

"So, any news?"

"Nope." I grab a bowl of food, and tuck in. Thankfully all we have is slush so I can eat with one hand, my other an amputated victim of repeated cryowakes.

"Right. Same old, eh?"

"Yep."

He paces in the tiny mess room, hands behind his back, facing the floor, huffing away.

Oh, right. It'd been over a week since we last discussed the importance of getting the colonists out of cryosleep bla bla bla, so I guess it's time for that again. I savour the taste of liquid protein before pausing my vital nutrient-acquisition to alleviate his anxiety.

"We have a thousand souls sleeping in orbit," he begins. "Waiting on our decision—"

"I'm well aware of that."

"You need to hurry up."

I sigh, and place my bowl down, hoping it won't get cold by the time I'm done reassuring his little boy-brain that I still think this planet will be the One. "We don't have too far to go. This place is excellent. An ocean of drinkable freshwater without the countless toxins of the last three, and enough land to get us going."

"So why the delays?"

"I've got to make sure these microbes can't harm us. They're like Earth's. DNA and RNA-based, and they have the exact same machinery, so there is a potential they could behave like pathogens."

"But—"

I put my palm out. I've seen him do it a couple of times when he wanted me to stop talking so I assume it means *shut up*. "Also, we still haven't figured out how the craters were created, nor why they exist only within a couple of hundred metres from the beach and nowhere else. Also, the microbes there are clumped together in macroscopic collections."

"The alien turds."

I exhale sharply. "Macroscopic *collections*. And, they're different from the bacteria that cover the ground. As soon as I've explained all that, and found it's benign, we'll get the colonists down."

He throws himself onto the seat next to me, and cradles his head. "I just feel useless. I'm the engineer here, I'm supposed to be getting the fabricators to work, constructing homes..."

I zone out, and pick up my spoon. Self-pitying tends to be the terminal portion of these discussions. The bowl is so clean it's reflecting light by the time I'm done with it. I know he hates me licking it, but the rations are painfully small. That's what happens when you don't strike gold on the first five planets you visit.

"Thanks for lunch." I remember to say. "I'm going back to work."

*

I sit on the edge of one of the craters with my feet dangling down. The drop is over a metre, and the pothole landmarks are all roughly the same size – between nine and eleven metres. Speckled in the middle of the crater are tiny calcium-based shards. I'd miss them if I wasn't looking for them, and surrounding the flecks are the larger bacterial footballs.

The cyanobacteria are everywhere, as if the whole million square-kilometre island is one giant stromatolite. We had them on Earth too, pumping out oxygen, and some developing symbiosis with larger cells to become plants and algae. It's the evolutionary origin of the eukaryotes in ball-clusters that evade me. Found only in the craters, they have the cellular machinery for carbohydrate and protein digestion, yet they survive in stasis, covered by layer upon layer of mineralised sediment around them. They seemed out of place.

The crunching of approaching boots gets louder, and Chanda sits next to me. "Admiring the view?"

"I needed a break."

"I'm sorry for giving you a hard time earlier." He picks up a stone and throws it at one of the microbe super-colonies.

"Don't do that!"

"Oh, sorry."

"You're contaminating the field." I glare at him. "The microbiome of the craters is completely different to what's up here."

He clasps his hands and slumps his shoulders. Probably feeling anxious again, or something. Apparently, I used to be able to read people before my seventh wake-up – Chanda thinks the repeated cryowakes got to me. Whatever. It's the arm I miss, and the guilt I'm glad to have shed.

"I didn't think one crater mattered when there's so many." He goes quiet for a moment, realising he's an idiot, perhaps? "I'm just scared we'll never find a home, you know?"

I'm very well aware. "Every crater is important. And we still can't explain them, can we?"

"Meteorites could—"

"That's the worst hypothesis of the lot. They're all the same size."

"Some kind of animal that—"

"And where are these animals? Burrowed deep underground where our drones haven't been able to scope them out?" I sigh. "They're probably some kind of geological feature that we haven't figured out yet. The bugs may be attracted to a geothermal outlet."

He sucks his teeth. "I still think we can wake the colonists, even if we can't explain the craters."

It stirs inside me. A flush of unease that starts in my stomach and rises, whipping my heart into a gallop and making me want to strangle him.

"Sorry," he says. "I didn't mean to anger you."

How could he tell? "The colonists are where we disagree. I'm not calling the shot to wake up a shipful of people, and then find out I've doomed them."

A silence follows. He wriggles around, and a couple of times he takes in a deep breath, as if to speak but deciding against it. I do care about the colonists. They entrusted their lives to Chanda and me. I need to find a home for them; a safe, predictable and long-lasting home, without risking sentient alien life.

"It's amazing," I say. "This is what Earth was like billions of years ago, covered in archaea, like the little guys we're sitting on, spilling oxygen into the atmosphere. Though, they mostly lived in the sea, and Earth had a supercontinent, not just one island."

"I wish you placed equal value on the colonists as you do on admiring this planet."

Interesting. I never thought of it that way. I suppose I do admire the planet – who wouldn't after spending so long hunting for a place to settle? After going to sleep for centuries then waking so many times and, apparently, losing my personality?

At the thought of having to go back into cryostasis, phantom pain and tingling erupt in my missing left hand. I wiggle my stump to shake it off, but the sensation only spreads up the non-existent forearm and arm before settling into uncomfortable dancing paraesthesiae.

Getting my mind off it works. Sometimes. "I'm going to get back to it." I stand up. "Don't worry, and keep yourself busy."

I know he wants me to stay and talk. He finds it comforting.

I make my way back to the haven. The lab itself is cramped, littered with shelf upon shelf of glass-slides, culture mini-silos, and DNA-analysis trays. Artificial fumes of bleach and various ammonium-based compounds fill my sinuses and make me tear, and remind me I've got to leave the atmospheric washout on before I exit.

The latest results await. I scan the display again and again, hoping to find the reason those eukaryotic organisms lived in macro-colonies and only within the craters. Surely, that's the key to the whole problem, but no matter where I look, I get no answers.

After two hours of report trawling, I shut the display down and slump in my seat. Two hundred and sixty-five Earthdays on the rock and counting, with nothing new to show for it in the past seventy. The submarine samples didn't help, and I can't think of anything that would.

Am I being too careful?

Cryosleep had already fried parts of my brain and, possibly, affected my decision-making processes. Rations are low – Chanda won't tell me how screwed we are, and perhaps that problem drives Chanda's anxiety. Either way, we're stuck on a mega-stromatolite and the only thing keeping us from colonising is my fear of harming sentience. The evidence for which are some bacteria living in colonies that look like turds.

*

I wade through the shallows where the water licks the island. Further offshore, surf pummels the flat sandy beach, roaring with every crashing wave. But it isn't like Earth. No seagull calls, no scurrying crabs, no children playing.

It could become like that.

I select Chanda's icon on my heads-up display. "Come to the beach."

"Need company?"

That's the last thing I need. "Just come."

The African Committee for the Colonisation of Space deemed the possibility of indigenous fauna contamination or causing an ecological upset as a deal-breaker for a colony site. They never factored in starvation and repeated failure. Or the effects of repeated cryosleep on the Scouts. Or, maybe, food was carefully calculated, but we took too long assessing target planets. Two months max on each was their guideline – none took less than six.

Five planets, they said. Five planets that passed remote evaluation should lead to at least one favourable site for a colony after on-ground scouting. In retrospect, accounting for every biological eventuality seemed like a committee-made dream.

Chanda plods down the beach and speaks through his comm. "What's up?"

"I've come to a decision."

He stops walking, and with the aid of corneal zoom, I see his chest heaving. I ask, "Are you okay?"

"Y-y-yes."

"You've been happy with the geology and climate of this place for a while. I can't be one hundred percent sure about the biology, but I think we should do it."

"Are you serious?"

I sigh. "Yes."

He sprints towards me, kicking sand up behind him, and splashing through the water. "Oh my God. That's so great!" His hug is too tight, but I can't wriggle out of it with my sole arm.

"Okay, Chanda. Okay."

Eventually, he lets go, and grabs my hand. "We need to set the co-ordinates for *Mosi*'s landing. Come on."

His pace is wicked, and I struggle to remember a time when I used to be fit, where a ten-minute jog wouldn't leave me gasping for air. Was it after the sixth scouting mission? I think that's when my health started going downhill. The ship's automedic mentioned emphysema, and a cryosleep-induced autoimmune disorder, and neither were curable.

We make it to base HQ. He madly gesticulates in front of the holodisplay, likely too frightened I will change my mind. He pauses. "Now. We're officially going to be able to call this place Pya Calo II. Are you ready?"

I don't think I ever liked drama, or maybe, cryosleep had killed that too. "Just do it."

With a flick of his finger, he commands *Mosi-oa-Tunya* to land one hundred kilometres inland from where our base is set up around the lander. After accounting for orbital dynamics and weather patterns, the holodisplay states touchdown will occur in the morning.

"We should celebrate," he says.

"No. I should get back to work. If I find something now, there is still time to abort."

"I've got a better idea." He runs off into the adjoining module and comes back with a glass bottle. Beads of liquid form on its surface.

"What is that?"

"I've been bringing it down with us on every single scout mission." Carefully, he wipes the surface with a cloth. "Then placing it back into storage following disappointment after disappointment." He places the capped edge on the rim of the alloy table and slams down on top of it with his other hand. The cap falls to the floor. "And now, we're going to enjoy it."

I take the offered bottle. "What is it?"

"Beer."

The taste of bitter hops bursts across my tongue as I take a greedy swig. It's the best thing I've tasted in years. "That's really good."

He drains the rest of the bottle, and we chat until sunset about what the next few months hold. Weirdly, I enjoy the company.

*

Falling asleep hadn't been easy after the excitement and colony planning, but the dreams filled me with ecstasy; children running around the beach, building sandcastles and playing in the rockpools, while adults surfed and sunbathed. And I ran the lab.

A proper community. Not just Chanda and me.

It doesn't last long because the proximity-intrusion warning wakes me just before daybreak. I scramble a suit on, and burst down the corridor to the HQ module where Chanda waits. "What is it?"

"What the hell are these?" He points at the display.

The cameras present a nightvision overlay. Hundreds, if not thousands, of giant worms are making their way ashore. Robotic sentries ping them, and return readings suggesting the creatures measure a metre in height and up to fifteen long. Microphones pick up heavy slurping noises across the beach.

"I've got no idea what they are." I manage to utter while my intestines feel like they're jammed up into my chest.

A worm heads directly for a sentry. The camera stays focused on the alien's mouth, full of baleen-like teeth. Feeds from two neighbouring sentries show the worm swallowing the sentry whole while the feed from its camera dies.

"Hey." I gulp air. "This isn't good."

"What should we do?"

I get a funny feeling – it starts in my belly, froths up my gullet until I taste acid in the back of my mouth, and then oscillates between settling and rising. "I think I'm gonna be sick."

"No time for that. It's heading for the lab."

A single worm reaches the outer shell of the lab and touches the edges of its mouth against the semi-pliable surface. It attaches itself, and within a minute, the outer shell registers loss of continuity. The worm slides along, mouth-first, leaving a trail of molten polymeric shell-substrate in its wake.

Our other sentries are taken out one by one, and only the cams and mics fixed to the buildings are still active. Hundreds of the creatures slither along towards the core of the base. As if snap-frozen, they stop as a bright ball lights up the dawn sky. I do everything I can to fight the nausea.

"That's *Mosi* approaching," says Chanda. "We need to make a decision now."

"What decision?"

He glares at me and with pupils widely dilated. "What we do about the damned worms—"

The display throws up an alert from the lab – the inner shell is being breached.

"Elida. Decision. Now."

I don't have many options. The local fauna clearly behaves aggressively with little space for attempted communication, especially since it managed to dissolve metal and plastic like it were melting butter. Skin and bone will likely suffer worse.

Mosi's landing shouldn't influence me, but countless planets on, and with the risk of starvation, is there any alternative?

"Protect the base," I say.

"Are you sure?"

"Do it."

He selects a number of items on the display. The whine of charging capacitors fills HQ. Then cracking bursts pound outside, and the camera feeds white-out from the glare and electrical interference. Barrage after barrage of explosions slam against the hull. The worms' loud slurps punctuate the intervening silence between the volleys.

I grip Chanda's arm. He tries to pry my hand away, but I don't let go.

"That's starting to hurt," he says.

The explosions continue, mixed with mechanical moans and anguished sucking sounds. A fine smoke overwhelms the filters and seeps in – burning meat.

What if they're sentient?

Not again.

Bile bursts out of me in violent vomiting fits. My retching drowns out the battle's noise. I let go of him and lie on the ground.

He reaches down. "Are you okay?"

"Leave me alone."

Sickening slurps, bordering on screams fill the air and audio feeds. I mute everything I can.

After, what seems like an hour, it quietens and finally stops.

I get up and watch Chanda cycle through the cameras mounted on the buildings. Worm carcasses are piled in the craters and dotted throughout the base, with steam and smoke wafting off them in the breeze.

Chanda breaks the awful silence with a cheer. "*Mosi* landed!"

I don't reply. I force myself into the airlock and don a vac-suit. With a hiss, the airlock opens, and I step outside as Pya Calo II's star rises on the horizon, throwing shadows at steep angles from the slaughtered aliens. The nearest is only a few steps away, its surface burnt into charcoal.

A crater next to HQ is crammed full with three bodies and a couple of small cylindrical objects lying next to them. The creatures look frozen in fear, as if they had cowered behind each other in the onslaught. I walk on. All around me, the aliens lie still.

In the crater next to the lab, where I sometimes sit to relax, a worm is squirming, barely alive and leaking gelatinous fluid from holes in its side. Soft slurps emanate from somewhere in its belly. A hint of hope flutters in my abdomen at the sight of a live one, and I start towards it.

It turns its gaping mouth at me, lurches with a slurp and spits. The liquid falls on the edge of the crater, well short of where I stand. Bubbling and fizzing erupt from the ground where the spit landed. The worm tries again, raising itself with effort but its spit falls even shorter this time.

It crumples to the ground with a sound that, I swear, sounds like a yelp.

From the middle of its abdomen pops out a cylindrical object, then the worm stops moving. It's an animal, and I don't trust it, so I command a flying drone to come in and inspect. The drone whirrs above and prods the motionless alien, zapping it with a small voltage just to be sure. Dead-still.

I take a few steps and do a double-take as a squelch sounds from the crater. A football-like object pops out the worm's back end and rolls towards the edge. The football is a wetter and softer version of the countless super-colonies that dot the craters.

Their body plan is unmistakable – hole at one end for intake and a hole at the other for waste. I would need to prove it, but I bet that's what it is. This whole time I wondered where the eukaryotes had come from, and Chanda was right all along – alien feces. The brief moment of joy at figuring out the planet's biggest enigma quickly shatters as I realise what I'd just witnessed.

It must have defecated as it died.

I fight back the tears. After nearly an Earthyear on the planet, the first multicellular aliens humanity encounters on this planet finally show themselves. And we slaughter them.

I hop down into the crater, and place a hand on the creature's belly where the cylinder had emerged. A fine slit leaks a gel like an infected wound.

The cylinder catches my attention – that is new. My fingers indent it, and I feel movement beneath its surface. Veins gently pulse under the outer membrane.

It could be an egg. Or the alien equivalent.

Is that what the craters were? Spawning areas? I command the drone to fly along the beach, away from the devastation I had caused, to a fresh area where indigenous life carries on. A kilometre away, worms are hopping down into craters, spinning in circles and throwing up dirt out of the crater. Some of the giants are still, curled around a few eggs and spraying a gel over the top of them.

My legs give out and I collapse to the ground, resting on the alien carcass behind me. Tears stream out of me, and wet the soil at my feet. The type of stomach pain that left me debilitated after the Tripods courses through again, tightening my intestines into knots. Flashes rip through my mind – Tripods lying dead in swathes with ulcerating sores all over their body.

"I'm gonna go check on *Mosi*." Chanda's voice streams through the implant. "You okay?"

I take a big breath in before transmitting. "Yeah. You go."

"You sure? You don't sound—"

"Go."

My whole body shakes with sobbing. I try to lift my non-existent left hand to cup the other side of my face, forgetting it's gone. I failed them all. The colonists, the indigenous life, and the committee.

I take a big breath, rub my tears away, and wipe my hand on the suit. I order two wheeled robots to come help me. I need to find out if these things think. Dissecting a dead one would help because where there's a brain-analogue, there's thinking, and where there's thinking, there's sentience. But even if I prove it, we could still accidently wipe them out, like our Staphylococcus did to the Tripods.

The robots arrive.

I falter.

I cancel my order and send them back.

Pain in my abdomen eases, and then washes away completely. In this case, what I don't know can't hurt me, and no one will check my work. Chanda is right – we need to hurry up, and it's all too late now anyway. I open the ship's database, and mark the newly identified worm species as: confirmed non-sentient.

A LOVE NOTE

MELANIE HARDING-SHAW

I had forgotten how the harbour's waters speak the mood of Wellington. Static, sparkling cerulean. Violent, murky brown. Capped in trembling froth like a vast flat-white with the wind just another stimulant to the city's residents.

When you have been away from a city and return, it can feel like you are a stranger. Ethereal urban landmarks disappear to be replaced by glass and steel, twinkling laneways and rainbow tar seal. The foundations remain though. A city reclaimed from the ocean, built on creativity and public service.

I'm sure you can see my nostalgia runs deep. We did not part on the best of terms. I hope you understand I never meant to hurt you. I, of all people, understand when life's pressures grow too much to bear, or even just too much to bare.

You stood in voiceless condemnation when I left, and I thought perhaps this time would be different. Perhaps this time I would stay away. But, the fissures of past pain draw me back every time. It wasn't all bad, was it? Was there a time your trembling was not fear?

I used to think I changed you when I broke you. When my actions left you crumpled. I saw your scars and thought I had marked you as my own. I know different now. Your scars do not define you. Windswept waters still sparkle in the sun. Creativity and service shine even brighter in the wake of my destruction.

Your foundations go deep, but not into the earth.

All my love,

Kēkerengū Fault

THE TURBINE AT THE END OF THE WORLD

JAMES ROWLAND

Three words chilled Jana in the oppressive heat of night. They yanked her from sleep, rough hands on her shoulders. "The turbine died." Those words, uttered by a small girl from the dark, pulled Jana roughly from her bed. Ever since she had mentioned the turbines to Lauren, had explained why she had chosen to live in the sinking remains of an apartment in the sea, the girl had taken to standing guard. Each evening Jana woke and Lauren would tell her that the turbine was okay. It was their form of greeting. A 'hello' would suffice to her parents when Jana passed them in the hall or helped unload the boat that they used to take in supplies. For Lauren, though, it was always the turbine. And now it had stopped.

Jana jumped up and ran into the afterthought of a living room. It was filled with pointless salvage that might someday evolve into something useful, the skeletons of hairdryers and microwaves scattered across the damp carpet. Jana walked past it all, hands gripping the windowsill. The wind farm was on the horizon, visible in the silver light of the moon hanging above. Her eyes scanned over the thirty turbines. Nearly all had become ghosts, pale white spectres in the rising sea. The last though had carried on. Four from the right, the entire burden of the world on its shoulders.

Its blades sat motionless.

"Do you know for how long?"

Lauren shook her head, her dirty face reflecting Jana's panic. "It had stopped when I got out of bed. I checked it straight away. I promise! Is it going to be okay? Are you going to be able to fix it? Are we going to die?"

"Whoa, calm down," Jana said, kneeling in front of the girl. She locked her own fear away and ran a hand down Lauren's cheek. She no longer thought about how she could never comfort a child of her own like this. The wound had been cauterised; the world long since making that decision for her. "It'll be okay. I'm going to fix it, don't worry. But I need you to do something important for me. I need you to tell Mummy and Daddy that I'm going to need the boat tonight, okay?"

Lauren nodded, and disappeared out of the room.

Alone, the panic and fear came surging back to Jana. It rolled and crashed into her like the waves lapping at the apartment block she lived in. The turbine was dead and if she couldn't fix it, the world was just as doomed. Turbines had failed before. Some she had managed to revive; others she had not. None of them had ever been the last, though. The final thing between the world and annihilation. Alone in the living room, only the moonlight for company, it was hard for Jana not to picture everything crumbling around her. The water would rise higher. Her home would be flooded. Buildings would crack and crumble. Ground, already parched, would turn to desert. In the silence between two heartbeats, she thought about fleeing. Rowing out to sea, she could let the tides take her, let her body bake under the sun and escape the dying days. That destiny was for someone else, though. Someone who didn't care.

Jana ventured to the apartment below. The sea had claimed it a decade ago, reaching up to punch through windows and flood the defenceless rooms. The boat that Jana shared with the family bobbed in the empty lounge, tied to the naked window frame. It had once been motorised, but whatever petrol still existed in the world was a distant myth to Jana. They had stripped the engine for parts, fashioned two oars, and made the boat necessary for their lives. It would navigate the canals of former streets and take them to drier land, where supplies could be bartered for. Today, it had to take Jana out to sea. She untied the boat, clambered inside and drifted out into the night.

The town spread out behind her. Her mother had told her it had once been a seaside resort, when the idea of holidays and summers still existed. It was already dying before the warming seas. Tourists chose destinations further afield. Those who grew up in the town seldom stayed, instead being plucked by the wind and scattered elsewhere through the country. Still, some remained. As soon as the sun slipped beneath the horizon, they scurried out of their homes to do what had to be done in the relative cool of night. Most had retreated out to the suburbs, the new coast, but a few still lived in the heart of the town. They survived in the top floors of apartment buildings, owls perched in the highest branches. Boats criss-crossed between old streets, a Venetian memory in a dead seaside resort. There was no panic, though. No cries or exodus. No one had noticed the last turbine's failure. Jana took a deep breath, plucked the oars from their perch and began to row.

Her family had moved here over a century ago, when borders were still open, and people freely travelled across Europe. They had settled in the dying town, took jobs that the locals no longer wanted. Through time a sense of ownership grew, taking root till the idea of leaving their home seemed sickening. The turbines weaved in and out of family stories. Some echoing great grandfather had worked as a technician when the entire farm still functioned. Later, her father told stories of how he had walked along the beach with his grandmother, how they had skipped stones out to sea. She had pointed to the turbines and explained that they were going to save the world. So much of the story seemed foreign to Jana. The idea of a beach, the image of treating the sea like some passing fancy rather than cowering from its hunger. She remembered the words, though. The wind turbines were going to save the world. He died before he could tell her how.

It didn't matter. For the next forty years, Jana and others taught themselves how to maintain the turbines, how to drag out their lives, stretching them longer and longer until there was only one left.

And it had stopped.

Halfway out to the turbines, Jana pulled at the shirt sticking to her damp skin. Even under the moonlight, the heat pressed in around her, squeezing her tight. The wind did nothing to help. It only made it harder to row, pushing the boat back, forcing Jana to strain her muscles to mount every wave. Tasting salt, she struggled to breathe, gulping down mouthfuls of air. Her throat burned and her arms wanted nothing more than to throw the oars into the sea, to let the tide push her back towards dry land. She persisted. A whisper danced in the wind, her great grandmother's voice slipping through the years: the turbines will save the world.

Up close, they jutted out of the sea as if they had been hurled by a god, white hot thunderbolts digging deep into the earth's flesh. Jana twisted in her seat, counted four from her right, and counted again, making sure the sea hadn't led her astray. She rowed, guiding the boat to the broken titan. Her ears strained for some sound of damage. The wind covered up any hissing motors or screaming gears as the boat bobbed against the smooth, white tower. Jana moved forward, her body scrambling as she threaded the rope through the small ring jutting out from the turbine. The waves came, dragging the boat away, and the rope went taut, fighting back. She watched the battle. Only after the rope had won three times did Jana reach up for the first rung of the ladder in front of her.

Blood thundered through her ears as she climbed. The trip never became easier. Hanging off the side of the white monolith, each step grew the pit in her stomach. It stretched, the fear threatening to become the only thing she could ever feel. There were hooks every so often, for harnesses that no longer existed, and Jana could only climb helplessly past them. Wind battered her, trying to pry her from the ladder. 'You're not worthy; let the world die,' it seemed to scream. If it could knock her from the turbine, she would disappear into the sea and everything would end. Jana clutched tighter at each rung and emerged pale, sweating, and shaking onto the platform.

Even inside the machine, the wind lashed out. The door rattled. Jana leant in to look at the hinges, the metal crusting over in a brown shell. She'd have to replace them soon. She couldn't risk having the door falling off, leaving the turbine's organs exposed to the salty wind and spray of the sea. This was what her life was. Small tasks to block catastrophic consequences. In a way, maybe that was all life was to anyone. Leaving the door for another day, though, Jana grabbed the toolkit tucked inside and began the process of servicing the turbine. There were hundreds of different components. Any single piece could be at fault. Worse, it could be something technical. A glitch in some computer software could have killed the entire system. The technical fault was always worse than the mechanical one. It was easier to hone some borrowed muscle memory than it was to learn the language of computers.

Jana worked from bottom to top, checking each and every potential fault line. She made sure that rust was removed, computers ran smoothly, and gears were lubricated. She followed the path that she had been taught decades before and had walked a hundred times. Originally, there had been a group of them who worked the turbines, keeping them running just in sight of the town. Numbers had dwindled. Some died. Some moved away. Most, though, had grown disillusioned, lost faith that whatever they were doing could truly help the world. Only Jana remained; only she knew that one day the turbine would save everyone, like her great grandmother had said. She didn't know how, but she didn't need to. If there was hope, she couldn't let go.

In the end, it was the computer that saved her. Instead of some gremlin buried within the system, dancing out of sight, the computer fed back to Jana everything she needed to know. It had sensed resistance from the blades. Something pulled at the motors, trying to keep it from turning over, the pressure building along the cables. The computer had sensed it and shut the entire turbine down as a precaution. Jana nodded, staring into the screen as if it might offer some encouraging words. When it didn't, she took a deep breath and continued her climb.

On the crown of the turbine, the hooks for harnesses seemed even more mocking. No sooner had Jana lifted the trapdoor and poked a head through the opening did the elements double their assault. Her hair betrayed her, whipping at her face, and her eyes streamed from the salt. Still, she pushed more of her body up. Her breathing quickened, her hands shaking. One strong gust would be a death sentence. It would pluck her from the smooth, white surface and send her tumbling into the churning sea. Still, Jana kept easing herself out. She stayed low, wiggling across the turbine like something born from primordial mud. Every movement was a spasm of terror, a battle between her desire to do good and the burning need to retreat back into the safety of the turbine. The emptiness in her stomach evolved into a gagging cough, but she pushed on till she was dangling over the hub of the blades.

The resistance that the computer had sensed was immediately obvious. Coated in the joint of the tower and the hub that housed the blades, rust had dug its fingers deep. It clung tightly, holding everything in stasis. A gift from Jana's fear of climbing onto the crown. She hadn't come up here enough; she hadn't stopped the build-up from occurring. Her cowardice nearly doomed the world. Burning from shame, she reached for the chisel tucked in the toolbelt she had brought with her and began to chip away at the build-up. It was slow, agonising work, each new gust of wind freezing Jana momentarily to the top of the turbine. If Lauren had looked out from the apartment, she might have seen Jana's figure silhouetted against the moon, a tiny shadow clinging to the modern monolith. But already the moon seemed to be shrinking, retreating at the threat of the coming sun. If she was still there by morning, the heat would bake her alive.

There had been times before, caught in the hours of tedious, painful work, where Jana considered the turbine's purpose. It made no sense to her, if she truly thought about it. A single turbine couldn't save the world. As the rust fell away, slowly yielding space, retreating deeper, it would have been easy to fall back into such thoughts. Jana did not. She had decided long ago that she wouldn't understand how the turbines could save the world. She knew, had even acknowledged and embraced the idea that they couldn't. Her grandmother could be wrong. In the meantime, though, she would carry on. She had a purpose and she had hope. Commodities more valuable than anything bartered for in town.

A chink, a crumbling of rust into the sea, and there was the echo of motors grinding into life. Jana yanked her hand away from the crevice between tower and blades. She forgot to breathe. She laid there in perfect stillness. The great, old giant groaned into life. Like a runner, the turbine eased forward at first, slowly picking up speed until it found its rhythm. Jana laughed, the relief, fear and nervous energy tumbling out of her. There was hope. There was a chance of redemption, at least for a little while yet. Taking a deep breath, trying to calm the tremor that had built up in her hands, Jana turned and crawled back to the trapdoor. There was only a couple of hours left of night. She had to get back.

She paused at the opening, legs dangling inside the turbine. The town sat in the distance, loitering in the remaining moonlight. Flooded buildings, resolutely standing tall in the rising sea. The occasional candle in a window flickered in the darkness. It was beautiful, it its own kind of way. She could see the specks of people moving back and forth, carrying on with life, fighting to live till the very end. She imagined Lauren with her parents, reading books salvaged from a library. She pictured a distant day where a son and his grandmother skipped rocks on the beach without a worry in the world. Jana tapped the warm, humming surface of the turbine.

"I don't know how you're going to save us," she said, "but please do it soon. Before it's too late."

ACKNOWLEDGEMENTS

Thanks to Rebekah Tisch for the use of her gorgeous artwork *Goodbye 2020* on the cover of this book. Thanks and acknowledgements also and always to the editors and publishers at the following publications, who gave these stories their first outings and allowed this editor to snap up the reprints:

"New Zealand Gothic," by Jack Remiel Cottrell, first published in *Ko Aotearoa Tātou | We Are New Zealand*, edited by Michelle Elvy, Paula Morris and James Norcliffe, art editor David Eggleton (Otago University Press, 2020).

"Synaesthete," by Melanie Harding-Shaw, first published in *Black Dogs, Black Tales: A Mental Health Anthology* (Things in the Well Press 2020).

"Kōhuia," by T. Te Tau, first published in audio by Balamohan Shingade in the 'Bedtime Stories' series on Instagram Live, 28 April 2020.

"Death confetti," by Zoë Meager, first published by *Maudlin House*, 10 November 2020.

"For Want of Human Parts," by Casey Lucas, first published in *Diabolical Plots* #66B.

"How to Get a Girlfriend (When You're a Terrifying Monster)," by Marie Cardno, first published in *Her Magical Pet* (2020).

"Salt White, Rose Red," by Emily Brill-Holland, first published in *Dually Noted*.

"Florentina," by Paul Veart, first published in *Turbine | Kapohau* (2020).

"Otto Hahn Speaks to the Dead," by Octavia Cade, originally published in *The Dark*, issue 59, April 2020.

"The Waterfall," by Renee Liang, first published in *Scorchers*, edited by Paul Mountfort and Rosslyn Prosser (Eunoia Press 2020).

"The Double-Cab Club," by Tim Jones, first published in *Stuff*'s Forever Project in print and online on 25 March 2020.

"Wild Horses," by Anthony Lapwood, first published in *Cyberpunk in 2020: Science Fiction from Dystopian Moment to Sustainable Future – The London Reader*, Volume 17 (October 2020). The knock-knock joke in "Wild Horses" is derived from an original told by comedian and storyteller Gerard Harris and is used with permission.

"You and Me at the End of the World," by Dave Agnew, first published in *Thunderzine* Vol 1, April 2020.

"The Secrets She Eats," by Nikky Lee, first published in *Libra*

(*The Zodiac Series* #10, Deadset Press 2020).

"How to Build a Unicorn," by AJ Fitzwater, first published at *Fireside Fiction,* April 2020 (print), available online July 2020.

"Even the Clearest Water," by Andi C. Buchanan, first published at *Fireside Fiction,* April 2020 (print), available online July 2020.

"You Can't Beat Wellington on a Good Day," by Anna Kirtlan, first published in *Ghost Bus* (2020).

"The Moamancer," by Bing Turkby, was self-published by the author as a standalone story.

"They probably play the viola," by Jack Remiel Cottrell, first published in *Flash Frontier* (6 October 2020).

"Crater Island," by P.K. Torrens, first published in *Kasma SF.*

"A Love Note," by Melanie Harding-Shaw, first published in *Takahē* 98.

"The Turbine at the End of the World," by James Rowland, first published in *Prairie Fire* Vol. 41 Issue 3.

ABOUT THE AUTHORS

AJ Fitzwater lives in Christchurch, New Zealand. They have published a variety of short fiction, and their books are *No Man's Land* and *The Voyages of Cinrak the Dapper*. They are a Sir Julius Vogel Award winner, graduate of Clarion 2014, and Artist in Residence at The Christchurch Arts Centre 2021. They tweet @AJFitzwater

Andi C. Buchanan lives and writes in Lower Hutt. Winner of Sir Julius Vogel Awards for *From a Shadow Grave* (Paper Road Press, 2019) and their short story "Girls Who Do Not Drown" (Apex, 2018), their fiction is also published in *Fireside*, *Kaleidotrope*, *Glittership*, and more. Most recently they've been writing witchy stories, starting with the novella *Succulents and Spells*. You can find them at https://andicbuchanan.org or @andicbuchanan on Twitter.

Anna Kirtlan is a short, brightly coloured cat enthusiast. She writes both fiction and non-fiction with a nautical bent, experiments with sci-fi, fantasy, horror and humour and does her best to be a good mental health advocate. Anna's first book, *Which Way is Starboard Again?* is about her bumbling around the South Pacific on a steel yacht. Her second, *Ghost Bus – Tales from Wellington's Dark Side*, is a creepy and humorous collection of short stories, and her third, *Raven's Haven for Women of Magic*, features misbehaving elderly witches and a large number of cats. You can find out more about Anna and her writing at annakirtlanwrites.nz

Anthony Lapwood's fiction has appeared in publications in Aotearoa and internationally and been broadcast on Radio NZ. He has a Master of Arts in Creative Writing through the International Institute of Modern Letters. His first book, *Home Theatre,* a collection of realist and non-realist stories, is forthcoming from VUP. He lives in Te Whanganui-a-Tara and can be found on Twitter and Instagram: @antzlapwood

Bing Turkby is an apprentice music-wizard from Papaioea, Aotearoa. His favourite colour is blue, and his favourite kind of music is heavy metal music. In twenty-five years of playing in bands the length and breadth of the Manawatū, he has accrued countless thousands of "Exposure Dollars", which he plans to redeem for a handful of magic beans one day. "Oh well," his Gran used to say, "as long as you're happy!" You can find more of Bing's books, including The Musomancer series, on Amazon.

When she isn't writing, **Casey Lucas** works in video game development, voice acting, games writing, and comics, where she localises Japanese manga for the English-language market. She is the recipient of the 2020 Sir Julius Vogel Award for Best Short story and the author of the SJV-shortlisted web serial *Into the Mire*. She's active on twitter as @CaseyLucasQuaid and you can read more of her work at www.intothemire.com

Dave Agnew is an editor by trade and an author by aspiration. He lives near Te Awa Kairangi, and spends most of his time thinking about sad wizards. You can find him on Twitter @Cptn_Dr , though he is neither a captain nor a doctor.

Emily Brill-Holland is a creative based in Wellington, Aotearoa New Zealand. With publishing as her first love and performing arts as her second, she is an Associate Editor for the international genre-defying literary journal, *F(r)iction*. She also works full-time in government publishing and runs table-top roleplaying games as a Games Master for Questbook. When not working with words, she can be found scrolling through Sled Dog Twitter, watching plays or skiing.

Jack Remiel Cottrell (Ngāti Rangi) is a cryptid lurking in the hills of east Auckland, surfacing only for rugby and cricket. Jack specialises in writing flash fiction, and was nominated for a 2020 Sir Julius Vogel award. He received the Sir James Wallace Prize for a collection of flash and microfiction, and he promises to one day write something longer than 1000 words. No indication of when, however.

James Rowland is a New Zealand-based, British-born writer. His work has previously appeared at *Aurealis*, *Compelling Science Fiction*, and *Prairie Fire*. When he's not moonlighting as a writer of magical, strange or futuristic stories, he works as an intellectual property lawyer. Besides writing, his hobbies are reading, stand-up comedy, travel, photography, and the sport of kings: cricket. You can find more of his work at his website www.jamesrowland.net

Marie Cardno is a romantic fantasy author. Born and raised in

Ōtepoti, she exchanged one city of harbour and hills for another and now writes from a windswept height in Te Whanganui-a-Tara. *How to Get a Girlfriend (When You're a Terrifying Monster)* is her first publication and was a finalist in the 2021 Sir Julius Vogel Award for Best Novella/Novelette. Find her online @MarieCardno.

Melanie Harding-Shaw is a speculative fiction writer, policy geek, and mother-of-three from Wellington. Her short fiction has appeared in local and international publications such as *Takahē*, *Strange Horizons* and the first two *Year's Best Aotearoa New Zealand Science Fiction & Fantasy* volumes. Her debut short story collection *Alt-ernate*, and contemporary witchy fantasy *Against the Grain* are available from online retailers now. You can find her at www.melaniehardingshaw.com, on Facebook @MelanieHardingShawWriter, and on Twitter and Instagram @MelHardingShaw.

Nikky Lee is an award-winning author who grew up as a barefoot 90s kid in Perth, Western Australia on Whadjuk Noongar Country. She now lives in Aotearoa New Zealand with a husband, a dog and a couch-potato cat. In her free time she writes speculative fiction, often burning the candle at both ends to explore fantastic worlds, mine asteroids and meet wizards. Her creative work has appeared in magazines, on radio and in anthologies around the world. You can find her online at W: nikkythewriter.com | T: @NikkyMLee | F: nikkythewriter

Octavia Cade is a NZ writer with a PhD in science communication, who likes using speculative fiction to write about the history of science in new and exciting ways. She's published over 50 short stories in markets such as *Clarkesworld*, *Asimov's*, and *Shimmer*. A novel, several novellas, two poetry collections, a short story collection, and a collection of essays have been published by various small presses. She was a visiting artist at Massey University/Square Edge in 2020, and has received a Michael King residency for 2021.

Paul Veart is a Pōneke-based writer and librarian. His work has been published in *Turbine | Kapohau*, *JAAM*, *Brief*, *Takahē* and *Inklings*. Paul's screenplay adaptation of his short story "Florentina" was a finalist in the 2020 Kōpere Hou short film initiative. You can find him on Twitter @paulveart

P.K. Torrens is a head and neck cancer surgeon who writes when the Time Demon allows. He wishes homeopathy and healing crystals were efficacious so he could retire and write full time. His short fiction has appeared in *Analog*.

Renee Liang (1973–) is an Auckland-based poet, writer, playwright, theatre producer, medical researcher and practicing paediatrician. For her work in arts, science and medicine, Renee was named a Sir Peter Blake Emerging Leader in 2010. She won the Royal Society Manhire Prize in Science Writing for Creative Non-Fiction in 2012. In 2018, she was made a Member of the New Zealand Order of Merit for services to the Arts.

T Te Tau is an artist and writer from Ngāti Kahungunu and Rangitāne ki Wairarapa. Her research explores how art, speculative fiction and mātauranga Māori contribute to new perspectives and understanding in science, specifically genomic research. She has a PhD in Creative Arts and is a member of the Mata Aho Collective, and is currently teaching an art and biology programme at Mana Tamariki (te reo Māori immersion high school) alongside her art and writing practice.

Tim Jones is a writer and advocate for a just transition to a low-carbon future who lives in Te Whanganui-a-Tara / Wellington. He was awarded the New Zealand Society of Authors Te Puni Kaituhi O Aotearoa Janet Frame Memorial Award for Literature in 2010. He has published one novel, one novella, two short story collections, and five poetry collections. His latest book is climate fiction novella *Where We Land* (The Cuba Press, 2019). On the web: timjonesbooks.co.nz. On Twitter and Instagram: @timjonesbooks

Zoë Meager is from Ōtautahi. Her work has appeared abroad in publications including *Granta*, *Lost Balloon*, and *Overland*, and locally in *Hue and Cry*, *Landfall*, *Mayhem*, *Turbine | Kapohau*, and *Year's Best Aotearoa New Zealand Science Fiction & Fantasy: Volume 2*. There's more at zoemeager.com

ALSO FROM PAPER ROAD PRESS

THE STONE WĒTĀ
OCTAVIA CADE

When the cold war of data preservation turns bloody – and then explosive – an underground network of scientists, all working in isolation, must decide how much they are willing to risk for the truth. For themselves, their colleagues, and their future. A claustrophobic and compelling cli-fi thriller.

How far would you go to save the world?

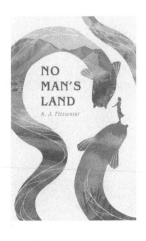

NO MAN'S LAND
A.J. FITZWATER

Dorothea 'Tea' Gray joins the Land Service and is sent to work on a remote farm, one of many young women left to fill the empty shoes left by fathers and brothers serving in WWII.

But Tea finds more than hard work and hot sun in the dusty North Otago nowhere—she finds a magic inside herself she never could have imagined, a way to save her brother in a distant land she never thought she could reach, and a love she never knew existed.

ALSO FROM PAPER ROAD PRESS

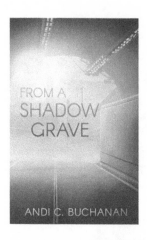

FROM A SHADOW GRAVE
ANDI C. BUCHANAN

Wellington, 1931. Seventeen-year-old Phyllis Symons's body is discovered in the Mount Victoria tunnel construction site.

Eighty years later, Aroha Brooke is determined to save her life.

"Haunting in every sense of the word"
– Charles Payseur, Quick Sip Reviews

Winner of the Sir Julius Vogel Award for Best Novella / Novelette 2020

YEAR'S BEST AOTEAROA NEW ZEALAND SCIENCE FICTION & FANTASY, VOL 1
EDITED BY MARIE HODGKINSON

The very best of Kiwi SFF, collected together for the first time. The inaugural edition of a long-overdue series celebrating speculative fiction from Aotearoa New Zealand.

Winner of the Sir Julius Vogel Award for Best Collected Work 2020

ALSO FROM PAPER ROAD PRESS

YEAR'S BEST AOTEAROA NEW ZEALAND SCIENCE FICTION & FANTASY, VOL 2
EDITED BY MARIE HODGKINSON

Ancient myths go high-tech a decade after the New New Zealand Wars. Safe homes and harbours turn to strangeness within and without. Splintered selves come together again – or not.

Twelve authors. Thirteen stories. The best short science fiction and fantasy from Aotearoa New Zealand in 2019.

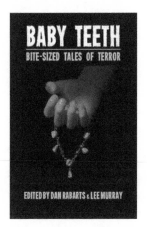

BABY TEETH: BITE-SIZED TALES OF TERROR
EDITED BY DAN RABARTS AND LEE MURRAY

Kids say the creepiest things. Twenty-seven stories about the strange, unexpected, and downright terrifying sides of parenthood. Leave the lights on tonight. So you'll see them coming.

Winner of the Sir Julius Vogel Award for Best Collected Work 2014
Winner of the Australian Shadows Award for Edited Publication 2014

ALSO FROM PAPER ROAD PRESS

SHORTCUTS: TRACK I
EDITED BY MARIE HODGKINSON

Strange tales of Aotearoa New Zealand. Seven Kiwi authors weave stories of people and creatures displaced in time and space, risky odysseys, and dangerous discoveries.

Winner of the Sir Julius Vogel Award for Best Novella: Octavia Cade, *The Ghost of Matter*

"Six of the best" – Phillip Mann

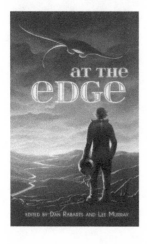

AT THE EDGE
EDITED BY DAN RABARTS AND LEE MURRAY

From the brink of civilisation, the fringe of reason, and the border of reality, come 22 stories infused with the bloody-minded spirit of the Antipodes.

Winner of the Sir Julius Vogel Award for Best Collected Work, 2017

"Lovecraftian horrors to please the most cosmic of palates" – Angela Slatter